# THE
# MISTRESS
# NEXT DOOR

BOOKS BY LESLEY SANDERSON

# THE
# MISTRESS
# NEXT DOOR

## LESLEY SANDERSON

bookouture

Published by Bookouture in 2023

An imprint of Storyfire Ltd.
Carmelite House
50 Victoria Embankment
London EC4Y oDZ
United Kingdom

www.bookouture.com

ISBN: 978-1-80314-681-2
eBook ISBN: 978-1-80314-680-5

*To The Mistress Moderately Fair aka Anne Williams, for being a wonderful friend*

# ANONYMOUS

Can you believe I'm living in Prospect Close? Eight exclusive dwellings and one of them is mine. I had to pull a few favours with the developer and get my hands on a large sum of money in order to secure the deal, but nothing was going to stop me from acquiring that particular postcode. Appearances matter.

I usually get what I want.

I hadn't expected to make friends here, but it's a really friendly community. The women soon started hanging out together; after all, they share similar tastes and backgrounds, some more similar than anybody could realise. The men rub along well together too – amongst the community they have some useful skills and it's that kind of place where people do one another favours.

Prospect Close is perfectly positioned for the village, with a playground, a school, a pretty high street with a choice of coffee shops. We buy our freshly baked bread and pastries and drink barista-crafted coffees together and discuss the merits of the local primary school under the new head teacher (who also happens to live on Prospect Close).

I hatched the plan to move here the moment I met him and set him in my sights. I liked the rather perverse idea of living virtually on top of them; it added to the illicit thrill. And he had the finances to make it work. I need that in my relationships; I lose interest pretty quickly once it becomes pedestrian and normal.

He calls me his mistress. I like it; it sounds quaint and old-fashioned and brings to mind a powerful woman, à la Anne Boleyn. Milk-white skin, dark hair and dangerous eyes, swishing around in her heavy brocade dress made from cascades of the ornate fabric, only her delicate shoulders and collarbones visible above her neckline, playing hard to get before eventually securing her prize.

I've already secured mine, and once that was done I set my attention on his wife. Who'd have thought that we'd become friends, popping in and out of one another's houses, stretching at yoga classes and sweating on the treadmill and sharing thick green gloop afterwards, believing it is good for us. I even get to spend time with their children, which is extra sweet, and there's no danger of them becoming mine. Children aren't part of a mistress's lot. But once I'm no longer the mistress...

The more these people trust me, the closer I am allowed to get, and the more mischief I can wreak. Part of the fun is that every day I walk a dangerous path. Our lives are becoming increasingly intertwined and the sense of trepidation at being found out paves that path.

However, what isn't part of my plan is that I'm beginning to suspect I'm not the only one. His only mistress. I'm not the kind of woman who belongs in a harem. I like to be the chosen one; I deserve special attention. This concern is becoming too prevalent in my mind and is in danger of distracting me from my carefully chosen route. Each move I make takes me closer to her, before I pull the ground from under her and watch her fall.

He dropped a bombshell last night. Said the wife wants to

move away, take him and their perfect little family with her, and he's running out of excuses. Which means it must be time. I've done the groundwork, got myself close to both of them, in an ideal position to ruin their lives.

Because it's payback time.

# ONE

'It's not too busy today,' Asha says, surveying the playground. Three children are racing one another around the climbing frame. A couple are standing around talking, one eye on their charges, a woman pushes her daughter on a swing, another woman sits on the bench. We watch Amira and Tess as they clamber onto the horse and the zebra, metal seats on springs on which they immediately bounce up and down as hard as they can. Tilly hovers next to me, watching her sister as she yells instructions to Amira.

'Doesn't Amira get fed up with Tess's bossiness?'

Asha laughs. 'You don't need to worry about that. My daughter can certainly hold her own. Don't you want to join them, Tilly?'

Tilly looks at me with uncertain eyes. I smooth her blonde hair back from her face.

'You do, don't you, go on.'

'No sitting on zebra,' she says.

'You don't have to do anything you don't want to. Go on, go and join them.' I nudge her back slightly and she skips over to join her twin sister.

'Where's Lucy this afternoon?' Asha asks, as we watch the children, ready to leap up at the slightest sign of trouble, as mothers always are.

'Mum's at home with her.'

'Such a shame about Kate. You're so lucky your mother is able to step in. I'd give anything to have my parents living nearby.'

'I know, she's a life saver.' Mum has always been there for me, more than Asha could ever imagine. Tilly is clapping and laughing as Amira and Tess bounce to a rhythm. They continue for a while until Amira stops and gets off.

'Look, Mummy,' she says, running towards us, so fast she trips over her feet and lands on the floor with a thump. She wails loudly, and Asha rushes forward to help her up. I keep an eye on the twins, who are still over by the zebra. I beckon them over.

'I've hurt my leg, Mummy, it hurts.' Tears are pouring down her face and she's gulping.

'Calm down, Amira, it's only a graze.' Asha sits her on the bench and Amira examines her leg.

'I'm bleeding.'

Asha rummages in her bag. 'Let me clean that up; it's not serious, honestly, darling. I'm sure I had a tissue in here.' She pulls a bunch of keys and a receipt out of her pocket, frowning.

'I've got some. Girls, come over here,' I call out to the twins, before turning my attention back to my bag. My phone is lit up with a message, but I ignore it, instead locating the tissues and my water bottle. 'Here, you can clean it with this.'

Amira calms down as Asha dabs at her leg with a wet tissue. Tess appears next to her.

'Does it hurt, 'mira?'

'No it doesn't, does it, darling? It's all better now,' Asha says. I look up at Tess, expecting to see Tilly behind her. She isn't. I stand up, look over to the zebra area, my heart beating a little faster.

'Where's your sister, Tess?'

'Behind me,' she says, turning. 'Oh. Where's Tilly? Shall I find her?'

'No, you stay here.' I scan the playground, trying to keep calm. She'll be playing quietly somewhere; it's what she does. Unlike her sister, she prefers peace and quiet and her own company. The children who were racing around earlier are on the swings now, and most of the other people who were here earlier have left; it doesn't take a minute to see that Tilly is nowhere in the playground.

'What's up?' Asha asks.

'I can't see Tilly. Stay here with Amira, Tess.' I run over to the other side of the playground, which isn't that large. *She'll be fine, she's OK, no need to expect the worst.* 'Have you seen a little girl?' I ask the woman on the bench.

'No.' She looks startled to be spoken to.

I repeat the question to a man who is watching two boys on the climbing frame. 'Blonde hair, she's three and a half, in denim dungarees and a yellow coat, black shoes.'

'No,' he says, looking around. 'Oh, look over there,' he says hopefully, indicating towards the bench where Asha is now standing, watching us, one hand on Tess's shoulder. My heart leaps, only to immediately realise his mistake.

'That's her twin. They're identical.'

'Where did you leave her?'

'By the zebra seat. I was watching her, I didn't leave her, I got distracted.' I would never leave my children. How could I have allowed this to happen? My heart is galloping. 'Tilly, Tilly' – I look around frantically – 'where are you?'

'I'll help you look,' he says. 'Boys, come with me.' He takes one by each hand and hurries them over to Asha. 'And I'll call the police. Just in case. I'm John.'

*Just in case.* A cold fear washes over me and for a second I'm rooted to the spot. This moment I've dreaded, since the day I dared to have children. Tempting fate. As if I could ever get away with it. Then I'm running around the perimeter of the playground. A single track separates the houses of Prospect Close from the playground. One glance tells me Tilly's not there. I yell her name at the top of my voice and people are stopping and staring, wandering over, relieved it isn't them that this nightmare scenario is happening to, as realisation dawns. People shake their heads, start looking around. Everyone wants to help.

'What does she look like?'

'Small, blonde shoulder-length hair, she's tiny.' She's beautiful and precious and my heart is ripping in two as my breath becomes ragged. I reach the gate and see John ahead of me.

'I'll check across the road,' he says. 'The police are on their way.' Only one path leads out of the close, but it joins a busy main road where cars move too fast, a road small children must be kept away from. A zebra crossing leads to a huge park. Tilly loves that park and if she crosses on her own... An image of a child lying on the ground flashes before me and my breath catches in my throat. I run back to the playground, stumbling over the uneven paving, my heart in my mouth. Becky, another neighbour, is by the swings on her phone, the chairs no longer creaking and flying through the air, but still, as is all the other equipment, as if the playground is in shock.

John is talking to the woman on the bench, who is shaking her head. 'I was miles away,' she is saying.

I can no longer breathe. I swallow huge gulps of air and bend over in panic, as terror sets in.

Tilly is missing.

Voices around me become a babble, everything blurs and my throat is closing. I'm in a dream and the world is spinning, I'm about to fall. Strong hands land on me and it's Martin, a neighbour.

'Take a huge breath in,' he says, 'you're panicking. We'll find Tilly, I promise. Lots of people are looking now. You need to stay where you are for when she comes back. Come on.' He leads me gently by the hand over to the bench where Asha and a small crowd of people are waiting, concern written on their faces, all looking at me when they should be looking for Tilly. I should be out looking too, but my body has frozen with fear.

'She's in shock,' Martin says, and my body *feels* shocked. It's juddering and Asha puts something warm and woolly around my shoulders. Tess puts her arms around me and holds me tight.

'We were with them in the play area. Tilly was on the zebra,' Asha is saying. She squeezes her daughter Amira's hand as she speaks. 'Amira fell over and hurt her leg. Harriet was helping her, her leg was bleeding and she had tissues, it must have happened then. Harriet had to hunt for the tissues in her bag. When she looked up, Tilly was gone. She can't be far,' she says, worried lines on her face. 'One minute she was there and the next she was gone.'

My Tilly, gone.

'No, Tilly,' I shout so hard my throat hurts. 'Tilly, where are you?'

'Harriet.' Mum is running towards me, adrenalin propelling her forward, Lucy in her arms. She appears at my side, her face flushed.

'Mum.'

'She panicked,' Martin says, 'I thought she was going to faint. The police are on their way.'

'Has anyone called Oliver?'

'No, you can't call him, not yet.' Calling him would make this final, mean that Tilly really is missing. 'He's travelling, let's wait. We're going to find her.'

Mum nods, understanding. 'We will, I promise you,' Mum says. 'I'll take Tess inside.' She's trying to sound upbeat but her eyes are full of fear.

'Tilly, Tilly, where are you?'

More of the neighbours come over, drawn by the unfolding drama in the quadrangle, anxious to know what is going on. It's late afternoon and the grey sky is rapidly darkening.

A huddle forms in the centre of Prospect Close, voices murmur, others call Tilly's name, and a few people go off to search the front gardens and neighbouring area. Asha is wringing her hands and desperate, trying to comfort me, but there can never be any comfort for me, not while my precious three-and-a-half-year-old Tilly is missing.

'She can't be far,' she says, worried lines furrowing her forehead. She hugs her own daughter tighter. Amira watches the grown-ups with solemn eyes, sensing something ill in the air.

'Where are the police?'

'I'll call them again,' Martin says, 'it's not good enough.'

'Listen, everyone.' A voice cuts through the babble of noise, making me jump as the owner is standing right next to me. It's Elliott, neighbour and head teacher at the local school. I'm relieved someone is taking charge. The noise dies down and heads turn to face him. He's wearing a suit and his deep voice always commands respect, even if you don't know who he is. Elliott clears his throat. 'Instead of all standing around I'm sure we could help. I want a few people to spread out and search while we're waiting for the police. We can't afford to waste a minute. We're looking for a three-and-a-half-year-old girl wearing a yellow coat and black lace-up shoes, she has shoulder-length blonde hair and her name is Tilly. She looks just like this little girl here as they are twins. Raise your hand if you're with me and I'll coordinate it.' Hands shoot up and a several people gather around him, before they head off towards the road that leads away from the playground and out of the close. Elliott is about to follow when a woman rushes over towards him. It's the woman who was on the bench.

'*Shit*,' he says under his breath and my stomach lurches.

What has he seen? An image of a lifeless child flashes before my eyes and a tremor runs through me.

'You were there when we were. Did you see what happened?' I ask her.

She shakes her head.

'What were you doing in the playground?' Elliott says, taking her to one side. 'I thought you were in France,' he says, lowering his voice. 'I can't talk to you now. A child has gone missing.'

Elliott strides over to follow the searchers and the woman runs behind him, remonstrating with him. I struggle to my feet. Sitting here won't help.

'Harriet,' Martin says.

'I'm going with them, I can't just sit here, Tilly needs me.'

The wail of a police siren cuts through my words and the uneasy murmur of the crowd, transforming it into a palpable sense of relief. 'At last,' someone says. Two police officers, one male, one female, spring out of a car, radios buzzing, blue lights flashing.

'Harriet Carlton?' the male police officer says.

'You have to find her, my Tilly, she's missing. I only turned away for a minute. She's so little.' I erupt into full-blown sobs and the female officer takes my elbow and guides me to a bench.

The other officer pulls out a notepad. Edward, another resident, briefs him, pointing to the play area, the metal post glinting in the sun. 'By the zebra,' he says. 'A few people have gone searching for her.' Someone brings out a mug of tea and puts it into my hands. Trancelike, I put it to one side, my eyes focused on the playground. The people who went out to search hurry back into the close. Two more police officers arrive and take control of the scene, identifying the key players, before asking the onlookers to disperse. Elliott returns and speaks to one of the police officers, gesticulating towards the road. A policeman is talking to Asha, pencil poised over a notepad.

'Let's go inside,' the policewoman says to me, taking my elbow. 'I'm PC Sterling.'

Mum's anxious face is watching through the window, Lucy in her arms. Feelings of love for my children well up inside me and I hurry down the path, willing Tilly to be found, wanting to check on the other two.

'Harriet, wait.'

Sienna jogs across the quadrangle, her sleek ponytail bobbing.

'What's going on? I just came from work, why are the police here?' She joins me on my doorstep. The policewoman goes inside and I hear her speaking to Mum.

'Tilly's gone missing.'

'Oh no.' She claps her hand over her mouth. 'What happened?'

Mum comes back out. I take Lucy from her and hug her tight. Her heartbeat flutters against mine.

'I'll talk to Sienna,' Mum says, and PC Sterling appears beside me and takes me indoors.

'They'll find her,' Sienna says. 'There's CCTV everywhere these days. She's probably wandered off the wrong way and someone will find her, you'll see.'

'I hope you're right,' Mum says from the doorstep.

Tess runs into the hall and I make a fuss of her.

'You're very pale,' PC Sterling says, 'you need to sit down.'

'I don't want to sit down, I want to be out there, looking for Tilly. Why aren't you out there looking for her?'

'Harriet,' Mum says, 'the police are looking; there are loads of them out there now. They know what to do best. Come inside and I'll make some sweet tea while you talk to PC Sterling.'

'I've been assigned to looking after you. I'm Fiona, please call me that. You can help me by telling me as much as you can about Tilly,' the policewoman says.

'Come back inside, Tess.' Mum shepherds her away from the open door.

Sienna hovers. 'Shall I come in with you?'

'Not this time,' Mum says firmly.

'No worries,' Sienna says. 'This is so awful. I was going to unpack my case from the weekend but I'll go and help with the search instead. Lots of love, they will find her, you know.'

Mum shuts the door on the terrible scene outside, and a shudder takes hold of me. My worst fears are being played out. It's all my fault. This time last week we had a nanny and she would have stayed with them, kept them safe; instead, I looked away. *I am responsible.* The cold sensation I normally experience every time I think about Kate and her sudden departure is totally eclipsed by my sense of desolation at missing Tilly.

Mum shuts the door behind us. Tess holds out her arms and Mum picks her up.

'I can't believe it,' she whispers, and holds Tess close.

'Nor can I.' My lip wobbles. The trauma of Tilly going missing has brought all the hard feelings I've kept at bay over the last week to a head. I swallow them down again, then turn to look out of the window at the police directing the start of the search party. 'They still haven't found her.'

'I'm sure she'll be OK; she must have run out of the square without anyone seeing her. She won't have gone far – she's so little. Someone will see her and get help; cameras will pick her up.' The possibility of the wrong person finding her hangs in the air, a man who will take her and... I shake my head to get rid of the thought, but how can I?

'I feel useless; we should be doing something.'

'Come away from the window,' Fiona says, 'I want to talk to you about Tilly. We're doing everything we can to locate her. This is a crucial time and anything you can think of that I may need to know is useful.'

Fiona updates me on everything that the police are doing; her photograph and details have been circulated nationally and a thorough search of the area is ongoing. She stresses how important it is for me to update her on our current circumstances, no matter how irrelevant any detail may seem. While I answer some questions, Mum gets some toys out for Tess and Lucy lies on her activity blanket kicking her legs, and gurgling. Mum puts the kettle on. My phone rings.

'You can answer it,' Fiona says.

It's Gabi.

'What's going on across the road?' she asks. 'I've just got back from my weekend away and there are police cars everywhere.'

I jump up and cross to the magnetic pull of the window.

'Tilly's gone missing. She wandered off from the playground. It's awful.' Talking to my best friend brings my emotions to the fore and I burst into tears. Mum takes the phone from me and speaks briefly before ending the call.

A dog handler is in the quadrangle now, the dog sniffing the air, straining on his lead.

'Come away from the window, love,' Mum says. 'You'll only upset yourself more.' I ignore her, keeping an eye on the quadrangle the whole time. 'I'm sure they'll find her.'

A sob lodges in my throat. Mum of all people should understand.

'It's bringing it all back, isn't it?' she says quietly. She gives me one of her looks and I know she sees right through me.

I turn my attention back to the window. Becky's husband, Ryan, has just arrived. He's wearing his work overalls. The ladder on top of his car shakes when he slams the driver door shut. My stomach churns. What if Tilly has been snatched, shoved into a van and driven away? What if something terrible is happening to Tilly?

I close my eyes, wishing I could unsee the little girl's face that haunts me.

But the face flickering before my eyes doesn't belong to Tilly.

# TWO

'We should think about informing you husband,' Fiona says. 'I know you didn't want to worry him, but it's important.'

*Now they are taking it seriously,* she means. Now Tilly is perceived to be in danger. I force myself to stay calm; getting hysterical won't help find my daughter.

'When is he due back?'

'Tomorrow evening.' My husband commutes to his job in a London city bank but he's been away this weekend at a conference in Paris. 'I'm not sure exactly when.'

'Give me his number and I'll try and get hold of him.' She dials the number and listens, frowning. 'It's switched off, no voicemail option. Can you message him, or send an email, anything that might get his attention?'

'I could try his PA. She might be able to locate him.'

The mobile rings, and a woman answers. His PA, Nadine – I'm relieved to recognise her voice.

'Hello, Mrs Carlton,' she says, recognising my voice too, a little surprise in her tone. She has worked at the bank with Oliver for years and I rarely need to contact her these days. 'How are you?'

'I need to speak to Oliver, it's an emergency, but he isn't answering his phone. What time does the conference end?' Today is Sunday, so I imagine it must be over or finishing today.

'It should all be ended by now; it was only one day,' she says, sounding surprised, 'finishing on Friday evening. He said he fancied staying on for a bit of sightseeing...' Her voice falters. 'Didn't he tell you?'

'Er...' I feel a flush spread up my face. He hasn't said anything to me. 'Oh of course, it's *that* trip... I have to talk to him. I don't know why he's switched his phone off. Do you have a number I can contact him on? Remind me – is he staying at the same hotel where the conference was taking place?'

'He is, I booked it myself. It's the Four Seasons Hotel George V. They gave us a special rate. He wasn't the only one of the staff to take advantage of the offer. It's a top-class hotel.'

'Do you have the number?'

I repeat the number she gives me out loud and Fiona dials the number. She goes into the kitchen to make the call. My legs feel a bit wobbly and I drag a chair over to the window. It's getting dark and I switch the fairy lights on, making the Christmas tree sparkle in the window bay. It feels festive and wrong and I switch them off. The police cars are still parked in the quadrangle and figures are moving about. A police officer stands outside our front gate and I go outside. Back inside, Fiona is still talking on her phone.

'Any news?'

'Not yet, I'm afraid. The team are out looking and an alert has gone out. We're doing our best to find her, miss.'

He only looks about twelve so I don't mind the 'miss'; it makes me feel young, unlike recently when I've been feeling tired and wretched, horrified by my haggard appearance when I look in the mirror, wishing Oliver didn't have to work so hard. And now this weekend away I don't know about. Is he up to his old tricks again? He promised me. *Tilly is missing.* Fiona is in the hall now, watching me; she's still talking to someone at the hotel. I fold my arms tightly across my chest. A man steps forward, pointing a camera at me.

'Mrs Carlton?' he says. 'How are you feeling?' Another journalist joins him. Fiona dashes out and stands in front of me.

'Go inside,' she says. 'I'll deal with this.'

A shout goes up from across the quadrangle and the journalists turn. My heart skips a beat. Have they found her?

'Excuse me,' the police officer says, hurrying across the street. The journalists run behind him.

Fiona takes my elbow. 'I've left a message with the hotel reception, and they will do their best to locate Oliver. They know it's urgent. Come inside.'

'I want to know what's happening over there.'

'I'll find out.' She speaks into her radio. 'It's nothing. We're going inside now; you're shivering.'

'Harriet, wait.'

I turn to see Ryan hurrying over. He lives across the street.

'Any news?' he asks.

I shake my head.

'Shit.' He's tall and lean and jittery. 'It must be so awful for you.'

I nod, biting my lip to stop myself crying. 'Becky was around earlier. Did she see anything?'

'No. She wishes she had. She wants to know if she can help.'

'The police are doing everything they can to help her, sir.'

'But are they? What are that lot doing over there just standing around the close? How do we know you're taking this seriously?'

'I can assure you that we are, sir.'

'I'm going to drive around the area, Harriet – they can't stop me.' He narrows his eyes. 'I'm worried some bastard's taken her.

Anyone who takes a kid deserves to be hunted down and strung up alive, made to suffer.'

'You're not helping.' Fiona glares at him. 'I'd advise you to let the police do their job.' She takes my elbow and propels me away from Ryan.

'You'd better look out for your kids,' he says. 'Nobody is safe round here anymore.'

His words send cold shivers down my spine.

Back inside my house, despite reassurances from Fiona, the talk with Ryan has unnerved me.

'He should never have said those things. Don't listen to him.' It's all stirring up inside me again. I sit in front of the window with my phone in my hand. Tess sits on my lap and I hug her so tight she squirms.

'I didn't mean to hurt you, love, I'm just happy you're here.'

'Where's Tilly?'

'Tilly is hiding,' Mum says. 'She's hidden so well that we can't find her yet. But we will, so you mustn't worry.' Mum and I exchange a glance.

'We will,' she mouths to me and I cross my fingers. *Please find her.*

Mum sorts out some food for the children, before taking them upstairs for bath time, after which Mum reads Tess a story in her room before settling her down for bed. My stomach rumbles.

'You should eat something,' Fiona says. 'You need to keep your strength up.'

'I can't.'

'I'll make some toast, see if you fancy that.'

'How can I eat toast when Tilly is missing? Where is she? What if she's hurt?'

Mum comes in and puts her arms around me.

'Lucy's asleep in her cot,' she says. 'Try and eat.' She rummages in the fridge and pulls out a portion of pasta bake from yesterday. 'This will do. Come on, love, at least go and freshen up; it will make you feel better.'

I go upstairs to the bathroom, not because I need to but to stop them making demands on me. I take my handbag, which is still on the table where I dumped it earlier. In the doorway of the twins' bedroom I watch Tess, who is fast asleep on her back. I'm relieved she can sleep, unaware her sister isn't back, unaware of how afraid I am. But there's no need to worry her because I have to believe Tilly is safe. Same goes for Oliver. I can't think about what he may or may not be doing in Paris; all my energy is needed for Tilly. I close my eyes and say a silent prayer that Tilly will be back with us by the time her sister wakes. Tears pour down my face.

In my bedroom I empty my bag to find a tissue. Car keys, a half-eaten tube of mints and a pack of tissues tumble out. As I take a tissue from the packet, a folded piece of paper falls onto the bed. I unfold it, expecting to see an old shopping list, written back when life was normal. But it's not my writing. Instead, written in capital letters are the words:

ARE YOU SCARED?

I sit on the bed, unable to move, transfixed by the note. Mum appears in the doorway and I jump out of my skin. I crumple the note in my hand, my mind working feverishly. If this is what I think it is, I have to be very careful. PC Fiona Sterling cannot know about this. One wrong step could be fatal.

———

'Any news from Oliver?' Mum asks, when we're back downstairs. She puts a plate of heated lasagne in front of me.

The note is in my back pocket, burning my skin through the material. Meanwhile my mind is racing, and I'm unable to keep down the rising anxiety three words written on a sheet of paper and shoved in my bag have caused me. Shoved in my bag when? By whom? Part of me wants to tell Mum everything, but then she will worry too and since having the children she's seen how much more settled I am. She's getting older and I don't want her making herself ill over worrying about me. I've caused enough hurt in the past. Oliver is my security blanket, but lately the edges are coming loose. I keep my scarred side hidden from everyone; it's safter that way. I try to convince myself the note is unconnected, kids messing about.

'No,' Fiona says.

'I don't want him to know,' I say.

'Of course he must know,' Mum says. 'He has a right to. He's her father.'

'Is everything OK between you and your husband?' Fiona asks, picking up on Mum's sharp tone.

'I've already answered your questions about my marriage. What has that got to do with finding Tilly? Either she wandered off, or somebody has taken her.' My voice catches in my throat. There it is, out there. My deepest fear. Fiona and Mum exchange a look and realisation dawns.

'You think he's got something to do with this?' I look from one to the other. 'That's crazy. Mum, you might not think Oliver is perfect but you know how much he adores the children.'

'I know he wouldn't hurt them, darling, but the police have to look at absolutely everything. It is strange that his phone is off.'

Mum can never quite hide the slight tone of disapproval with which she speaks about my husband, specifically the amount of time he spends with the children. 'And he spends far too much time at work.'

'Mum.' It's all very well for me to criticise my husband, but not other people. Especially in front of a police officer. 'He's always busy at this time of year. But he's due some time off over Christmas. Anyway, he can't possibly have taken Tilly.' The words sound ridiculous spoken aloud. 'He's not even in the country.'

'Exactly my point. He needs to change his priorities. Aside from all this, you look shattered. You're working too hard, aren't you?'

I sigh. 'It's a double-edged sword, Mum. The business has really picked up over the last few months, at the worst possible time.'

I'd started my business by accident, making baby clothes when I was pregnant with the twins, unable to find the exact type of clothes I envisaged my children wearing, my mind full of design ideas. My grandmother had always made her own clothes, and Mum had kept some of the baby dresses she'd made and I wanted to replicate her designs. Friends and acquaintances had praised the clothes I made, asking where I'd bought them and begun placing their own orders once I'd told them I'd made them myself. The business grew organically, and by the time the twins were born, I was fantasising about not going back to work once my maternity leave was up, growing my business, with the eventual aim of opening my own shop. Today has decided me.

'I know, Mum, I'm going to talk to him, as soon as Tilly is home. We need to move away from here. There are too many people around and I don't feel safe. He can't put me off any longer.'

Moving to Prospect Close had been Oliver's idea, and I agreed to compromise. Make no mistake, Prospect Close is wonderful and I've been happy and couldn't ask for a better community to live amongst, counting several of my neighbours as good friends. But it's not where I want to be. Oliver has known from the moment we first met that my dream is to live in the country, a rural hideaway, just me, him and the children. Just like the farmhouse where I spent the first fourteen years of my life, before we moved and everything unravelled. I'm convinced if we'd never left I'd be a completely different person now, not having this threat hanging over me. Hidden away, I'd feel safer. Here in Prospect Close I feel too visible, the way the buildings all face inwards towards the central quadrangle. The windows are like eyes, watching me, waiting to find me out and expose my secret. No matter how good a person I am now, it would only take one person to reveal my sins and expose me to my neighbours and friends.

'Just for a couple of years,' he'd cajoled me, and how could I resist the shiny brochures he laid in front of me, the plan of a brand new luxury complex of a mixture of eight apartments and houses. The small number of dwellings persuaded me, that and knowing it was for a limited period of time. Oliver knew I would be persuaded when I stepped into the extravagant show home with its designer kitchen, the large windows and light-filled rooms. We were young, and it was only for a couple of years. Plus, Oliver had his career to think about.

Oliver had just been offered his promotion in the city bank and it was unusual for someone so young to be offered a managerial position. His star was on the rise; it was too good an opportunity to turn down.

And now it's been five years. The 'couple of years' stretching ever further. Oliver and I need to talk. I've been trying for the last few months. Every time I mention it he manages to wriggle out of having a conversation, and it's possibly this that has driven him to spend more time at work, avoiding a showdown. Driving him away was never my intention. Now, with this note, I can't help wondering whether something more sinister is keeping him away. Or someone.

Ever since the twins were born three and a half years ago

I've been restless, wanting to move away, convinced that someone will recognise me and set about destroying my life. Oliver knows nothing of this, knows nothing of my renewable New Year's resolution that this year will be the one where I take myself out of danger.

Fiona's radio crackles and we all look at her. Hope is keeping me alive. She listens to a male voice but it's impossible to hear what he's saying.

'What is it, any news?'

'We still haven't had any luck tracing your husband. We're currently getting contact details for his colleagues. Otherwise he will get back to the hotel at some point and find our message.' She looks at her phone. 'It's an hour ahead over there so hopefully he'll be back soon. Does your husband keep late hours?'

'Mostly he goes to bed around midnight. But over there who knows?'

'It's a work trip, though, so hopefully not too late,' Mum says.

If only I could be sure it was.

The plate of lasagne is congealed in front of me. I push it away. A text arrives from Sienna.

*Any news?* I text back on autopilot.

*Not yet.*

Tilly going missing.

*ARE YOU SCARED?*

I sink down onto the sofa and cover my face with my hands. I'm absolutely bloody terrified.

# ANONYMOUS

When she lost her daughter, she lost everything. As fast and shocking as a lightning bolt, her ground was hit, cracking the surface and destroying her foundations. When she resurfaced she'd lost everything.

The church gave her comfort, where nothing else could. A cold building full of unknown people, who took her into their warm embrace and strove to fill her with kindness. She read the holy words and tried to forgive those who had sinned against her, but she couldn't do it.

The hole inside her grew larger and she abandoned the church, as she'd abandoned her family and friends when her child was lost. Her world grew smaller, despite the love of her family, and she gave up.

I saw what happened to that woman, the way she lost her own life along with her child's, and understood the tie that binds a mother and daughter. It strengthened my resolve.

Being a parent could never be part of my life plan.

I bided my time.

Until I saw that she dared to conceive, she who didn't

deserve to ever know the love of a child. Once I knew that I devised my plan. Seize her children, and fashion their minds. Take what is most precious for my own and let her see how it feels to lose a part of yourself. To understand what she did to that woman, and to everyone who knew her.

# THREE

A shout in the street brings me out of my trance, then more shouts and a car door slams. Fiona's phone rings. She goes into the hall and Mum and I stand up. Mum puts her arm around me.

'Perhaps they've tracked Oliver down.'

'It's not him I'm worried about.'

Fiona comes back in. 'Some possible good news, but I don't want you to get your hopes up too much. A child fitting Tilly's description has been brought into the station. She's being checked over. I'll know in a couple of minutes for sure.'

Mum and I hug tightly. A loud knocking at the door splits us apart and I run to the door. Fiona gets there before me.

Have they found Tilly?

We all step outside. The police officer on duty outside our house is at the end of the path.

'Stay here please and I'll find out what's going on.' A police car drives into the close. Darkness has filled the sky since Tilly went missing. Asha and Mohammed are outside their house next door, craning their necks to see what's going on.

'Have they found her?' Asha says, wringing her hands. 'Oh please let them have found her.'

Two more police cars pull into the close, their flickering blue lights lighting up the scene. Officers jump out, slam doors and talk into radios. With only the streetlights lit, it's difficult to make out exactly what's going on. My heart rate accelerates. Please let them have found Tilly. Other people come out of their houses, drawn by the unexpected commotion.

'What's going on?' I ask Fiona. 'Tell me. Is it her?' Please let it be her.

'Something's going on that's for sure,' Asha says, holding her cardigan around her.

'Come with me,' Fiona says.

As we hurry across the quadrangle we see Sienna talking to a police officer and we arrive to hear the tail end of the conversation.

'We should have news very soon,' he is saying. 'I'm not at liberty to divulge any details.'

'But we're her friends,' Sienna argues. She gives a tight smile as the police officer is accosted by another concerned individual. 'He won't tell me anything.' I'm surprised by how many people have amassed out here, desperate for news, mobiles lighting up the scene.

'Oh, Harriet.' Everyone turns and stares. A man holds his mobile aloft, anxious not to miss a moment. I want to swipe it from his hand; this isn't entertainment, this is real life. My life.

Suddenly the police officers get busy as another car pulls into the close. The car doors open and a policewoman clambers out, clutching a large bundle. I yell, breaking away from Fiona and run to the woman who is grasping the bundle, which moves and transforms into Tilly, covered in a blanket. I gasp out loud and Fiona puts her hand on my back to steady me. The policewoman holds out the bundle and her reassuring smile is the sweetest thing I've ever seen.

'She's safe and unharmed.'

Then Tilly is in my arms and we look at each other and I check her over and she looks as she always does and best of all she is smiling and then I am too. I hug her close and her warmth becomes mine. My shoulders sink with relief and Mum appears and puts her arms around us.

'They've found her, Mum.' I sob with relief into her shoulder.

A cheer goes up from the crowd, somebody claps and the fear dissolves and the tension snaps. A babble of conversation erupts around us and I can't take my eyes off Tilly. Her face is unblemished and she's smiling.

'Where did you find her?' I ask, my legs suddenly jelly. Sienna appears behind Mum. 'You're still shaking,' she says.

'I've been out of my mind with worry.' It's as if I've been wound up tightly for the past few hours and have suddenly been released. The heaviness leaves my limbs. I look around, marvelling. A television camera crew is parked up behind us and cameras have been flashing ever since the car pulled up. Last time we were all gathered out here in an evening it was Bonfire Night, everyone waiting for fireworks to shoot coloured lights into the air. The tension is as palpable this evening, the same sense of expectation hanging in the air, but tonight faces are tense, tinged with fear, not excitement.

'Does anyone know what happened?' a neighbour asks.

'She's unharmed,' someone says. 'I heard the policeman say so.'

'Let's get her inside,' Fiona says and we are escorted back into our house, as the crowd slowly disperses, people going back into their own lives. Two of the police cars drive away, while another stays stationed outside our house. The reporters follow us, calling out questions, taking photographs of the house. The man with the camera is talking into his phone. Police officers keep them away from us. Sienna follows us.

'Is Oliver back? Do you want me to stay with her?' she asks.

'Thank you, but we need to speak to the family,' Fiona says and I'm relieved. Much as I like Sienna, she will want to talk and probe, and I don't have the energy. 'Her mother is here.'

'I'm so happy for you, and for little Tilly. Can you imagine if she hadn't been found, how everything would have changed around here? We're such a tight community; it would have spoilt everything, having to lock our doors.'

My door is always locked. The worst hasn't happened, and she may think we don't need to be hypervigilant all the time. But we do, I've always known that. I know what can happen if you lose your focus, how a life can change with one mistake.

Fiona is frowning as she closes the front door. 'Are your neighbours always so insensitive?'

I shrug, not caring. I only care about finding out what happened to my daughter. I check her over, but she's unhurt and gives me a smile. I stroke her hair and inhale the peachy smell of her skin. The sweetest smell.

Two more police officers follow us in and close the front door and I breathe a sigh of relief that for now we're all safely locked inside. At moments like these, I have to wonder whether I was right to risk everything by having children. I had underestimated how tight the bond would be and the lengths I would go to in order to protect them. Whoever sent that note will have a battle on their hands.

Mum fetches Tess and brings her downstairs where she is reunited with her sister. They sit on the floor and chatter together. Mum pulls me into a hug and I hold onto her tight, my eyelashes damp, my body enveloped by her softness. Mum's the only person who knows everything, and she will understand how frightened I have been.

She guessed the first time I was pregnant before I had even told Oliver. It was during those heady days when we couldn't bear to spend time apart, and when we were together we wanted to talk and touch and find out everything there was to know about one another. Mum had tried to warn me to take things slowly.

'Be careful,' she'd said, and I didn't need an explanation. We never talked about what had happened, not then and not now. I knew what she meant; she wanted a normal life for me but she was terrified I was going to fall for someone, take them into my confidence and reveal more than could be coped with.

One of the police officers who followed us in sits down with us at the kitchen table and introduces himself as DS Murray. Fiona sits by the children, but I sit where I can watch them at the same time.

'Where did you find her?' Mum asks. My stomach churns with anxiety.

'A woman found her in the woods, not far from here. A Mrs Jennifer Bird. She took her to the nearest police station, which is on Washington Road, at six-thirty. She hadn't heard anything about a child going missing. We're satisfied she's telling the truth.' He flips his notebook open.

'The woods? How did she get over there?'

'We were working on the assumption she wandered over there of her own accord. Is it somewhere you take her?'

'Yes, we quite often go for a walk that way.'

'When Mrs Bird found her she was sitting on the ground playing some sort of game. She seemed quite happy.'

'She does that,' Mum says, rolling her eyes. 'She goes off into her own little world. She's such a dreamy thing.'

I glance over at Tilly, who is laughing at her sister. The relief feels like cooling balm.

'You said you *were* working on the assumption... What do you mean?'

DS Murray picks up his notebook. 'The police officer who was given immediate charge of Tilly says she said that, and I quote, "a nice man took her".'

'What?' I almost jump off my chair. 'What man? That changes everything.'

'We'd like to ask her about it again in your presence if that's alright with you?'

'Of course. I want to know exactly what she's saying.'

'We can come back tomorrow if you think it's too late.'

'Tilly.'

She looks up and toddles over.

'Are you tired?'

She shakes her head.

'Why did you leave the playground?'

She stares at me. The only sound in the room is the kitchen clock ticking.

'A nice man held my hand and we walked in the woods.'

'Do you know this man?' I ask. 'Is he a friend of mine?'

'No. A new man. A nice man.'

'He didn't hurt you?'

'No. A nice man.'

'Why was he nice?'

'We crossed the road and held hands.'

My stomach is twisting at the idea of her holding hands with a stranger. I look to DS Murray for guidance.

'What did he look like, Tilly?'

She shrugs. 'He was big. Nice big man.'

'Nice.' Mum mutters under her breath.

'Bigger than Daddy?' I ask.

She shrugs.

'What was the nice man wearing?'

She shrugs again and rubs her eyes.

'She is tired,' Mum says. 'This should stop.'

DS Murray closes his notebook. 'Of course. Thank you, Tilly. You've been a very brave girl.'

I pick her up and stroke her hair. Her eyes are already closing.

Tess tugs at my jumper. 'Was she hiding in the forest, Mummy?'

Mum and I lock eyes.

'Yes, she was hiding in the forest.'


Mum takes the girls upstairs to put them to bed.

'Thank you for finding her,' I say.

'It's my job. It's the outcome we hoped for. My officers will be doing some door-to-door enquiries and we'll be checking any CCTV and other cameras in the area to see if we can find out who this man is. The doctor checked her over when she first came in and she isn't physically hurt and doesn't seem to have suffered any ill treatment.'

'It's bizarre,' I say. 'Why would someone do this?' An image of the note flits into my mind and my hand drifts to my back pocket. Now is the time to tell them about the note. A cold sensation creeps down my spine. If the threat is real, and refers to what I think it does, then I need to tread very carefully. I pull my hand back.

'I'm afraid we come across many different behaviours that are difficult to fathom, but I promise I will do my best to get to the bottom of this.'

'Thank you.'

He nods. 'I'll leave you to get some sleep.'

My phone rings.

'It's my husband.'

'What's happened?' he says as soon as I connect. 'I've had all these messages and missed calls. They said it was urgent.'

'Everything's OK, the children are safe in bed and Mum is here. Tilly wandered off and we couldn't find her for a while.' I'm aware of the attention of Fiona and DS Murray, who is getting ready to leave.

'She's OK, you say?'

'Yes, safe and well and cheerful. She just got lost. I'll tell you everything later but you don't need to worry.'

'You must have been going out of your mind.'

I grip my mobile and turn away from the police. 'Why didn't you answer your phone?'

'My battery died and I didn't have my charger.'

'Right. When will you be back?'

'Later tomorrow.'

'OK, text me when you know the time.' I hang up. 'My husband,' I say to the police and plonk down on the chair, suddenly swamped with exhaustion. 'His battery died. He's back tomorrow.'

'He's not coming back tonight?' Mum asks.

'There's no point. Tilly's safe and that's all that matters. I didn't want to worry him unnecessarily.'

Mum frowns. 'You need to sleep.'

DS Murray leaves, followed shortly by Fiona. She offers to stay if we need her but I want to be alone with my family now.

'What did Oliver say?' Mum asks, as she makes us some cocoa.

'Not much, but I didn't want to alarm him.'

'Probably sensible. Tilly is fine, thank the Lord. No need to worry him unnecessarily. Although I do wish he was here more to support you. He was such a good parent when they were born, it's unfortunate.'

'Mum, don't. He has to work, you know that.'

Tess was born in hospital after hours of labour, followed a few minutes later by Tilly, every detail the opposite of my ideal birthing scenario, but none of that mattered in the moment. All I wanted was for my babies to be healthy and safe. Oliver was working from home the week they were due, doing very little work and instead attending to me. He was jumpy like a startled cat, wanting to whisk me off to hospital at the slightest twinge. When labour finally happened, in the early hours of the morning, Oliver drove like a maniac to the hospital, his entire focus on me and the needs of our children. When the twins were placed on my chest and I felt their warmth for the first time, Oliver gathered the three of us into his arms. He looked at me and I didn't need words to know he felt that massive love too, that sense that everything we had known in life had completely changed. Our babies now took priority in the world. They united us, bringing us closer than ever.

Oliver had no idea that our children were in jeopardy; he knew nothing about my past and I wanted to keep it that way. Despite coming close, wanting to reveal my soul to him during the early heady days of our relationship, Mum always warned me against it and she was right. I made the correct decision. The revelation from his secretary that he lied about the conference being a one-day affair has got buried underneath the trauma of Tilly. Only now does it come to the fore and demand my attention. If Oliver is having an affair then who knows what secrets he lets slip from his lips. It was a risk I'm so relieved not to have taken.

# FOUR

The Prospect Close WhatsApp group is up and buzzing the following morning. It went quiet last night after Tilly's disappearance out of respect for us and I'm touched by the concern of the neighbours. I messaged them last night to let them know Tilly was safe and well. Sienna and Gabi messaged me privately and I gave them more of an update.

Sienna: *In case you haven't heard Tilly is safe. Harriet and Oliver want to thank all of you for yesterday's support. Got to be careful everyone. Keep hold of your kids just in case.*

Holly: *Such a relief! Thanks hun. I'm keeping Jack strapped to me!! Is coffee time still going ahead?*

Sienna: *I'm still up for it.*

Holly: *Great! See you then.*

There's no chance of a lie-in. Lucy slept through until three and then it's been on and off ever since. The twins wake up full of energy as they do every day. I can't wait for Oliver to get back, although the anticipation is spoilt by the tinge of anxiety that hangs over me since I spoke to his assistant.

I don't want to send the girls to preschool. The note has got under my skin and poisoned my thoughts. I shouldn't let them out of my sight. But Tilly is her usual cheerful self, both girls devour their cereal without any fuss, chattering with excitement about seeing their friends and I manage to get them dressed. We all bundle into the car with enough time to get them to nursery. Not sending them would require too much explanation and I have so much work to do. I grit my teeth and carry on – after all, I've done it for years. Becky's daughter Dolly comes flying across the playground when she sees the twins arrive and I know I've done the right thing carrying on as normal, even though I'd prefer to keep her right where I could see her. When I hand them over to Ms Almond, reassured by the security around the building, I'm grateful for having a bit of time to think about the note and what it could mean.

———

I'm playing with Lucy on the carpet when the doorbell rings. We spend hours together like this, as I did with the girls, missing them dreadfully when they began going to nursery. These hours together are so precious and watching Lucy kicking her legs and gurgling with delight when I tickle her tummy makes my heart sing. It drops when I open the door to a policeman, but he's come to collect a few more details regarding who was in the playground. Lucy wriggles against my hip as I tell the police officer, the young one from last night, the little we saw yesterday afternoon. He takes notes in a small notebook, concentrating hard as he writes. He's been sent to double check some details from yesterday. As I give him a list of the people I saw outside in the quadrangle, I'm making my own mental list of who could have put that note in my bag. It must have happened then. It has to be related to Tilly going missing, otherwise it's a hell of a coincidence.

'Have you had any more thoughts about this "man" she referred to?'

I shake my head. 'But it's worrying me.'

'Try not to worry; we'll let you know when we've checked all the CCTV in the area. She's safe, that's what matters.'

I know I should tell him about the note, but it would mean having to answer questions, and I'm no good at lying. My neck blotches and holding eye contact becomes impossible. He'd see I was hiding something straight away and I can't risk digging all that up again.

The police officer utters some platitudes before thanking me for helping and scuttles off down the path. Someone shouts my name and I look up to see Gabi calling me from her terrace.

'Such a relief about Tilly,' she says. 'Are you busy? Fancy a coffee? You can tell me exactly what happened.'

'OK. I'll just grab Lucy's things.' Talking will help; work will have to wait.

I settle Lucy into her carry basket and make sure everything she needs is in the huge bag full of baby accessories I take everywhere with me, before locking up the house and going next door. Gabi is in the large apartment block next to our house, the block forming one end of the quadrangle. Her duplex apartment is underneath Edward and Martin's penthouse. At this time of the morning her apartment is filled with light, and we sit in her large kitchen, as it's too cold to sit out on the terrace. Lucy's carrier is in the middle of the carpet, where she wriggles around, chatting in her own language. She must be tired after last night. Hopefully she'll get a good couple of hours' sleep in. My intention to be an organised mother with routines for the children goes out of the window in practice. No matter what advice I imbibe from the two shelves of parenting advice books I own goes awry with the reality of having a baby. Any sleep she gets is good when I'm tired. The room is warm. An undecorated pine tree leans against the wall, next to a large cardboard box labelled 'Decorations'. An enormous bunch of red roses is displayed in a vase on the glass coffee table. Gabi's in the kitchen area, pouring coffee into china mugs. I tell her everything that happened last night.

'I'm so sorry I wasn't here,' she says. 'I didn't get back until late.'

'Mum was here – that helped. And Oliver is due back later. These roses are beautiful, Gabs.' I stroke a velvety petal, it feels as lush as it looks, and inhale the rich smell. 'Did you buy them?'

'No,' she says, handing me a mug and setting a tray with the milk and sugar onto the table. 'They arrived half an hour ago.' She's blushing as she sits down.

'Wow. Who from?'

'I don't know. There was no card with them. Honestly, look at these boxes; I'm so disorganised as usual,' she says. 'I took the day off with the intention of decorating my tree, but somehow the morning has slipped away from me.'

'Late night, was it?' I raise an eyebrow and she smiles, her cheeks flushing pink.

'You could say that.'

'You must be exhausted after the weekend. How was it?'

'It was great. Already it seems like ages ago. How was Tilly today?'

'She was perfectly normal, as if nothing had happened. She wanted to go to preschool so I let her. Security there is excellent.'

'I was so relieved when I got your text. It must have been terrible for all you parents. If anything had happened you'd all be scared to let your children out of your sight.'

'Exactly.'

*I never let my children out of my sight.*

Other than the tree and decorations, Gabi's flat is immaculate as usual. The surfaces gleam, the cabinets are sparkling white and the chrome beautifully polished. Gabi matches her kitchen, looking just as polished as the chrome in her denim jumpsuit, styled with a large leather belt. Her long chestnut-brown hair is pulled back in a sleek ponytail and she wears silver hoop earrings. For a day off. But this is Gabi, who's seen me at my worst, and today's ribbed polo neck and wrinkled jeans certainly isn't my worst. At least I'm clean and free of baby sick and spilled food for once. Purely luck, given how rushed breakfast was.

While Gabi makes me a Nespresso, the comforting drone of the coffee machine makes me wish for a second I was in her position, living the single life without all the responsibilities hanging over my head. Immediately I check myself; I wouldn't be without my children for anything, and I wouldn't be without Oliver either. I can't be losing him, but if he's having an affair... He wouldn't do that to me, surely, not with Lucy being so young. Throughout my pregnancy he couldn't do enough for me; we were so close, talking about our hopes and dreams for the future. When I went into labour he was ridiculously excited and terrified, forgetting to put his shoes on as he rushed out to the car to drive me to hospital. Would the anxiety about my past still be happening if I was childless? That's the question that is haunting me. Have I tempted fate, by daring to allow myself a normal family life, a fear I have never been able to chase away, ever since I first looked at those two lines on the pregnancy test? Me, pregnant.

*How dare you?*

'Harriet! Are you listening?'

'Sorry.'

'I said I only have soya milk. Will that do?'

'Sure, whatever.'

'Are you OK? You looked like you'd seen a ghost for a minute there.'

'Yes, I'm fine. I can't help thinking about Tilly, that's all.'

'That's understandable.'

Gabi brings the coffees over.

'There's plenty of CCTV around to capture her movements. They could check with residents too, given the vantage point we all have from our balconies.'

'Yes, they're on it at the moment. They were doing house-to-house visits this morning. That's a good point, though, especially the penthouse terraces; Edward was there at the time and Elliott organised a search before the police came. I guess we're lucky to have him.' Elliott is the headmaster of the nearby independent school that all the children from the development attend, both nursery and primary. He lives in one of the two penthouses. He's friendly enough if you pass him in the street but avoids actively participating in anything organised in the close.

She sips her coffee and gives a contented sigh. 'It's a shame about your nanny,' she says, 'I liked Kate.'

'Me too. I thought we were friends, despite the age difference. That's why the way she left is so strange.'

'What do you mean?'

'Well, I had no warning. Everything was normal. She was fine in the morning, got the kids their breakfast and took them off to preschool. I was meeting a friend for lunch and she wanted to meet Lucy so I took her out with me, and I collected the girls on the way back. When I got home all Kate's stuff was gone and she sent me a text saying she had an emergency at home and was sorry but she'd had to quit. Obviously I was concerned for her, never mind anything else, and I've called her and sent texts but apart from once to tell me not to worry she hasn't got back to me. It's so odd.'

I drink some coffee. It's bitter and makes me flinch.

'It's bound to be man trouble,' Gabi says. 'Are you getting a replacement?'

'I've contacted the agency but no luck so far. I don't suppose you know anyone? I've just had a big order of dresses for a new client and I can't imagine how I'll manage without help at home.'

Gabi shakes her head. 'I'd ask around Prospect Close. That's great news about the order.'

'I know, and I shouldn't get so stressed.'

'How's Oliver?'

'He's fine, he's due back tonight, but…' I fiddle with my hair, wishing I wasn't having these thoughts.

'What is it? He went away for a work thing, didn't he?'

'He did, it was for what I thought was a weekend conference but… something strange happened.'

'Oh?' Gabi raises an eyebrow.

I explain about the phone call yesterday with his assistant. 'I'm sure it's all innocent, but she mentioned other staff had stayed on and there are some very attractive women in his team.'

'You think he's cheating?'

'It's got me thinking, that's all.' I hesitate, my gaze settling on the roses and to my horror, my eyes fill with tears. 'Oliver hasn't bought me flowers for ages. It's not that we don't get on, more that we never have any time together. Oliver has this glamorous part of his life which he leads in London, wining and dining his clients and then he's back to drudgery out in the sticks with me and three small children, who require a humongous amount of attention. How can I possibly compete with that? He's bound to meet other younger, more beautiful woman all the time.'

'Stop torturing yourself,' Gabi says. 'You're an attractive woman; you're just tired out with the children. Drink some coffee and let's think about this. You don't know anything for sure. It's not as if he's done it before, is it?'

My face drops.

She looks uncomfortable and sighs. 'Oh. I'm so sorry, I didn't know.'

'If it was the first time then maybe I wouldn't have jumped to that conclusion.' I drink some coffee. 'It's happened before, you see, a long time ago and we went through a difficult time.' I stare into my cup, my throat tight.

'Do you want to tell me about it?' She leans forward, her expression kind.

'The last time – at least the last time I know about – was just before we moved here.'

It was more than five years ago now which is why I'd dared to believe he had changed – a new house, a new start. Plus, his career had been on the ascent and with each increasing responsibility I figured he barely had time for his family, let alone anyone else. It was also before we had children. I could come up with all number of excuses to justify his behaviour and my subsequent decision to stay with him. I'd found out after his other woman, a young secretary from his office – such a cliché – telephoned me to tell me they'd been sleeping together for six months and she thought it only fair I should know as he was about to leave me. Oliver broke down when confronted, admitted everything and we had many long, emotional heart-to-hearts, saw a marriage guidance counsellor and after about a year we were in a much better place. The secretary left the company, and I believed Oliver when he vowed it would never happen again, and swore he would never leave me. For ages after I was on constant alert for signs, but then we had the children and that gave me a new focus.

'Oliver loves being a father, but for the last two years since his work has been so full-on, I must have missed the signs. I doubt we'll survive this.' Putting my thoughts into words eases the pressure on my chest. 'I won't go through that again, not now, especially as we have a new baby together. I can't bear to think he would do that to us.'

'Ask him straight out when he gets back. Put your mind at rest; there's no point in letting it fester.'

I hesitate. 'Not until I've got more evidence. But I won't let him get away with it.'

'Pay me a decent rate and I'll follow him to London; I wouldn't mind hanging out in the big city for a bit.'

'Idiot.' I'm grateful to her for trying to make me laugh.

'Have you talked any more about moving?'

Since the arrival of the note the move has been back on my mind. If Oliver knew the real reasons behind my wanting to move to somewhere more remote, he'd understand why I'd be prepared to sacrifice my friends, this life I've built up. Without this knowledge, he can't understand my reasons. If he's having an affair, however, and he wants to make our marriage work, then taking himself out of our present community could help the problem, give him less temptation.

'No, we haven't had a chance to talk much lately, but I'm hoping we'll get time over Christmas; he'll be home for a couple of weeks.'

'You're always making excuses for him. Doesn't he know how hard it is for you at the moment with three little ones, an up-and-coming business and no childcare?'

'Mum helps when she can.'

'That's not the point. They're his kids too; he should be pulling his weight, not swanning around the city eating fancy lunches on expenses and drinking champagne.'

It helps to be able to share my worries about him with her in a way I can't with anyone else. We keep each other's secrets. Or some of them. I consider the red roses. Gabi sidestepped my questions about them, as she always does when I probe her about her love life. And I haven't had a chance to ask her about her weekend away. But I won't push her. Everyone has a right to privacy. I should know. Some things are just too dangerous to reveal.

*ARE YOU SCARED?*

I can't tell her about the note. I can't tell anyone about that. But what I can do is find out who sent it, and what it means.

Although I have a horrible feeling I already know.

# FIVE

I text Oliver.

*What time are you due back?*

*Eight thirty*

*Still in Paris?*

*?? Where else?!*

*Nadine mentioned you'd stayed on after the conference.*

*Nadine? Yes, a few of us did. Why are you speaking to Nadine?
How's Tilly today?*

*She's fine.*

My sister-in-law Holly has taken the twins back with Jack to
her house after nursery and Lucy is asleep. Oliver and Ben are
super close, and at first I'd been wary about living in such close

proximity to them, but having him and his family so close has been great since the children were born. I take a cup of tea out onto the terrace before I cook some food for Oliver's return later. There's no guarantee we'll get to sit and eat it without interruption but it's worth a try.

My skin goosepimples sitting out here despite the shawl I drape around my shoulders. I pull it tighter around me. A half moon glows in the dark sky and the quadrangle below is calm, the streetlights illuminating the empty space, this focal point of our community. It's hard to believe that this time yesterday a crisis was unfolding. Looking down at the quadrangle makes it easier for me to map out the scene from last night – who was there, who stood where... *Which of you did it, got yourself into position and slid that note in my bag?* I'm cold despite the shawl.

Sienna rushing over to me last night. How close was she, did she slip her hand in my bag? Becky and Ryan were there, Asha and her children in the midst of it all. Edward was there also, reassuring people. Edward is a natural leader, like Elliott; they're the ones I'd look to for reassurance, they instinctively know what to do. I should know appearances can be deceptive. Did anyone come up behind me? My memories are blurry; my mind was in panic mode, focused on Tilly. That's the problem, the terror of losing a child hitting me like a bolt of lightning. One arm around Tess hugging her close, much like I'm hugging my shawl now. Warm bodies as opposed to soft cashmere. Asha was with her children in the same place, right where I could see her, looking after Tess and the man... John, was it? His children too. Did anyone come too close? Martin, the hand on my shoulder, the squeeze of reassurance, everything in me screams *no*. Martin is my friend.

Martin, the kindly designer with the fluffy beard and gentle smile, we've always got on, but it's only since he started coming to book club that we've seen each other outside of that group. We often go for coffee in the high street. Lately, I've been confiding in him more since Oliver is away so much. No, it can't be Martin.

I visualise last night again; so many friends and neighbours were here, plus other bystanders who'd wandered over, attracted by the commotion. Obviously Elliott was organising the search and I wonder about the woman who tagged on the end. She seemed to have some kind of beef with Elliott and she hadn't paid me any interest. We were all so preoccupied with the unfolding drama that anyone could have come up too close to me and I wouldn't have noticed.

Looking down over the quadrangle, empty of bodies save for a black cat running across the playground, I'm struck by the contrast to last night – people crying, shouting, police sirens, fear. Me in the midst of it all, the focus of attention. Exactly where I don't want to be.

Shaking my head, I go back inside, locking the door behind me. If only I could lock the fear outside too.

I check in with Holly before I start cooking.

'Everything OK with the twins?'

'Of course. They're rolling on the floor at the moment, bags of energy as usual. How are you feeling after yesterday?'

'Shaken up, even though she was found. When will you bring the twins back?'

'Ben will drop them back at about seven, OK? I bet you can't wait to see Oliver. I heard he was away at the weekend. I hope he's pulling his weight.'

'Of course he is.'

Why does everyone feel the need to point this out to me? Holly thinks Oliver is away far too much, but Ben won't hear a word said against his older brother. Oliver is only doing his job, after all; he will argue that he's working all hours to keep us in this luxurious lifestyle and accuse me of being ungrateful. He's done it before.

'Do you know how lucky we are to live in a place like this?

Some people would give anything to be where we are.' I picture her standing in front of her bifold doors, her feet sinking into the luxurious carpet.

Oh I do know, that's why I do as much for the local community as I can, to atone for my past behaviour, but since the arrival of the note I'm beginning to think some people would do *anything* to make me pay, no matter how I've behaved since.

———

Ben waves as he crosses back to his house, the twins safely deposited. How much does he know about what Oliver gets up to when he's away? My stomach cramps as it always does when I'm anxious. He'd made a comment once, years ago when Oliver had recently been appointed to his role and hadn't yet started the occasional trip abroad.

'You know what they say about Frenchmen having mistresses? I wonder if it's true. You don't want Oliver becoming too French in his customs when he goes over there,' Ben had joked. 'You know what a Francophile he is.' Oliver had done a degree in French and business studies, later qualifying as an accountant. Landing a job at the London branch of a French bank using his language skills had long been an ambition of his, and he swore he didn't resent sacrificing a life abroad for me. He loved working in London, but lately I wasn't so sure about it, sensing an increasing distance between us, and not just a geographical one.

I hadn't found Ben's joke about the mistress at all funny, given the affair Oliver had had. It had stuck in my head, cropping up on unwelcome occasions, whenever I was feeling threatened. Like now. I didn't expect to enjoy living at Prospect Close so much, but moving might be the only answer to resolving the problem. Persuading Oliver, however, is proving difficult.

The twins are tired after spending time with their their cousin Jack. Bath time runs smoothly, and they both fall asleep mid story. I check Tilly closely for any signs of distress but she is the same as she always is. Lucy takes longer to settle and it isn't until she's finally stopped grizzling and I'm rocking her to sleep that I catch sight of the clock. It's almost nine. Oliver said he'd be back around eight-thirty. Sitting here in the semi-darkness with Lucy, the sound of her regular breathing comforts me, and I wish I could preserve this moment forever, warmed by my love for my children, which burns fierce like a flame.

I creep downstairs, my eyes heavy, desperately hoping Lucy will stay asleep for a while. I check my phone, but Oliver hasn't texted to say he'll be late. He knows about Tilly; OK, I played down the scale of her disappearance but even so, I'd have expected him back early if anything.

*Where are you?*

He doesn't reply, but if he's on the train, reception can be patchy. I try and call him but get his voicemail. My stomach rumbles. The casserole is in the oven and I turn the heat down low so as not to spoil it. There's half a bottle of white wine in the fridge and I pour myself a glass, resisting the urge to snack. I don't want to spoil my appetite and it's only now I realise how much I've been looking forward to seeing Oliver, sitting down with him and having a proper conversation. Last time I attempted to talk to him, Lucy woke up and refused to settle after that. Oliver says I should leave her alone but leaving her to cry gives me physical pain. The children always come first and I'd expect him to feel the same. The following morning he'd been back off to work again.

I'll give him half an hour, otherwise I'll eat.

During that time I send a message to the Prospect Close WhatsApp group asking if anyone knows of any nannies who are looking for work. I'm loath to place an ad; I want to be able to vet whoever is going to come into our house carefully. If anyone should know what can happen if you leave your children in the wrong hands, it's me. Tears prickle behind my eyes and I drain my wine and deposit my glass in the sink. No more of that, or I'll melt into a mess of self pity, stress catching up with me. My stomach roars again and my head pinches with the beginnings of a headache. I need food. Oliver still hasn't been in touch and I take out the casserole, slamming the oven door. I'm not waiting any longer.

Once I've eaten, I switch the television on and scroll through the channels, finally settling on a wildlife documentary which doesn't require much concentration. A lion is stalking a wildebeest, the poor animal oblivious to the slavering creature behind it. I try Oliver again. He picks up. Finally.

'Where are you? Why haven't you been in touch?'

'I'm having a nightmare. We got delayed for over an hour, stuck at the Gare du Nord.'

*We?*

'Everyone had to get off the train because of a security alert. Pretty terrifying, I must admit, the gendarmes herding everyone off with machine guns strapped to their waist. We had to wait for another train and it took an hour before they cleared the replacement to leave. We've just got through the tunnel. Your message has only just come through. I won't be home for a couple of hours, and that's if the train from London is on time.'

He sounds exhausted and immediately I regret going on the attack.

'It sounds awful, poor you.'

'How are the children?'

'Tired out. They've been at Ben's, playing. They're all asleep now. I've already eaten as it was getting late. I'll keep your food in the oven.'

'I've had a sandwich. I'm so knackered I'll probably just crash out when I get back.'

'OK.'

When he's gone, I let out a huge sigh. It's not the first time this kind of thing has happened but before I've had Kate to complain to and spend the evening with. The house feels so empty this evening. I try and call her, hoping this time she'll pick up. Her lack of communication is worrying me. It's so unlike the Kate I've grown to see as a friend. I click off when I get her voicemail, pride kicking in. I've left several already. For whatever reason, she's not interested in getting in touch. Time to stop wallowing and put my energy into finding a replacement.

I'm in bed, just falling asleep when I hear the front door open and the sound of Oliver moving around downstairs. Footsteps, cupboard doors opening, the creak of the fridge door. The murmur of his voice. My limbs are too heavy to get out of bed and I drift off wondering who he's talking to so late at night.

# SIX

The sound of running water wakes me. Oliver is in the shower. The events of the previous night come back to me. When Lucy's crying woke me in the early hours of the morning, he was fast asleep beside me. I fed Lucy and then we both dozed off on the couch, until a cough startled me awake. It sounded like Tilly. I settled Lucy into her cot, praying she'd stay asleep and I checked in on the twins before going back to bed.

The noise of the shower stops. A rush of annoyance sweeps over me, remembering last night, waiting for news of Oliver's return. He appears, a towel around his waist, rubbing his hair dry with another.

'Hello,' he says, leaning in to give me a kiss. Water drops onto my front. My nightdress is clammy against my skin. 'I missed you last night. Sorry it was so late.'

'I'm surprised you're up so early.'

'I've got to go into the office.'

'What time?'

'Ten.'

'Oh Oliver, I never see you. We really need to talk.'

'What about?'

'Everything. The nanny situation, for a start. And aside from all that, it would be nice to have a conversation. I haven't even told you exactly what happened the day before yesterday.'

'You can tell me now.'

Feet patter outside the room just as I finish telling him about the events with Tilly.

'Why didn't you tell me a search was going on? That's huge. You made it seem she'd wandered off for five minutes.'

'I didn't want to worry you when you were so far away. The police called you; didn't you realise then? Besides, by the time they got hold of you she was safe.'

'I guess you're right. Obviously I'd have come straight back if she had still been missing. I looked in on her last night and she was fast asleep.'

'Mummy.' Tess appears in the doorway.

'Yes, darling.'

She squeals when she sees Oliver. 'Daddy!' She rushes at him and he swoops her up in his arms.

'How's one of my favourite girls?' he asks, grinning. I can't help smiling, despite the vanishing opportunity for a conversation. The girls adore their father, and like me they want to make the most of him when he's home. I didn't sign up to be a single parent but that is how family life feels at the moment. Something has got to change.

Tilly sidles into the room on hearing her dad's voice and Lucy wails from her cot. I hug Tilly tightly, before I go and fetch Lucy, snuggling my nose into her warm body, a rush of love overtaking me.

'Come and see Daddy,' I say.


Oliver takes the girls downstairs to set the table for breakfast.

'Let's see who can eat as many soldiers as me,' he says, making them giggle. He switches the radio on and sings deliberately off key, and they beg him to stop. He settles them at the table and makes boiled eggs and soldiers for the girls while I feed Lucy. Tess is overexcited and keeps up an incessant babble, wanting her dad's complete attention. He entertains them by slicing his own toast into soldiers and pretending to dip it into their eggs, making them giggle. Tilly concentrates on chewing her toast, taking her time, while Tess eats hers at breakneck speed, smearing butter all over her mouth.

'Look at you, messy pup,' Oliver says, trying to wipe her face with kitchen roll.

'That tickles,' she squeals, chuckling and pushing him away.

'I'll drop them off on the way to the station,' he says, 'leave you with Lucy.' He takes her out of the chair for a cuddle. 'You're right that we need to sort out a new nanny. Have you asked around?'

'Yes, no luck so far.'

'I'll mention it at work, see if any of the guys know anyone.'

I take the calendar down from the wall, turning to this week.

'Let's have a catch-up when you're back,' I say.

'OK. Don't forget I'm hoping to get leave over Christmas.'

'Christmas is about three weeks away. I thought next Wednesday; I'll see if Becky can have the children. Failing that I'll ask Mum. We could go out for a meal? We haven't done that for ages and it would be nice to have a proper chat.'

'Wednesday is squash night. You know that.'

'You can miss it for once, surely? It's the only night I can do this week because of being without a nanny.'

'I'd rather not. It's the only exercise I get, plus I get to catch up with Ben.'

'You mean seeing your brother is more important than catching up with your wife? He's only over the road so it's not as if you hardly ever get to see him.' I make my comment sound light-hearted, but I can't help being disappointed that he doesn't make more effort with me. Any little gesture proving he still loves me is welcome this morning. He wasn't very forthcoming about the weekend when I asked him about it and I can't help wondering why. 'I wouldn't ask if Kate was here, but being without her this week has made me think now might be a good time for a change and think about moving. We've been here five years now and you promised me...'

He sighs. 'I'm not sure it's the right time for me work-wise. I certainly don't want to discuss it now.'

'*Now* is the first conversation we've had in person all week. That's exactly my point.'

Lucy's face crumples at my raised voice, and she starts to cry.

'That's all we need,' Oliver says, jiggling her up and down to try and placate her. 'You take her while I get the girls ready,' he says. 'Come on, you two, let's see who can get ready as quickly as me.' The twins scramble to get out of their chairs, the legs scraping against the floor, the squeal making me flinch. Oliver hands Lucy to me and kisses me. His hair smells of mint. 'We'll catch up very soon, I promise. I can't wait until my Christmas leave starts.' Lucy stops crying as soon as she's in my arms.

The next hour is taken up with looking after Lucy and we play with her plastic bricks until she loses interest and settles on her play mat gurgling happily, waving her arms at the bees which bounce around on the mobile above her head. Once the twins have gone to nursery I can appreciate the calm of the house. Oliver's already told me he'll be back late this evening. I fetch the washing basket and sort out clothes for the washing. Oliver's clothes from the weekend are on the top of the basket and I sort out piles for whites and different colours. Oliver's white shirt is at the top and as I unfold it and shake it out, I notice a red mark on the collar. Has he cut himself shaving? After closer inspection, I freeze, peering at the mark to make sure. It's lipstick. I sniff the collar, inhaling a hint of a familiar aftershave, and is that something else I detect? A faint musky scent, similar to one of my perfumes, only I haven't worn any perfume for ages. I hurl the shirt at the wall, a futile gesture as it carries no weight and flops to the floor.

I knew it.

Oliver is having an affair. Again.

I need proof. Who she is, where she is and how long it's been going on.

I abandon the washing, put Lucy in her carrier and take her upstairs. Oliver has left the suit he was wearing yesterday out for dry cleaning. In the pocket I find a receipt. Careless. Or arrogant? Does he think I'm so out of my depth in my current nanny-less state that I won't even notice? The receipt is for a Parisian brasserie on the Champs-Élysées, at 7pm last night. When he was supposedly stuck on a Eurostar or at the station. Lying to me, despite knowing the Tilly situation. How could he? I wrench at the material, tempted to try and rip it apart, but manage to talk myself out of it. *Don't do anything rash. Take control of the situation; he won't get away with it this time.*

A lump sticks in my throat and tears are welling in my eyes. So much for my bravado; I'm crushed.

Part of me wants to shove the shirt in Oliver's face the minute I see him and demand an explanation, but what if I've got it wrong? I need to be sure of my facts. By challenging him, I risk everything. Other than Oliver working too hard, I am comfortable in the security of my marriage, having a good home and settled routine for the children. Divorce would mean breaking our little family apart and a custody battle. What if things got nasty, and Oliver hired solicitors to delve into my past? I shiver at the thought. Not only would I lose him but I'd lose the children and the thought makes my throat seize up and I can't breathe. It's not just losing the children but the thought of losing Oliver that devastates me. I love him and hope I've got this all horribly wrong.

To take my mind off it, I follow up the few remaining leads I have left to try and find a replacement nanny, but to no avail. From where I'm seated at the kitchen table it's like sitting in the centre of a junkyard. Oliver is great at entertaining the children but he causes chaos in his wake. There is stuff everywhere. Kate was contracted to do some cleaning too. Sighing, I set about cleaning the room from top to bottom, knowing it will make me feel better.

An hour later the kitchen is pristine and Lucy is crying. Cleaning didn't stop me worrying, and I can't stand being in the house any longer. I strap Lucy into her baby sling, begging her to stop pummelling me with her sturdy legs and arms. It's distressing seeing her so agitated, and I talk to her in a soothing voice, desperate for her to calm down. Her cheeks are rosy red and her throat must be sore from crying so much. Seeing her in such discomfort tears me apart. We walk outside into the quadrangle and cross over towards the play area. It's been relatively quiet since Tilly disappeared. Ryan appears on the path coming towards me. Lucy's crying has subsided to a whimper, and we exchange a few words.

'How are you all doing?' he asks. 'I'm so sorry you had to go through all that.'

I hug Lucy tighter against my chest.

'We're OK, now, thanks. She's unhurt, that's what matters.'

'And is she OK? Has she said anything about where she went?'

'She wandered away and a lady found her.' I shiver at the thought of her crossing the main road.

He cranes his head as if trying to get a glimpse of Lucy, who's snuggled into my chest now.

'How's the little one? Lucy, is it?'

'Yes. I've just got her off to sleep. She's hard work today, lovely though she is. I can't believe she's actually stopped crying. It's hard when they can't tell you what the matter is. I'd do anything to make her feel better, but when you don't know what it is...' I raise my hands in a helpless gesture.

It's good to be out in the fresh air and I need some milk so set off in the direction of the shop. My mind inevitably turns to Oliver and what he was up to in Paris last weekend. Ben's comment about the French mistress has been lodged in my head ever since I sorted the washing. There's something slightly lofty about the word 'mistress', giving the woman a status in life. I'm all for empowering women, but when it directly affects you it's different. Have there been other mistresses and I just didn't notice? Particularly when the girls were small, that was such an unbelievably stressful time. Magical, but they occupied me totally, I could barely stay awake let alone keep tabs on what Oliver was doing. I just didn't allow my mind to even consider that a new father would do such a thing, as devoted to the three of us as he seemed to be. No, I'm sure this new affair is the first since the one with his secretary, and he's kept his promise – until now.

I'm so engrossed in my thoughts that I don't see the protruding paving stone until my toe slams against it, causing me to stumble over the uneven slab, and for a few terrifying seconds I do everything I can to regain my balance and stop myself falling over and crushing Lucy. My chest seizes up with panic. The sudden jolt wakes her and she lets out a loud wail. I'm shaking all over at how close I came to falling and I lean against the wall of the park shelter and try to control my breath.

'Are you alright there?'

The voice startles me.

'I didn't mean to make you jump.' It's Martin, and I'm so relieved to see him I burst into tears. Lucy is screaming now, her little fists curled up hard in the air and she drums her feet against me, arching her back.

'Let me help,' Martin says, seeing my distress. 'I saw you trip just then, no wonder you're so shocked. Edward's already complained twice about these uneven paving stones. They're so dangerous, especially for pushchairs and small children running about.' He takes my elbow and guides me to the bench, where I unstrap Lucy.

'You must think I'm pathetic.' I loosen the papoose, desperate to get Lucy out and make her more comfortable. 'And what with Tilly, the other night... It's not about the fall, although that was a huge shock; I thought I was going to squash Lucy.' I wipe my eyes, so relieved it's Martin and hadn't happened a few seconds earlier when I was with Ryan. Becky is such a natural, competent mother, I can't imagine her in this situation. 'She's been crying for ages and I came out to try and get her to stop. She'd just dropped off when I fell. Now look at her. What is it, Lucy darling? Are you hungry?' I jiggle her up and down. 'She shouldn't be.'

'Shall I take her? You know how my beard fascinates her.' He raises an eyebrow. 'It's worth a shot.' I hand my wriggling child over, desperate to try anything. Maybe it's me she doesn't like; maybe she can sense what a bad person I am deep inside no matter how much love I bestow on her. I shiver.

'There, there,' Martin says, beaming at her and she immediately stops crying and grabs hold of his bushy brown and white beard. 'Ouch, you little urchin. That's what you were after all along. You'll have to get Oliver to grow a beard. It works wonders.'

I smile, relieved that she's stopped and that Martin is such easy company. 'Shall we take your mummy over to the café and buy her a cup of tea? And a large piece of chocolate cake, which I know she likes very much. It's time you learned how to talk so you can tell her what the matter is; you're not giving her much to go on and she's a very good mummy, I know she is.'

'Thanks,' I say, as we head for the café, which is five minutes' walk away from Prospect Close. We sit down at a table outside. 'I didn't know you were such a natural with children.'

'I love them,' he says. 'Not enough to want any of my own – for which Edward is heartily relieved – but other people's are wonderful. My niece Kelly was such an adorable baby, but that was the last baby in my family and she's sixteen now. Speaking of Kelly, she lives just in that street there' – he points to a side street just across from the main road – 'and she's an experienced babysitter. If you're interested, I'd recommend her. You look as if you could do with a night out with that dashing husband of yours. Kelly could stay at ours after, so you wouldn't even have to worry about her getting back home. Even though it's only five minutes away, it's not a nice walk in the dark.'

'I can't help thinking about Tilly when you say that. That's the area she wandered off to. It really shook me up.'

'Me too. You have to be so careful these days.'

Stella from the café appears with two slices of cake and a pot of tea and a bottle of tap water. Lucy is sitting on Martin's lap and I take charge of pouring tea, relieved to cover up the surge of anxiety the thought of a babysitter gives me. An image flashes through my mind, a woman shouting, crying.

'That's very kind of you, but Oliver and I barely get time for a conversation at the moment, let alone an evening out together.' My pulse quickens, remembering the incriminating shirt.

'Well, the offer's there if you want it.'

The slab of cake on my plate looks enormous, and I cut it into small pieces, my throat suddenly thick with emotion. Tears prickle at my eyes.

'You're in shock,' Martin says. 'Let me pour you some water. You had a bit of a scare there so I'd be surprised if you weren't.'

I drink a glass of water, which soothes my throat. 'Excuse

me for a minute, I'm just going to the bathroom.' I force a laugh. 'I need to sort myself out. Are you alright with Lucy?'

'Sure, you go ahead.'

A woman is staring at me as I make my way to the bathroom but she averts her gaze as I pass her table. I'm not surprised I'm attracting attention, looking as if I'm about to burst into tears. I splash my face with lots of water and pat it dry with a paper towel, gazing at my flushed cheeks in the mirror. My fringe is so long – I must make an effort and try and get to the hairdresser. Sienna has an excellent hairdresser who comes to her house; I'll ask her tomorrow. I feel better for the breather and once I re-join Martin my appetite has returned and Lucy has fallen asleep. The cake is delicious and the rush of sugar is just what I need. That and Martin's easy conversation. He tells me about the Christmas party they're planning to hold in the penthouse. 'Edward will have finished his latest renovations by then,' he says. 'No doubt he'll find another project to start in the new year.'

A queue is forming at the counter and we decide to make a move. As I gather my bag, I sense that someone is watching me. I look up and lock eyes with the woman who I noticed earlier. I turn away from her.

'Don't look now but there's a woman over by the bathroom,' I say in a low voice to Martin. 'Do you know her?'

'No,' he says, when we're outside the café. 'Should I?'

'She seemed to be watching us, that's all. I thought she might know you.'

'She looks vaguely familiar,' he says. 'Maybe I've seen her around the area. I use this café a lot. Or she could just be watching Lucy; she's very cute.'

The thought of someone watching my baby makes me want to bolt home and lock the door, and I can't shift this sense of unease. When I get back home and put Lucy into her carrier to sleep, I go round the house making sure all the doors and windows are closed, my mind constantly returning to the note. I lie down on the sofa, my hand rocking Lucy's carrier, close my eyes. Exhaustion sweeps through my body. Weeks of broken nights combine with the discoveries I've made today about Oliver, and with the threat contained in the note; I try to block out my thoughts. Images flicker behind my closed eyelids, a baby crying without making any sound, tiny fists clenched and twisted face, a girl's face, her sweet looks marred by a snarl. Adults running, flashing lights. My stomach twists and I bolt towards the downstairs bathroom, make it just in time to empty my guts into the toilet bowl. I stare at my bloodshot eyes in the mirror.

A babysitter, a young, irresponsible girl, is out of the question.

# SEVEN

Later that afternoon after I'd collected the children from preschool, I spent a quiet evening at home and was asleep in bed by the time Oliver got home. The following morning is the street's regular coffee morning. I'm half expecting the café to be full this morning, our usual table taken by another group, the young mothers from the estate across town, throwing glances and sneering looks our way. 'The Yummy Mummies', they call us, hardly original, but there's a sense of resentment towards those of us who live in Prospect Close, those lucky enough to be able to afford a property here. The queue snaked around the block when the last house and two-bedroom flats were released for prospective buyers. Becky offered way over the asking price, determined to get the one remaining house. She'd been single at the time, pregnant with Dolly, having recently split with the baby's father, and she wanted stable housing for her daughter, plus the school opposite had an outstanding reputation. Her parents had helped with the purchase.

'It's like being back in school,' she'd told us, when she'd first joined our Prospect coffee group which Sienna had set up as soon as she'd moved in. Once a week a group of us meet for coffee on Wednesday mornings in the village high street. The group is open to anyone who can make it. Unfortunately, Gabi is always at work, hence the group has free licence to discuss her rumoured affair. It puts me in an awkward position. The group can be quite judgemental, despite their claims to being open-minded.

Becky's one of the most reliable attendees, ever since that first time she joined us and fitted in like a comfortable slipper. She almost makes me feel inadequate as a mother; she's only in her twenties with a wise old head on her shoulders.

Sienna and Asha are already there, Sienna's at the counter while Asha is fetching a couple of additional chairs for the long wooden table we usually sit at. They must be expecting a few more – I wasn't sure whether anyone would turn up today after this week's events. Wanting to keep up with the gossip, the cynic in me thinks. Sienna beckons me over from the counter and gives me a big hug. 'I wasn't sure you'd come.'

'I'm carrying on as normal. Nothing happened after all.'

I wish I could believe that, though.

'Asha and I are going to the gym after, why don't you come?'

'I'm not dressed for it, and besides, I've got Lucy,' I say, stating the obvious.

'That doesn't matter, there's a creche there. You'll be fine in that jumpsuit, and they have mats there you can use. Please come, we haven't had a good old natter for ages.'

'That's kind, but it's OK. I'm not really in the mood for exercise. And I'd probably need to check out the creche first before leaving Lucy there.'

'Honestly, you do fuss.'

I try not to let my irritation show. *Wait till you have children.* Immediately I feel churlish. She's only being friendly, and being pushy is in her nature.

'We can catch up now over coffee.'

'Fine,' she says, her lips pursed. 'What can I get you?'

I ask her to get me a flat white and a piece of lemon cake. I feel a bit deflated as I push the buggy over to the table. It was nice of her to ask me and somehow I appear to have offended her. I wish Gabi wasn't at work so she could join us. I'm most comfortable in her company. She's only ever made it to one of these when she had a week off. Hopefully, Martin will turn up. Lucy is asleep and I move a chair so that I can park her next to me.

'Hi,' I say to Asha. She's wearing baggy yellow harem pants and has her yoga mat beside her.

'Hello, Harriet.' She flashes me a smile. 'Isn't Lucy adorable? It's good to see you; we weren't sure you would come. How are you doing?'

'I'm OK,' I say, 'and so is Tilly, that's the most important thing. We thought it was important to carry on as normal.'

'How have you been since the other night? You were so brave.'

'I didn't feel brave, I was terrified. But Tilly is unhurt and that's what matters.'

'I can't stop thinking about her, how lucky she was. I had to get a grip of myself. I didn't want to let the kids out of my sight, but as Mo says, ours are old enough to know what they should and shouldn't do. I can't mollycoddle them forever. If mine were your age...'

'Tilly is safe, don't forget.' *And Mum calls me paranoid.*

'Of course, I'm sorry. I bet you're sick of talking about it.' She looks around the café. 'Becky should be joining us. Oh hello.' She waves to Holly, who has just arrived. 'Is Martin coming?'

'I don't know. Oh look, there's Becky.'

Sienna brings the coffee over. 'Hello, everyone. What do you want, you two?' she asks Holly.

'Hi. It's OK, I'll get mine.'

'Cheers. Let me sit here next to this gorgeous baby.'

'She's asleep,' I say, 'please don't wake her, it's taken me ages to settle her.'

'Don't worry, I'll just look.'

'How are you?' Becky asks. 'You don't have to talk about it if you don't want to.'

'I don't mind. It helps, actually. Being out of the house is good for me, and Oliver's back.'

'How is he?'

'To be honest I toned down what happened. He couldn't do anything being so far away and Tilly was unhurt.'

'What exactly happened?' Asha asks. 'The police wouldn't tell me anything.' There are murmurs of agreement.

'We think she wandered away from the park when I was attending to Amira. A woman found her alone in the wood and phoned the police. But...' I hesitate. 'She also mentioned a man, so the police are looking into that.'

'Not that man John who was helping Elliott?' asks Sienna. 'I've never seen him before.'

'I don't think so, he was really helpful.'

'I was looking after his boys,' Asha says. 'They were in the playground when we were.'

'Still, a man sounds way more sinister than what we were led to believe,' Sienna says, the rest of us nodding in agreement. I experience a surge of anxiety. I'd hoped it was just a case of Tilly wandering off and getting lost, a kind stranger finding her and alerting the police. *A man* is the stuff of nightmares.

'Did she say anything else?'

'"Nice man" is all she will say.' I stroke Lucy's hair. 'That's all we can get out of her, that he was "nice".'

'I presume the police have checked CCTV?' Sienna asks.

'Yes, they still are. You'd think the playground would be protected.'

'Let's bring it up to Edward at the next residents' meeting,' Asha says and everyone agrees.

'What would we do without Edward?' Sienna says and everyone laughs. I pretend to laugh along with them, but the thought of needing security in the close makes me feel nauseous. Edward is, however, a godsend.

'And Elliott,' Asha says. 'He was great before the police turned up.'

The WhatsApp group was set up by Edward in the first week of everyone moving in. One of the best things about living on Prospect Close is the sense of community. Living here in the Home Counties is so different to the Yorkshire farm I grew up in, but we look out for one another, this motley group of people who all happened to choose to move here at the same time five years ago. There had been an enormous amount of publicity around the building of Prospect Close, an exclusive new development on the fringes of a Surrey village, surrounded by green space but close to the beautiful high street of the village. The plots were sold off-plan within days of being released, and we were able to work with the developer to adapt the proposed specifications should we wish to. Hence Edward, a trained architect, helped to design the most beautiful penthouse flat which has featured in magazines and property programmes. Only one new resident has moved in since then, and the atmosphere remains the same.

I feel another wave of nausea and remind myself what the police told me when they brought Tilly back. 'She wasn't hurt, or traumatised as far as we can tell, and was seen by a child psychologist affiliated to the police, and they couldn't detect anything to worry about.'

'That's what matters,' Asha says, 'but it's given you a terrible fright and I'm not surprised. It's brought out the protective mama bear in me.'

'You can never be too careful where children are concerned,' Sienna says.

'Let's talk about something else,' Becky says. 'I'm sure

Harriet came here to take her mind off it. What's everyone doing for Christmas?'

'Talking of Christmas,' Sienna says, 'have you all had your invites yet?' Her eyes sparkle as she looks around the group. 'The Penthouse Party invite? You'll all be invited so I'm not speaking out of turn. Mine arrived yesterday.'

'Oh yes,' Asha says. 'It's on the twenty-third of December, which is nice and festive. I can't wait to see what it looks like since the latest redecoration. Edward has such style.'

'He should do, given he's an award-winning architect,' Sienna says.

I smile. 'Martin was saying Edward's already wondering what he can change next.'

'He's never satisfied,' Becky says. 'I wish Ryan was more interested in interior design. If it was a car, that's a different story, he's always tinkering with his out in the garage. I bet the terrace looks fantastic.'

'Never mind the room,' Sienna says, 'what are we all going to wear? I've been looking on Instagram already for some inspiration. I want something really sparkly that stands out.'

Asha rolls her eyes. 'You always stand out.'

'Talking of standing out,' she says, 'did anyone notice Gabi going out the other evening? She was obviously going on a date, wearing an extremely slinky dress. She looked great,' she adds quickly when she sees my face. 'Has she told you where she was going, Harriet?'

I take a bite of lemon cake.

'No.'

'You're hopeless. I'm sure she's dating. What I don't get is why she's so secretive. We're all dying to know who he is.'

'Maybe she just values her privacy,' I say. 'Why should she tell us? We're just her neighbours after all.'

'We're more than that and you know it. Especially you, you're really close.'

'Just because she was dressed up it doesn't mean she was going on a date,' Becky says. 'Her job has a busy social calendar. Remember when she went to that film premiere with all those A-listers? Even I would make an effort for that.'

We all laugh. Becky lives in sportswear. I'm grateful to her for sticking up for Gabi. I'm sure Sienna knows Gabi confides in me, but I wouldn't dream of breaking a confidence. Not that I know much more than she does, except that he definitely exists. Privately I'm as intrigued as the others are, but she's my friend. To me she always stands out. She has an effortless chic, perfect poise, like a French woman. *Oliver is in Paris this weekend.*

'*Didn't he tell you?*'

The cake sticks in my throat, making me splutter. At the same time Lucy cries out.

'Steady,' Asha says, 'shall I take Lucy for you?'

I nod, coughing, resisting the urge to keep her close when Asha eases her out of the pram, clucking baby talk at her. Tears have sprung into my eyes and I drink some water, my throat settling down. The cake is an uncomfortable wedge in my stomach. My discomfort in the group makes me think about the note, slipped into my bag right under my nose. It's hard enough to shake off my past and feel relaxed in a group of people, especially women, who can be so catty. Suspecting everyone around me just puts me more on edge. Any one of these women could have put that note in my bag, just like anybody could have been the one who lured Tilly away. Meanwhile my husband is away doing goodness knows what.

'She's getting so big,' Asha says, as Lucy stops crying and gazes at this new face. 'It's such a shame about your nanny, such bad luck; she was fantastic with the children.'

'What happened to her? I thought she seemed so settled,' Becky says.

*So did I.* 'She had an urgent family commitment that came up; that's why it felt so sudden. Can any of you recommend anyone? I've not had much luck so far through my contacts and with Oliver being at work I don't get much time to look. I'd prefer to have someone who is recommended.'

'You can't be too careful,' Becky says, smiling ruefully.

'I can't think of anyone who isn't employed right now. The good ones get snapped up, that's the trouble,' Asha says.

'If you could all ask around, I'd appreciate it. Qualified, with good references, obviously.'

Chatter returns to the party, and the holidays in general and the plans everyone has made. It's lunchtime when we all leave; Sienna and Asha head off to the yoga class at the nearby gym, mats tucked under one arm, water bottles in the other.

'Sure you won't change your mind?' Sienna asks.

'I'm sure. Do a downward dog for me. I'll try and come next time.' I don't know why I say this as I'm not a yoga person. I'd rather thrash a ball against a wall to let off steam, or go for a fast run. It's ages since I last ran. Maybe over Christmas I'll be able to make a bit of time for some exercise.

Becky and I walk back together.

'Are you really OK?' Becky asks, coming to a stop. 'Only you looked a bit upset back there. Is Tilly really OK?'

I feel a rush of warmth towards Becky for her kindness; she always puts others before herself.

'She is. It's just stress; Kate leaving me so suddenly has dropped me right in it. But Oliver should get some leave soon, so that will help.'

She goes back to pushing the pram. 'I understand. We're programmed to be protective, aren't we?'

She waves before she unlocks her front door, and my chest tightens.

I look around at all the buildings, so many windows; who is behind them? I shiver. Is one of them centred on me?

# EIGHT

Oliver is home at a reasonable hour this evening and he has news.

'I've found a potential contact for a nanny. Her name's Danni, and one of the women in our Guildford office recommended her. I'll text her details over to you. She's worked for her sister and one of her friends and is happy to give you a reference, if you need it.'

'That's a relief. Fingers crossed she's free to start straight away. I thought I was never going to find a replacement.'

'Heard anything back from Kate?'

'Nothing. It's so weird. But I'm not going to dwell on it anymore. For whatever reason she wants to sever contact and I just have to accept it. I just hope she's OK, that's all.'

'It's the best you can do,' Oliver says. 'She knows where we are if she needs us. Hopefully the twins will like this Danni and they'll soon forget Kate; you know how fickle they are.'

'Maybe.' He doesn't acknowledge I've lost a friend. 'How was your day?'

'Busy. Good news about my leave: I've got the two weeks off over Christmas and New Year.'

'Oh that's great. We really need some time together as a family.'

'Hopefully we might have a nanny by then and we can go out for a meal one night. If not we can make it happen some other way. We could find a babysitter.'

'Mum will do it,' I say quickly. 'She doesn't mind, as long as we give her enough notice. Her social life is far busier than mine.'

'We'll have a good Christmas. I see we've had the invite to the Penthouse Party.'

'Yes, on the twenty-third. Make sure you keep it free. When's your work do?'

'We're not having one this year.'

'Really?'

'What I mean is nothing fancy, maybe a meal or something, a few drinks before we head off over Christmas. Do you want a coffee?'

'Please.'

He whistles as he puts some coffee in the machine and locates some cups. He moves with his usual confidence and I watch him closely for signs that he's lying. Is the company do really not taking place? They usually have a meal at a London restaurant, a really splashy affair, partners invited, waiting staff, the works. Is he just trying to fob me off?

'That's unusual, isn't it? Why not?'

'No idea. To be honest I'm relieved. I'd rather get back here and forget about work for a couple of weeks, spend some time with you and the children.' He brings the coffee over and joins me at the table, loosening his tie. 'Work's been so full-on lately, and what with all the commuting, I'm starting to feel old.' He laughs.

'You've just had a weekend in Paris. Didn't that give you a chance to unwind?'

'Not really. I was with colleagues. You know that guy

David, he's a nice guy, but he's very serious. We spent a lot of time visiting galleries when I'd far rather have spent the day outside a café, watching Parisians going about their business. And it would have been much more fun if you were there.' He leans forward and kisses me. 'When was the last time we went away together, just the two of us?'

'Barcelona. How could you forget?' Oliver had surprised me on my thirtieth birthday, told me to pack my passport and a bag for a weekend in the sun. We'd stayed in a five-star hotel and he'd spoiled me the whole weekend. Shortly after that break I'd started feeling nauseous and discovered I was pregnant with the twins. I still remember the way my skin tingled all over when I dared to look at the pregnancy test, knowing I was undergoing a momentous moment.

'That long ago? I'm shocked. If only I could cut my hours, but it just isn't possible at the moment with the mortgage on this place, but it won't be like this forever, I promise.'

I watch his face closely. He's relaxed... and tired yes, but is he lying to me? I can't get the image out of my mind of him sitting at a long table, his arm draped around a woman's bare shoulders, a woman who isn't me, a chic, French woman – or is it somebody closer to home, one of his attractive colleagues? I decide not to challenge him yet, stick to my plan of gathering evidence. It's too easy for him at the moment to deny it, and if I let him know I suspect something he'll be more careful. If, that is, my suspicions are true. From the way he is with me tonight I'd say he's telling the truth and I'm reminded of the memories we share and why I married him.

My mobile rings. It's PC Sterling. She tells me they haven't found any footage of Tilly with a man, but the playground exit isn't covered so it's impossible to verify Tilly's story. She assures me they will continue to appeal for witnesses and keep me updated. My phone rings again as soon as she ends the call. Gabi.

'Hey,' she says, 'are you busy?'

'Kind of. Oliver's home.'

'Yes, I noticed his car. I wondered if you fancied coming over for a cheeky glass of wine or two?'

'Not tonight, thanks. Not with Oliver being home. And I'm still monitoring Tilly closely. We'll catch up soon, though.'

'Sure, no problem.'

'What did she want?' Oliver asks.

'Me to go for a drink, but I'd rather stay home with you. Do you fancy a film?'

'There's a thriller on Netflix that's supposed to be good. David recommended it.'

'Dull David from work?' I raise an eyebrow.

'Yes, that one. He's not the only one to recommend it. I can't promise to stay awake, though. I'm knackered.'

'And I can't promise the children will stay asleep. Tilly's sleeping well, which is a relief. I was worried she might start having nightmares.' I update him on the phone call from Fiona.

'I wonder if Tilly imagined it,' he says. 'It's impossible to know without evidence.'

He puts his arm round me on the sofa and I try to relax. He doesn't seem fussed that I'm not going out. Surely if he was having an affair he'd want me out of the way so he could pick up his phone the minute I left, and speak purring French that I wouldn't understand to a mistress who may not exist? I hate thinking like this. I snuggle into his shoulder and will my body to relax. An outsider looking in through the window would see a loving couple, happy in one another's company, three well-loved children asleep in a comfortable home. It's all I've ever wanted, more than I deserve. Is that why I'm searching for reasons to derail my life?

When Oliver and I had been dating for a few months, one of our favourite ways of spending a weekend was to stay in and watch a film together. By that time I was virtually living in his flat, my flatmate and I maintaining our relationship by leaving notes for one another on the kitchen table. I'm sure she was happy to have the flat to herself and she was genuinely thrilled for me. 'It's so obvious how much you love one another,' she said. 'I wish my boyfriend was half as romantic.'

Even though it was established that I'd spend my weekend at Oliver's flat, which was bigger – plus he lived alone – every Friday a huge bunch of roses would arrive at the reception desk of the company I worked for, causing the women in the office to tease me no end. It was a leap year that year and there were several suggestions for me to propose – they'd met Oliver one night when he picked me up from the bar, and declared him a catch on his good looks alone, never mind all the romantic gestures. The roses would be accompanied by an invitation to dinner, requesting that I dress up. I'd spend hours getting ready, the excitement building, and he'd treat each occasion as if it was the first time he was trying to impress me with his cooking. Beautiful culinary smells would tickle my nose as I entered the flat, my dress would often be removed before we attended to the meal, and afterwards we liked nothing more than cuddling up in front of a good film, just the two of us, and we'd spend most of the weekend holed up together. I'm not sure when that routine changed; when I moved in officially he was still romantic, but in a different way, leaving little surprise notes for me around the flat. A card saying 'I love you' was a special surprise in my underwear drawer when I was rushing to get dressed for work.

The film is complicated and requires concentration. Oliver falls asleep after about half an hour and my thoughts continue to wander. By the halfway point Oliver is snoring gently, when something clonks onto the ceiling above. I move gingerly to extricate myself from his shoulder without waking him and I run upstairs to check on the children. All of them are fast asleep; Tilly's breathing is a little laboured with what seems to be the beginnings of a cold. Lucy is on her back, her angelic face looking peaceful. I feel a burst of pride. We made these together, Oliver and I. Would he really risk everything for someone else? I hope desperately that my suspicions are wrong. I need to have concrete evidence before I challenge him. If I ask him now after we've had a comfortable evening together, it will just provoke an awkward discussion and I have nothing to back up an accusation. I hope I'm proved wrong.

Downstairs he's still asleep. I pause the film and he opens his eyes.

'What did I miss?'

'Not a lot. There are too many characters and I lost track of what was going on. I just went up to check on the kids and they're fine.'

'I'm sorry,' he says. 'You might as well have gone next door for all the company I've been.'

'Rubbish. I like having you here, just being with you. I haven't got the energy for Gabi tonight.'

'Is she seeing someone?'

'Who told you that?'

'You did.'

I sit back down on the sofa. I don't remember telling him. I turn the television off.

'I don't know, to be honest. She's very cagey about it. But somebody sent her some gorgeous flowers.'

'Bit strange, isn't it? I thought you women told each other everything.'

'We're all different. You can't just lump us all together. Would you tell Ben if you were having an affair?'

I'm still holding the remote control and I grip it so hard it hurts my hand. The question popped out before I could decide whether it was a good idea or not.

'I wouldn't tell Ben anything. We don't talk about personal stuff. Most of the time it's impossible to get him to talk about anything other than Chelsea. You're lucky I'm one of those rare men who doesn't get wildly excited about football.'

Lucky? Is that what I am?

'When are you going to call this nanny?'

Another neat change of subject?

'First thing tomorrow. I'm praying she will be free. I'm going up to bed now.'

'I won't be far behind you. You go ahead and I'll lock up and make sure everything is switched off down here.'

I check the back door before I go upstairs; despite Oliver's assurances I need to make sure for myself that the house is well and truly locked. I thought Tilly was safe, I lost attention for the moment and look what happened to her. You only need to be distracted for a moment, that's all it takes. One lapse to lose your children.

———

Danni is well spoken and friendly and I like her immediately. She sounds confident as she talks me through her last two work placements, one for three five- to eight-year-old boys, and one for a baby girl and her two-year-old sister. I've already made up my mind I'm taking her if she's free, but I maintain a professional charade. Obviously I'm going to check the references she gives me, both from families in Kensington, which further reassures me. Good area, good families, good nanny.

'I heard that you needed someone soon and I'm available whenever you want me to start. You caught me at a good time as I'm between jobs; I've just had a week's holiday in the Seychelles and I was going to call the agency when I got back.'

'Which agency is that?' I ask, wondering why our paths haven't crossed sooner.

'Angels, it's over in Kensington.'

'Ah, I see. When could you come over and meet the children?'

'This afternoon?'

'Gosh, that would be perfect. I'm so grateful to you; what with it being so close to Christmas, I didn't expect to find anyone until New Year. Give me your mobile and I'll text you all the details of where we are. Around three?'

'Three it is, see you then.'

———

Danni is willowy, with long pale blonde hair and a warm tan, sun-kissed skin from her holiday. Everything about her is natural, no makeup and a winning smile showing her even white teeth.

'Come in,' I say, leading her through to the kitchen. 'Did you find us OK?'

'Yes, fine thanks. Wow... Nice house,' she says.

'Thanks. We have plenty of room here, if you take the job. The twins are at nursery and my mother collected them today so we have a bit of time together before you meet them. But this is Lucy.' She leans over Lucy's carrier where she is asleep, head turned to the side, her fingers clenched into little fists. 'Afternoon nap,' I say. 'She doesn't sleep much at night so I take advantage when she naps during the day.'

'She's adorable.'

'Tell me about your experience while I make some coffee. Or would you prefer tea?'

'Coffee is fine. White, no sugar, thanks. I've got my paperwork here too, CV and details of my referees. My last employer was Nathalie. Her sister works with your husband, I believe.'

'Yes, that's right.'

She outlines her career and she's warm and witty and I like her immensely. I'm praying the twins won't do anything terrible when they come in. Tess can be a real handful if she's in a bad mood.

But all is well. Tilly clings to me and takes a while to overcome her shyness, but Tess takes to Danni immediately, engaging her in chatter. Mum has brought one of her homemade chocolate cakes over and reacts with pleasure when Danni reveals she is a keen baker too. I'm beginning to think Danni is one of those women who's accomplished at everything. Mum cuts her a generous slice, smiling. Tess and Tilly take Danni on a tour of the house and garden.

'What a lovely young woman,' Mum says. 'She seems ideal. Did you hear from Kate yet?'

'No, I don't think I will now. Thank goodness I might have found someone. I was beginning to despair.'

'I know you were, but I told you not to be so pessimistic. Something good is usually around the corner.' Mum has a strong faith, but I'm not so convinced. I almost tell her about the note; she out of anyone would understand. But Tess comes in dragging Danni by the hand.

'Mummy, can Danni be our nanny?' she asks.

'Tess,' Danni says, flashing me an apologetic smile.

'That rhymes. I did a rhyme, Danni the nanny.' Tess looks up at Danni for approval. Danni smiles again.

'I'm off now, girls,' Mum says. 'Come and wave me out while your mother has a quick word with Danni. She might not want to be a nanny to you two cheeky ones.'

'Nana,' says Tess, pouting.

'Come along.'

'They're adorable,' Danni says, as they disappear into the hall.

'What do you think? Your references look good; I'll check them out but it's merely a formality. I think you'd be ideally suited. If you'd like the job, that is?'

'Oh I would. Tess showed me the attic bedroom with the ensuite?'

'Yes, that would be your room if you prefer to live in. It would suit us. Most of the time it's just me. When I had the children I quit my job, and I'm setting up my own business making and selling children's clothes, hence the need for a nanny.'

'What a lovely job to have. Did you make the gorgeous dungarees the twins are wearing?'

'I did.' My cheeks go pink with pleasure at her words. 'It started as a hobby but I'm getting lots of orders in at the moment and I hate turning business down. You'd be looking after the children throughout the day, taking and picking them up from preschool.'

'What about your husband?'

'He works in London during the week and travels quite a bit for work. He's a banker. You'd have evenings and weekends free unless we mutually agree otherwise. You can have full use of the kitchen. I'd say eat with us but our mealtimes are a bit chaotic what with Oliver having such an irregular schedule and these three little handfuls with their differing needs. We could do a trial for a month. How does that sound? We'd pay the going rate for the agency.'

'It sounds great, thanks, I'd love to accept.'

# NINE

The following week, when Oliver is at work, Danni arrives in her chilli-red car, neat shiny cases in the boot. I give coffee morning a miss this week, to be there when she arrives. The twins fall over themselves trying to show her around her room and finally I manage to get them to leave her to settle in. She soon proves to be a huge asset, picking up the children's routines quickly. She's mainly employed to look after the girls, leaving me to look after Lucy. I managed to contact one of her referees, who gave her a glowing report.

On her first full day I walk to the twins' nursery with her, to help her orient herself, leaving her to pick them up that afternoon and she offers to take them to the park afterwards. I tell her about the incident the previous week, stressing that she has to be ultra-careful. My instinct is to not let them out, but I've been taught how to let go, and not get too paranoid.

Finding myself alone in the house, I wander into the study with a mug of tea, placing it on the windowsill. 'Study' is a bit of a fancy name; it's where we keep all our paperwork, and books line the walls, but it's not organised enough to warrant the word 'study' and there isn't a desk, just a couple of inviting armchairs.

Although we do most of our business in the Cloud these days, any paperwork we do get is kept in a metal box file. Most recent documents are left on an in tray and it's these I look through, determined to find out more about what Oliver is up to.

Of most interest is his credit card bill. The last month proves extremely interesting. There are many restaurant and café transactions, for amounts that to me look like two people are dining. I google one of the restaurants and pull up the menu to check prices, and I'm convinced I'm right. It's not clear whether these were morning or evening transactions, and Oliver eats out a lot as part of his job, wining and dining clients and putting the bill on the company's expenses, as do all the managers working at his level, so it's impossible to know for sure. There are also quite a few payments to restaurants and bars in London. A London mistress who jets to and from Paris to see him? My jaw is stiff with tension. I work my way through the list of amounts, one of which catches my eye. It's listed as Greenwood Lettings Company and is for a large sum of money.

Putting the bill to one side, I work through the rest of the pile until I find the same credit card statement from the previous month. On the same date, the same amount was paid out. In the box file, which is well organised due to Oliver having a sort-out last summer, I find an older statement from last month. What I'm now seeing as a regular transaction is listed. I work my way back through the statements until I find one marked 'first payment'. The date is nine months ago, not long before Lucy was born. How could he? I slump back into the chair and the pile of papers slides to the floor.

Oliver is renting another property, which is significant. Is that where is he carrying out this affair? Does he whisk his mistress away for the weekend like he did with me? His romantic side won't have gone away, just because he is married. I kick the pile of papers and stare in dismay at the floor.

The front door slams. 'Hello,' Danni's voice calls out and

four small feet stampede on the wooden floor, heading for the living room, which is where they'd normally find me. I'm too late to react and before I can close the study door, Tilly and Tess run into the room calling me.

'Mummy, Mummy.' Tilly throws herself at my legs.

'Are you OK, darling?' She smiles and I'm relieved.

'Oh Mummy,' Tess says, hand over her mouth. 'Messy Mummy.'

Danni appears behind them. 'Oh dear, what happened?'

'I was sorting out some bills and I dropped the pile. It looks worse than it is.'

Danni squats down to help pick up the sea of paper which covers the floor.

'Please leave it,' I say, grabbing the documents from her, not wanting her seeing our personal stuff. 'I roughly know how it goes and I need to sort it all out anyway. I'll do it later. Let's go into the kitchen and have some tea. I want to hear all about nursery, and whether you two behaved for Danni.' I take the girls' hands.

'They were very good,' Danni says, leading the way into the kitchen. Her long hair is loose, reaching halfway down her back, and she's wearing a navy jumpsuit. She moves with a catwalk elegance. 'Their teacher said they'd both had a good day and she's given me a letter about the end-of-term arrangements. She said all parents should be getting a text message about it too. Here you are.' She hands me a letter, which I glance at and leave on the kitchen table.

'Thanks. Would you like some tea?'

'Yes please. I can make it if you like?'

'No, it's OK.'

Lucy, who has been asleep in her carrier, begins to cry.

'I'll get her,' Danni says. 'We haven't had much of a chat yet, have we?' She eases Lucy into her arms and sits at the table with Lucy against her shoulder and strokes her back. The cry becomes a whimper and she stares at Danni, her eyes wide as she takes in this unfamiliar face, tiny fingers exploring it. Danni smiles and Lucy smiles back.

'You're very good with her,' I say. 'Sometimes she takes against people immediately.'

'Have you been without a nanny for a while?' she asks. 'It must be hard with three under-fives to look after. My mother runs a nursery and she's always exhausted, although she loves her job.'

'A few weeks,' I say.

'What happened to the last one?'

'She had a family emergency and had to leave. It was unexpected.'

I make the tea and place the mugs on the table.

'Are you alright with Lucy for a moment? I just want to pick those papers off the floor in the study.'

'Of course,' she says. 'I can see the twins from here too.' The twins are playing with their toys on the floor, Tess keeping up a stream of conversation.

As I go into the hall, the front door opens and Oliver comes in, startling me.

'You're early. You're in time to meet Danni; she's in the kitchen with the children. I'll be down in a minute.'

I race up the stairs and gather the statements from the floor, my eyes drawn to the name Greenwood Lettings. I need an explanation, and now. I head for the door, statement crumpled in my hand, ready to present him with the evidence and see what he says, when a cold sweat trickles down my back and stops me. Danni is in the house and I don't want to scare her off by ranting at my husband the first time she meets him. Besides, if I accuse him again and I'm wrong it could do untold damage. I force myself to calm down and think back to last time.

It had begun with Oliver working late, not just one night but consistently. At the same time he'd got a new colleague and was constantly talking about how efficient she was and how much easier she was to work with than her predecessor. I'd been so intrigued I'd looked her up on the company website, expecting to see a woman of my age, and was alarmed to see how attractive she was, and so much younger. Her image began to haunt me. Oliver had talked to me about the important project he was working on and how important it was for him to make a success of it as he was hoping it would help him progress to the next level. It felt as though he was too eager to give me a reason for his sudden dedication to work. I convinced myself he was cheating on me. I asked him outright if his colleague was working late, and he was hurt at my suggestion. Too hurt, I decided. One night I arranged for Mum to come over and mind the twins and I turned up at his office, convinced I'd catch him in the act with his secretary. The security guard informed me he was the sole worker left that evening, but I believed he must be in on the secret too. The building was eerily dark, one light from Oliver's office giving off the only light. I confronted him, convinced she was hiding somewhere. Oliver was shocked that I had doubted him, and it had taken us a while to get back to trusting one another again. Of course, this was prior to the actual affair he had with his secretary, but still, the humiliation I get from just thinking about that scenario confirms my decision to wait until I'm sure.

I shove the papers into the back of the file. I'll sort them out into some sort of order as soon as I get a chance. Oliver rarely comes in here during the week.

Danni's laughter rings out as I run back downstairs. I catch sight of my pink flustered face in the mirror in the hall and I'm struck by Danni's contrasting looks when I go into the room – the sleek au pair versus the harassed mother. She's laughing at something Oliver has said, her face lit up, attractive, and Lucy is clutching her hand. Oliver doesn't see me come in and I catch a look on his face which I don't like. Clearly, he's captivated by

Danni, and I see her through his eyes: flawless skin and shiny long hair, beautiful bone structure. *Pretty* is the only word to describe her. Her jumpsuit fits snugly to her curves and her top button is undone revealing a hint of a cleavage I hadn't noticed earlier. I smooth my creased sweatshirt down, resolving to make more of an effort from now on.

'Dan was just telling me about the last family she worked with,' he says. Dan, *already*? 'You'll find our lot a doddle after that, as long as you can cope with Tess's stream of consciousness.'

'Of course,' she says, beaming at Tess, who looks up at the mention of her name. Tess beams back.

'Nice to meet you – I'm going up to get changed. Squash club tonight,' he tells Danni, before heading upstairs.

'I won't be a minute,' I say to her, following Oliver to the bedroom. 'Are you sure you won't change your mind about squash? Especially now that Danni's here, it would give us some time to catch up.'

He pulls his tie off and throws it on the bed, unbuttoning his shirt.

'Has something happened?'

'No.'

'Then it's not urgent. I'm not cancelling Ben. We've been through this already. I need to speak to him; we have some work stuff to sort out.' Ben runs a building company, which Oliver has invested some money into.

Everything is *work stuff* lately; it's too convenient.

'Besides, I've confirmed my holiday leave, so I don't see what the urgency is. And you've got a nanny sorted out. You're just stressed, that's all this is. Danni seems great; everything will get easier now, trust me.' He opens the wardrobe and rummages inside.

'I could see how much you liked her.'

'What?' He stops searching through the coat hangers.

I shrug. 'She's very beautiful.'

'As you are to me. Come here.' He pulls me into a hug. 'I know you think I'm being selfish, but this one hour of squash is the only exercise I get all week.' I hug him back and relax. He pats his stomach. 'My job entails so many rich lunches and I don't want to end up with a huge belly or you won't fancy me anymore. We'll talk soon, I promise. I know we've got decisions to make about our future, but time is on our side.'

'Sure. You go and enjoy your squash.'

It would be so much easier if I could tell him about the note. Time is precious. If somebody is after me then I need to get away and fast. If it weren't for my suspicions about his infidelity then I would trust him with my secret, but I can't risk him revealing it to someone else. Not being able to trust and confide in my husband makes my chest hurt. It's imperative I can get through to him that a change is necessary. I need to feel safe in my own home.

I run back downstairs. Danni is crouched down, playing on the floor with the twins, Lego bricks strewn across the floor. Lucy is watching from her carrier, eyes large, legs kicking. Danni has one hand on the carrier. They're all one little unit.

'If I was in any doubt about you being right for this job, it's totally gone. They're never this quiet, especially if their dad comes in from work – they get overexcited when they see him. They've transferred their interest to you.'

'Suits me,' she says, flicking her long hair over her shoulder. Wisps of it catch Tilly's face and she puts her hand to her cheek, giggling.

'Do it again.'

'I'm just going to make a quick phone call and then I'll take over.'

'I'm in no hurry; you go ahead.'

'OK, but I won't be long. You need some time to settle into your room, and have a bit of time to yourself.'

I take the phone into the study and close the door. Before I make the call, I retrieve the credit card statements I stashed in the back of the file earlier, scanning the dates to check when the UK meals took place, bringing up a calendar on Google. Sure enough, a couple of the dates fall on Wednesdays. Oliver's supposed squash nights. Gabi answers after a couple of rings.

'Are you busy?' I ask.

'If you call sitting on the sofa with a coffee thinking about the exciting prospect of cleaning the kitchen, then yes, I'm busy.'

'That sounds perfect. I was wondering whether you'd do something for me.'

'Possibly,' she says slowly, 'but I'm not committing myself until I know you haven't got something horrendous in mind, like going for a jog or some other evil.'

'It's going to sound mad, but bear with me.' I lower my voice. 'You remember what I told you about Oliver last week?'

'About him having an affair?'

'Yes.' My stomach twists at the reality of somebody else acknowledging it. 'Could you pop over for a couple of hours and mind the children? I need to nip out for a bit. Our new nanny has started but she's settling into her room this evening and I don't want to dump this on her.'

'This is all very mysterious. Where are you going?'

'I'll tell you later, but I won't be too long, I promise.'

'Sure, I can do that. Might as well sit on your sofa watching television instead of mine. What time do you want me?'

'Six-thirty? Oliver doesn't know I'm going out, by the way.'

'This is all very mysterious.'

'I promise I'll explain later.'

————

Gabi arrives promptly and Oliver leaves at quarter to seven. I head off immediately, promising to update Gabi as soon as I get back. Oliver has gone into the garage to get his car and I run around to the next street where I parked my car earlier. I'm wearing a jumper but I wish I'd grabbed a coat on my way out. I sit inside keeping the lights off, shivering at the cold, until I see him drive out of the close and off towards the traffic lights. He's heading in the direction of the leisure centre, but he could be meeting anyone there. If Ben knows he is having an affair, then he wouldn't hesitate to cover for his brother.

Loud music blares out from the radio when I switch on the ignition, making me cry out in shock. My hands are trembling as I drive off and pull up at the first set of traffic lights behind a taxi, which is one of two cars behind Oliver. I turn the heating on full blast and huddle down as low as I can in the seat, my heart beating fast. The thought of Oliver spotting me makes me feel cold all over. How would I explain myself? I can't make the same mistake twice.

It isn't far to the leisure centre and I park on a side street just outside the car park and walk down the road adjacent to it. I can see the entrance to the club from this position. Lights illuminate the way in, but the rest of the car park is dark. I never normally have cause to come here at night, and the quiet darkness unnerves me. Oliver parks up close to the entrance, gets out of his car and takes his racket and sports bag from the boot. He puts his stuff on the roof of the car and gets out his phone, checking the screen. I can see the light from where I'm standing. I position myself behind a tree, holding onto the trunk for support, taking a quick look around me. If anyone can see me, I must look incredibly suspicious.

The sound of a car driving fast makes me jump and cling onto the tree, a piece of bark digging into my hand and making me cry out. The sound is swallowed by the car, which is in the car park now, sliding to a halt and I recognise it as Ben's. I close my eyes and experience a wave of nausea. What am I doing? Oliver is playing squash with his brother, exactly as he said he was.

Or is he?

Oliver and Ben go into the leisure centre and disappear from my sight. I wait a few moments before heading back to the car. Gabi has sent me a text.

*Everything OK?*

Something is bugging me. I switch the engine back on to warm up the car and drum my fingers on the steering wheel. If Ben were in on the affair he could still be covering for him, having a workout while Oliver meets someone else. The steam room and Jacuzzi area is very conducive to romance, particularly in the evening, I would imagine. Suddenly the thing that is niggling me hits me; Ben was carrying a small gym holdall but he wasn't carrying a racket. It's possible the leisure centre hires them out, but this discrepancy niggles me. I know Ben has his own racket; Ben is all about owning the best of whatever he does. His excessive spending on gym equipment drives Holly mad.

I check the time. The squash courts are booked out for forty-minute periods; add on a shower and they'll be out within an hour. If they are playing squash, that is. After their game the routine is to stop for a pint at the Green Dragon. He's usually back by nine-thirty. I text Gabi.

*Yes. Is everything OK there? Will you be OK if I'm not back for another hour?*

*Take as long as you like. I'm watching your tv and eating your biscuits. What's not to like?*

I switch the radio on in the car, trying not to watch the clock. Time crawls by. I can see both their cars from where I am parked. I find a chat station so that I can occupy my mind while I keep my gaze trained on the entrance. I don't hear a word of the show. When I try and switch my mind away from Oliver having an affair, I can't stop thinking about the threatening note, the main reason I asked Gabi to come over. It's Danni's evening off, but she's in the house. Gabi I trust, and with two of them in the house I know my children are safe.

Eight o'clock finally arrives. The squash game will be over. I switch the radio off and focus, thankful the street I'm parked in also isn't well lit, and my car is pretty nondescript. Oliver won't notice it. At about ten past Oliver and Ben emerge, both laughing. They get in their cars and drive off. I tuck myself in behind Ben, but keep my distance, balancing the need for secrecy while keeping him in sight at the speed he drives, which is way faster than the limit for the area, which has recently been lowered. My stomach churns as we take the road towards the Green Dragon. They're heading into the pub as I arrive, and I drive off. I should feel relieved that I'm wrong in my suspicions, but I just feel stupid. Imagine if they had seen me.

I don't stop and head back home. Gabi will want an explanation and I wonder what to say to her. On the short drive home a sense of unease returns, and I wonder if I can be sure nothing bad was going on; I didn't actually witness them playing squash, likewise I didn't follow them into the pub to make sure they weren't meeting someone else. But I don't really believe it.

I remove a bag from the boot of the car which I've been meaning to bring inside for a while, but I've always had too much to carry when I've got the children with me. When I let myself in, I hear animated voices from the living room. Danni and Gabi are chatting, the television playing in the background with the sound turned down low.

'Hi,' Gabi says, 'I've just been getting to know your lovely new nanny. Fancy Oliver coming up trumps.'

Danni smiles. 'It was perfect timing for me too. But you could have left them in my care; I wouldn't have minded – next time just ask.'

'Where did you go?' Gabi asks. 'I hope everything is OK?'

'I just had to collect this parcel from my mother's; she's been on at me for ages.'

I can tell Gabi isn't convinced by the look she gives me. I put the bag on the counter and switch the kettle on. 'Does anyone want a drink?'

'A peppermint tea, please,' Danni says. 'I'll take it upstairs if you don't mind, ready for my early start. Lovely to meet you, Gabi.'

When she's gone, I close the door behind her and in a low voice tell Gabi what I've been doing.

'I feel like a bit of an idiot now. I really appreciate this.'

'So what if it proves you wrong – that's the best outcome, surely? I didn't mind coming round. And I like Danni, she's lovely. But I'd suggest you have it out with Oliver over Christmas when he's home.'

'Are you seeing anyone over Christmas?'

She shakes her head. I wait for her to elaborate, tell me about her mysterious new lover, but she remains silent. Given that I've told her my concerns about Oliver, I'm surprised she doesn't want to tell me more, but she must have her reasons. In the grand scheme of things, it doesn't matter a jot. I've enough on my mind as it is.

'I'd better get off,' she says. 'Work for me tomorrow too. Let me know if I can do anything else to help. I'm sure you're worrying about nothing, though, but I understand; I'd have done exactly the same.'

I watch her as she goes down the path, deep in thought. I wonder if her lover is married, and that's why she's keeping schtum, because she's not the girlfriend, but the mistress. If Oliver is having an affair then it would be me who is the Other Woman. I'm in the way.

The thought makes me shiver.

Gabi waves and disappears into her building. Her words come back to me. *'She's lovely.'* What if she was trying to tell me something? Am I mad to invite such a beautiful young woman into our house? But they've only just met. The spinning thoughts in my head are like bees buzzing around, driving me mad.

Maybe she's right and I should challenge Oliver. Our relationship can't continue like this. We need to be honest with one another. A car drives into the close and makes me jump out of my skin. When I tell him about my fears I'll tell him about the note too, and what I am afraid of. Then he'll understand why I need to leave the close. I look around at the buildings, most of which are in darkness now. I lock the door behind me. I no longer feel safe.

# TEN

Thursday morning, Danni offers to take Lucy out for a walk, which means I'll be able to make my favourite spinning class, before spending the rest of the day working on the new order. It's the first time I've exercised in weeks and releasing a bit of energy and focusing on myself is just what I need after all the emotional upheaval of the last few days. Oliver got in at his usual time and I felt a complete chump for checking up on him. He was off early again this morning but is due back this evening.

The kitchen is gleaming when I fill my water bottle – Danni is like an angel sent from heaven, whisking the children away to nursery and somehow cleaning the debris from the kitchen. When I used to return from taking them to nursery the kitchen was always in complete disarray. Having a nanny is a godsend but also makes me feel completely inadequate. I jump into the car and try to focus on my morning off.

I park opposite the entrance to the gym, experiencing a cold sweat when I look across to the tree I was hiding behind last night. What was I thinking? I picture myself in the semi darkness, the entrance lit up, revealing Oliver and Ben going in,

Oliver with his racket, both with bags slung over their shoulders. From behind they're a similar build, although Ben has lost most of his hair, whereas Oliver's is short and thick. Ben must have hired a squash racket. My fear around my demons from the past is making me behave irrationally.

I'm fumbling in my bag for my gym pass when the receptionist calls me over.

'Mrs Carlton? I have something here for you in lost property.'

'For me? Are you sure? I haven't reported anything missing.' Even I'm not that forgetful, besides, I haven't been here for two weeks, ever since Kate's sudden departure. Today I'm going to treat myself to a spa session after class and I can't wait to sink into the Jacuzzi, before relaxing in the steam room.

'Let me see, ah, yes, here it is.' She hands me an envelope with my name on. 'You must have dropped this in the changing room.'

I take the envelope, frowning. 'I've never seen this before.' I turn it over: nothing on the back; my name is printed on the front in a handwriting that isn't familiar.

'That's funny, but it's definitely you; we don't have another person here with the same family name, I checked it myself just now. I was about to leave a note on your membership record.'

'Do you know who handed it in?'

'No, but it would either be the cleaners or another member. Don't look so worried, it might be good news.'

'Yes, I hope so.' I fake a smile but the note in my bag is ever on my mind. Is it the same writing? It could be.

I head down to the changing room, which is empty, and get changed, stashing my bag into my locker before confronting the mysterious piece of lost property. I open the envelope and find a sheet of paper inside.

YOU'RE NEXT

I crumple the piece of paper in my hand and chuck it into the locker, my heart pounding.

*Somebody knows.*

I'm convinced now. It has to be the same person who left the note in my bag. Immediately I think of the children. They're safe, I know they are. I phone the nursery on a pretext, text Danni. They're all safe. Danni will think me neurotic if I'm not careful. No, she's a nanny. Children are precious; she wouldn't do her job if she didn't understand that.

The phone call has taken up valuable time and if I go to the spinning class now I'll be late and I don't want to draw attention to myself. It takes me ages to tie the laces on my trainers as my hands are trembling so much. Nervous energy is pumping around inside me so I head to the gym floor instead, programming the treadmill for a pacy run. Sweat pours off me as I follow the inclines set by the programme, up and down imaginary hills as I turn over in my mind who could possibly want to scare me like this. The person has to be a member of the gym, or work here, although anyone can enter on a casual basis by purchasing a day pass. Every house in Prospect Close has automatic membership to the gym and spa.

After my run I'm exhausted, see my face glowing red and shiny reflected back at me and I head down to the spa area, grateful the spinning class is still in progress so none of my usual classmates will see me like this. Most of the women who attend are flexible and model slim and I feel like an interloper wearing the wrong gear whenever I catch sight of my curves in awkward poses in the mirror which runs round the side of the room and from which there is no escape. I shower and change into my swimming costume, collect a fresh towel and head off to the spa area.

I choose the end of the Jacuzzi where the bubbles are most forceful and close my eyes, enjoying the full force of the water pummelling against my legs. It's so long since I've had five minutes to do something like this and I can't remember the last time I was in this Jacuzzi. Two women are sitting on the loungers chatting in dressing gowns, one of them throwing her head back and laughing as the other recounts a story, and I envy her that moment of pure happiness. My lack of results last night is still bugging me – is this what I'd imagined, Oliver and his mistress snuggling under the bubbles, sneaking a kiss in the sauna... The bubbles stop and start again on the opposite side of the pool and I shiver, decide to spend ten minutes in the steam room before heading back to the changing room. I'm so relieved to have found a nanny that I may as well make the most of it.

The steam room is thick with clouds of vapour, and I choose one of the hidden corners, fumbling my way across as I've taken my contact lenses out after having problems once before from wearing them in here. I can make out the form of a man in the central area, and a woman on one of the higher levels across from him. The heat makes my skin prickle as I acclimatise to it, lying down and closing my eyes. I'm almost dropping off when the sound of the door opening startles me and women's voices invade the silence, loud at first then lowering as they move further into the steam room. As my ears adjust I recognise one of them, the unmistakable voice of Sienna. A higher-pitched voice answers, and I recognise Asha. Much as I appreciate the community feel of Prospect Close, at times it feels so intrusive and this is one of them. I pull myself up into a sitting position to reveal myself to them, swinging my legs down to the floor, when I hear my name mentioned. I freeze. I hope I'm mistaken.

'I know. She's the last person I expected this to be happening to,' Sienna says. 'I feel sorry for her.'

It must be another Harriet. Why would they feel sorry for me? Maybe because Kate left, that will be it. I was complaining about not having a nanny at the coffee morning last week. I really must make more of an effort, stop being such a moaner. These are hardly life-or-death problems. I resolve to give more to charity, and shut up about moving, just make it happen instead of talking about it. They all know about my aspirations to move to the country, even if they don't understand it, and I don't want to alienate them.

'Tell me again what he saw.'

'He was at a restaurant with his workmates, and they came in and sat in a corner, one of those booths that are tucked out of sight.'

'Is he sure it was him?' Sienna asks.

'Pretty sure. And this is Mo, you know how he hates gossip, and he was upset by it.'

'I feel so sorry for her,' Sienna says. 'Everyone knows he has a mistress, but I had no idea it was her. But what Mo says confirms what I saw. I'm not surprised, what with him working long hours. It must be very difficult to sustain a relationship when you hardly ever see one another.'

My head feels woozy, the hot steam becoming oppressive. I could do with dunking myself under the ice-cold shower outside, but can't risk them seeing me, not until I understand what I'm hearing.

'Are you sure you've got the right person?' Asha asks.

'Of course. It was definitely him, and he was walking fast as if he didn't want to be spotted. Which is frankly ridiculous as every property looks out towards her house.'

'That's so brazen. Then what happened?'

'He knocked at number ten and she opened the door. I saw her, lit up by the hall light.'

'Did they kiss?'

'No, but they didn't have to. He looked back over his shoulder before he went in, to check nobody was around.'

'I can't believe he'd be so brazen. And she's supposed to be her friend.'

I'm finding it hard to breathe, my chest tight, the steam hissing in the background. But it isn't the heat that's stopping me from breathing, or even the thought of Oliver having a mistress, or everyone knowing about it. What's gripping my chest and squeezing hard is who she is, Sienna seeing Oliver go into number ten.

Gabi lives at number ten.

Gabi, my so-called best friend.

# JUNE 2006

This babysitting lark was alright. The first time she'd been reluctant; babies weren't her thing, they cried too much and threw up all over your clothes and her wardrobe was her passion. She'd wanted to wear her new jeans because she just had to wear them all the time; she loved the way they stretched and made her feel better about her lumpy thighs. Mike said they made her look sexy and she tingled all over when she thought about what that meant. He did fancy her.

She sent him a text, told him where she was going. She didn't actually ask him to come over, he probably wouldn't want to hang out with her, but you never knew with boys. She didn't understand them at all. What she'd noticed about the male species was that they said one thing when they were with you on your own and acted completely differently with their mates. Regressed to ten-year-olds. Laura said that boys were way more immature than girls and that they should stick together in a sisterhood. Make no mistake, she was well into feminism but she fancied Mike like mad. She couldn't help her feelings, it was basic chemistry, the way her body reacted when she thought about him.

Mum was happy about her going because it was a Friday night so she didn't have to get up for school in the morning, plus she was earning money and Mum was always on about her not having a Saturday job like most of her friends. Erin and Sam both worked in shoe shops, but she hated the thought of handling other people's smelly feet, touching socks and wrinkly skin. Her friends spent all day on their feet and were full of stories about rude customers, who treated them like skivvies. Her way was much better. Alright, it wasn't as regular and reliable as Saturday work but thirty-five quid for a couple of hours – she knew which she'd rather do. Plus babysitting fitted in perfectly with the childcare course she was studying at school. These were the arguments she gave her mother whenever she complained about her lack of commitment.

The couple she was babysitting for lived across the road and had always been friendly with her mum. They had two children, a five-year-old from the wife's previous marriage, and a baby but the older girl usually stayed with her father, so she babysat their daughter Lydia, who was six months old . The two times she'd babysat her before she'd slept right through. She was disappointed; she'd stood in her bedroom doorway watching her. The room was entrancing enough in the moonlight with silver stars glowing on the ceiling, highlighting the pink tones of the wall and the cute mobile with jumping lambs hanging over her cot. She liked to watch her sleep, marvelling at the way her eyelids flickered, her skin smooth and unblemished. She willed her to wake up so she could take her downstairs and cuddle her, feel that little warm bundle against her skin. She was going to have at least four children when she was older. She wondered what Mike would be like as a dad, conjured up a picture of him with Lydia on his knee, pulling faces at her to make her laugh. His sense of humour was one of the qualities she most liked about him. He had a friendly face, slightly round with lots of freckles and a wicked grin. He hadn't replied to her text and he probably wouldn't but she'd only sent it five minutes ago. Plenty of time from now until Friday.

# ELEVEN

I stay in the steam room until Asha and Sienna leave, moving to a lower level where the heat is less intense, waiting for what feels like an age until I hear them go, talking about being hungry, thinking about lunch, my situation forgotten and discarded like the damp towels they leave in the laundry bin provided. I cling to my towel as I make my way over to the showers, wishing I could cover my head and make myself completely invisible. The Jacuzzi is empty and I stand under the ice-cold shower, punishing myself, wanting to drown my thoughts away. It's so cold it makes me gasp aloud, but I welcome being unable to focus on anything other than survival, wishing in that moment that it would shock the life out of me so I wouldn't have to know what I've just heard.

Oliver and Gabi.

Gabi is Oliver's mistress.

Gabi, my friend.

Until now.

It makes sense. They must be laughing so hard, at my getting Gabi over so I could spy on Oliver last night, me being so easy to fool. She knew full well he was at the gym with Ben playing squash last night. My blood feels like the ice of the steam room shower. That doesn't mean that's where he always goes; she would have warned him somehow. He's been supposedly playing squash for months. Is Ben in on it too, his brother? He has to be, and no doubt Holly as well. All taking me for a fool. Tears run down my face and I wipe them away with my towel, bolt into one of the toilet cubicles where I lose it completely.

*Everyone knows he has a mistress.* Sienna's lilting voice is killing me with her words. How can I face anyone in Prospect Close again? I hate that my world has become concentrated around this square. A thought hits me like a punch in the face. Book club. It's tonight, and it's my turn to host. I have to welcome people from around the close, give them food and drink and make them feel welcome. Sienna and Asha will be there, and I'll have to look them in the eye and pretend I'm happy to see them. I can't do it. I won't.

I cancelled last month when Lucy was ill. I can't cancel again. But I don't have anyone to turn to because my life has become so small that since having the children, all my friends are drawn from this claustrophobic community. I have to get my children out and away from here. Away from her. Away from their father too. I can't stay with him this time. It's not going to be easy. In the past I made the decision to stick by him, not wanting the children to only have one parent, but I'm no longer prepared to be treated as second best.

Gabi will be at book club too.

I must have been out ages and Lucy will no doubt be crying and Danni will regret taking this job already. I don't leave the cubicle until my breathing is under control. Instead of being rejuvenated and re-energised, my skin is on fire and my heart is racing.

On my way home I worry about the note. How did whoever sent it know I would be there? I haven't had a chance to go to a class for a while. I keep looking back over my shoulder, sensing a presence behind me, but it's the ghosts of my past, which I can never shake off. Asha or Sienna could easily have left it there; they would have been in the changing room before the spinning class. But no, why would they do that to me? Or it could have been Gabi, last night, or even Oliver. The women are my friends, I've never had any reason to doubt that, and as for the other two, who knows what they wouldn't do?

I walk to the high street where I shop on automatic pilot and pick up some food and drink for this evening's book club. We have plenty of good wine in the rack at home, but I make sure to include some soft drinks as not everyone drinks and I have to get everything right this evening. It's probably best if I don't drink alcohol tonight, otherwise I might say something I regret. In the deli I choose a selection of cheeses, delicate biscuits and crisps with unusual-sounding flavours like cracked pepper, horse-radish and gunpowder. Any of these delicacies would stick in my throat if I were to try and eat one now. It's tradition with the book club that the host feeds back on the book first. This month's read is a contemporary romance and all I've read is the blurb on the back.

Laughter greets me as I let myself into the house and I find Oliver in the kitchen, engaged in a conversation with Danni. They're both seated at the kitchen table, mugs of coffee in front of them and Lucy is in Danni's arms. A stab of pain surprises me and I want to empty the contents of Oliver's mug over his head. I dump the large paper bag full of shopping on the counter.

'You're back early,' I say, surprised to see him.

'I thought I'd surprise you. I finished my work and I've done a lot of evenings lately. Plus I wanted to see how Danni is getting on.'

Danni flashes me a smile. 'Oliver has been telling me all about his job. It sounds exciting, working abroad, but I'd get sick of all that travelling.'

'It's not the easiest life,' I say, sticking a coffee pod in the machine and adding some water. The machine splutters and churns out the welcome aroma of coffee. I join them at the table, taking Lucy from Danni, needing to feel the warmth of her body against mine.

'Have you been a good girl?' I ask. She fixes me with her large blue eyes and I stroke her cheek, loving the warm feel of her against me.

'She's been so good,' Danni says, 'and Oliver was making her laugh.'

'I didn't realise you were going shopping,' Oliver says.

'Me neither. I suddenly remembered it's book club tonight and it's my turn for everyone to come here.'

'Oh god,' says Oliver. 'A house full of women drinking wine.'

'Don't be so sexist. It's not just women, fewer men, yes. In fact, it's better when Martin comes because he helps us stay on topic. Although I haven't read the book at all this month so maybe it's better if we don't.'

'Just 'fess up,' Oliver says. 'You've got a small baby, perfect excuse.'

*So you've noticed?*

'What's the book you're reading?' Danni asks. I lean back and grab the book from the counter behind me. '*Her Beloved Husband*,' she reads the title aloud. 'I haven't heard of it.'

'You'd have lost me at the title,' Oliver says. He gets up, putting his cup in the dishwasher. 'It's great to see you settling in, Danni. You're a life saver.'

No doubt he's thinking of the help she'll give me and how I'll be less stressed meaning I won't fret about him so much. I vow to do the opposite. I'm going to find out exactly what he's up to.

'It's not my kind of book. Holly, Ben's wife – Oliver's brother – chose it. They live over the road.'

'That's nice, at least I hope it is. Do you get on?'

'Oh yes, she's lovely, a lot younger than me, but she has a baby too, Jack, he's six months old, she's a great support. It's their first, so she asks for advice a lot. Although I'm not sure what I'm doing half the time.'

'Nonsense, your children seem very happy, and they're well looked after,' she says. 'It's a privilege that you let me into your household to be their nanny. I hope I can live up to your expectations.'

To my alarm my eyes fill with tears, and I nuzzle the top of Lucy's head so that Danni doesn't notice. I don't want her to know about any problems I have with Oliver. She might not be so keen to stay if she thinks we're not a stable household.

'You're doing great so far. And thanks for the compliment.'

'What time is your book club?'

'Eight o'clock.'

'How many are you expecting?'

'Anything from four to about eight. It depends who comes.'

————

Oliver offers to take charge of the children's bath and bedtime. It's the first time he's been home in ages to do that, another reason I resent his squash night commitment. It enables me to focus on sorting out the room and getting the refreshments ready. Danni offers to help but I insist she doesn't need to and must do her own thing. It's hard to get the balance sometimes when you're living in the house which is also your place of employment and I don't want her to think we're taking advantage of her. So far, I think she's going to fit in just fine.

I set the food out on the kitchen island and light some candles, dimming the lights and switching the fire on. White lights shine from the Christmas tree and silver baubles catch the light and add sparkle to the room. Relieved to have got everything ready in time, I open a bottle of red wine and pour myself a generous glass, all thoughts of restraint forgotten. I'll be too busy being a hostess to drink much later, never mind eating. As long as everyone enjoys themself, that's the main priority.

I take advantage of the half hour before guests are due to have a look at the book. Romance isn't my preferred reading choice, I prefer a cosy crime, nothing too dark and secretive, or a good old-fashioned whodunnit. I read the blurb on the back of the book.

*Sally has had her heart broken more times than she cares to remember but all that is in the past now she's been happily married to Gerald for the last few years. But when he gets a promotion and a new secretary, he becomes increasingly distant.*

*When he stays out late, acquires a new wardrobe and takes up running, warning bells begin to chime. Is her beloved husband having an affair?*

The woman on the cover is standing in front of a window, eyes full of angst. I chuck the book onto the sofa. To read that book now would be like rubbing salt into a wound. A peal of laughter filters down the stairs. I go into the hall. The deep murmur of Oliver's voice is coming from the bathroom, and I can just see Danni standing on the landing outside, her shapely ankle in a dark stiletto. A pain grips my insides. Is this why he was so keen to look after the children? Is his roving eye not satisfied with a wife and a mistress?

# TWELVE

The sound of laughter reaches my ears, accompanied by footsteps coming down the path. The doorbell rings. I check my face quickly in the hall mirror, making sure no traces of my earlier tears are showing. I've found it hard to stop crying today; the thought of Gabi cheating with my husband is breaking my heart. Earlier, after I'd reapplied my makeup after a bout of tears and got myself together, ready for the evening, I'd spotted her car sliding into her driveway and I'd ducked out of sight, hurting as if I'd been knifed in the chest. Gabi is the only friend I've allowed myself to get close to, and I was convinced our relationship was one that would last – frequent nights out when the children are older, maturing and changing together. If I do ever move away from here, I'd envisaged her coming to stay for weekends, taking long country walks, our cheeks rosy with the country air. Now our relationship lies in tatters. My eyes harden as I scrutinise myself in the mirror, and the sadness and devastation are replaced by white-hot anger. How dare she get close to me, worm her way into my life, only to take what is mine and laugh at me behind my back. I grit my teeth, more determined than ever to get the proof I need and present them with it. I straighten my shoulders and give myself a final stare, telling myself I will get through this evening, before opening the door. Martin stands outside in his camel coat, huge mustard-coloured scarf thrown around his neck.

'Hope you've got the heating on, darling,' he says, pulling me into a huge bear embrace. His scarf smells of expensive aftershave and his beard scratches my cheek as we exchange four kisses, as is his manner. He and Edward lived in the South of France for years before moving back here. 'Oh look at that lovely fire, so welcoming on this winter night.' He shrugs out of his coat, which I put in the cloakroom. I quickly check my phone to see if Gabi has replied to my text asking her if she's coming. My stomach lurches every time I think about what she's done. If only it wasn't book club and I could sit down with Martin and pour my heart out.

Martin is admiring the Christmas tree and I fetch him a glass of wine. We sit down in front of the fire and he picks up the book from where I discarded it on the sofa.

'Dreadful book,' he says, 'but I've passed it on to my mother. She loves a good romance. The writing's not bad but the plot is all over the place.'

'I haven't read it.'

'Naughty,' he says. 'I missed you at coffee this week.'

'I had to meet our new nanny. I missed you last week, too.'

'I had a work meeting which overran and by the time I finally escaped it wasn't worth going.'

'How was it?'

'We talked a lot about Tilly and what happened last week. Edward is on it, of course. He's looking into upping security on the development.'

'He's so good. It's not as if he hasn't got enough to do. There was a lot of talk about your party, by the way. Dresses were discussed. Will Edward have finished his redecoration by then?'

'It's a bit more than redecoration, but that's the plan.

Setting the party date gives him a fixed deadline so that's when he'll finish; you know he likes to stick to a schedule.' He rolls his eyes.

'Don't knock it. I wish Oliver could catch the schedule bug.'

'Speaking of Oliver, Edward is inviting Gavin Lord to the party. Oliver might be interested to know his employer will be there. He'll have to be on his best behaviour.'

'Of course, I forgot Edward is friends with them. He's here this evening, actually; he's putting the children to bed.'

'I thought I heard voices. I bet you miss Kate.'

'I do. But I've got a replacement, she's here too but she isn't working tonight. At least, not officially.' I've been aware of the continuing murmur of conversation upstairs. Perhaps Oliver is reading a story.

'You don't sound thrilled. Is she not working out?'

'Oh no, she's great so far, although it's still early days.' That reminds me I need to check the second reference she gave, just to be on the safe side. The doorbell goes again.

'Hello,' Becky says, her face hidden by a huge hood pulled down almost covering her eyes. She's clutching a bottle of wine and her hands are pink and mottled. 'I reckon it's going to snow, you know, it's so cold. I've only walked across the road and my toes are icy already.'

'A drink will warm you up,' I say. 'Martin's here, he's the only one so far.'

I check my phone again. Not a word from Gabi.

I pour Becky a glass of wine and bring some more glasses to the table. Asha arrives next, and I'm just closing the door when I hear my name and recognise Gabi's voice. She comes tripping down the path in her high heels.

'Don't shut the door.' She pulls me in for a hug and I can't help tensing my shoulders. 'That bad already, is it?' she whispers in my ear, and I experience another bolt of anger, followed by sadness for our friendship that it is slipping away from me.

But for now, I don't want her to know I'm on to her. I loosen my shoulders, smile at her.

'So glad you're here.'

'Ben can't make it,' Becky is saying as we go into the lounge. 'I bumped into him on the way over.'

'Ben,' Asha says, laughing. 'He says that every time and I don't think he's been once. What about Holly?'

'He didn't say.'

'It would be nice not to be the token male,' Martin says.

Asha checks her phone again. 'I reckon that's everyone, apart from Sienna, and she just texted to say she's on her way.'

'I saw you at the spa earlier,' I say, watching Asha's face carefully. Not that I think for a minute she'll have left that note in my bag. She looks genuinely surprised.

'Oh, I didn't see you. Shame, you could have joined us.'

'I was just leaving when I saw you go down to the spa area.' The doorbell rings, and I get up to answer it. Sienna is wearing a soft-looking hoody and a thick scarf. She kisses me on each cheek and holds her hands out.

'I come bearing gifts,' she says. 'No gold or frankincense, but this wine is a good one and I found this on your car. Lazy postman couldn't even make it to the letter box.' She hands me a bottle of red wine and a white envelope. I shiver. 'Let's get inside, you're shaking,' she says. I don't want to take the envelope, already sensing what the writing on the front looks like. I can't help looking. My name is handwritten in capitals. It looks much like the others I've had and I shove it in the letter rack. I won't let it spoil this evening. I need all my strength to put on a friendly facade with Gabi.

'I'm looking forward to hearing what you all thought about the book,' Asha is saying. 'I finished it last night. Hi, Sienna.'

'You've started without me,' Sienna says. 'Hi, everyone. Sorry I'm late.'

'Only just,' Asha says. 'You haven't missed anything.'

'I'm not talking about the book,' Sienna says. 'I mean the wine.' Everyone laughs as Martin pours her a glass. My phone beeps with a text and I'm glad of the excuse to fiddle with my phone, willing my pulse to calm down.

'It's Holly,' I say, 'she's running late, says not to wait for her.'

'We might need another bottle already,' he says.

'Good job I brought one then. And I'm afraid I haven't had a chance to read the book. I forgot and my copy only arrived last weekend.'

'You should have saved your money,' Sienna says. 'I couldn't get on with it at all. The bad choices the protagonist made drove me insane. And the happy ending was unrealistic.'

'You're so cynical,' Asha says. 'Don't you believe in love?'

'Depends on the man.'

'Help yourself to food,' I say, indicating the table where the food is laid out.

'Did you like the book, Becky?' Martin asks.

'It was quite good, not her best. I chose it because I've liked all her others, but this one was a bit of a let-down. The husband was a complete pig, though. I'd like to think most men aren't like that.'

Sienna laughs. 'You mean you don't believe married men have affairs? Please.'

I top up people's drinks to avoid having to participate in the conversation.

Footsteps are heard coming down the wooden stairs. Oliver sticks his head around the door.

'Hi, everyone.'

'Oliver! I didn't realise you were here. Are you coming to join book club?' Asha says.

He grimaces. 'Reading's not my thing, I'm afraid, unless it's non-fiction...'

'He means work-related,' I say. 'Give him a thick book on economic trends and you won't get a word out of him for hours.'

'Can I get anyone anything?' he asks. 'Need any wine from the cellar?' He directs the question to me.

'No, we've got plenty. How are the kids?'

'All asleep. I helped Danni with the stories. She coped with them admirably. Come and say hello to the neighbours.' He gestures to Danni, who I hadn't realised was behind him. She appears in the doorway. The lights from the tree pick out the golden highlights in her hair.

'Hi,' she says, 'I'm Danni, the new nanny.'

'Hi,' Asha says, 'you didn't tell us you'd found someone, Harriet.'

'It happened quite fast. Oliver found her through a work contact.'

'That must be such a relief.'

'Come and join us for a drink,' Sienna says, as if it's her house.

'Thanks, but I'm a bit tired and I've got some phone calls to make. Nice to meet you all.'

She goes upstairs and Oliver goes into the kitchen and gets himself a drink. His phone rings and he takes it outside.

'So Oliver found her? I'm sure I've seen her over in the park before. You can't help noticing her. She's a bit gorgeous,' Sienna says. 'I'm not sure I'd want someone so attractive living in my house.'

'Wouldn't you trust your husband?' Martin asks, and I want to hug him. How can Sienna be so insensitive, given what she knows about Oliver and Gabi? I risk a glance at Gabi out of the corner of my eye. She's eating a piece of cheese, apparently indifferent to the conversation going on around her. Clever, I think. If it hadn't been for overhearing Asha and Sienna in the spa earlier I really would have had absolutely no idea. Of course Oliver would help Danni; any partner would have done the same. And it's natural that Danni wouldn't want to join us. I can't help remembering last month, when Kate joined us after expressing an interest in the book I was reading. I wonder what she's doing now. The doorbell rings.

'That must be Holly, excuse me a minute.'

'I'm so sorry I'm late,' Holly says, 'Ben was called out for work and I had to wait until he was back. I'm so mad at him; he knows I look forward to these meetings.'

'It's fine, we're just glad you can make it.' I hug her. Her hair is lank and she has dark circles under her eyes. 'Come and get a drink.'

Holly's arrival breaks up the group discussion and I fetch her a glass, my hands unsteady.

'You alright, Harriet?' Martin asks.

I nod.

Becky puts the paperback down. 'Can I have a glass of water, perhaps.'

'I've got still and sparkling in the fridge,' I say.

'I'll come with you.'

We move down to the kitchen end of the room.

'You looked a bit lost there for the minute,' she says. 'Are you sure you're OK?'

'I keep getting flashbacks to the other night. Tilly is totally unscathed, but she can't really tell us what happened. I just have to believe nothing traumatising took place.'

She grips my wrist. 'It was terrifying. I'm paranoid as it is about anything happening to Dolly, and since that happened to you I'm even worse.'

'You don't have to justify anything to me. I know exactly what you mean. Any time you need to talk, you know where I am.'

'Thanks.'

'Still or sparkling?'

'Still please.'

I sort out her water and she goes back into the other room. Everyone is laughing and I catch sight of the envelope where I hastily shoved it into the letter rack. I can't resist a quick look. My hands are shaking a little as I tear the edge off the envelope. I must be the only person who would prefer it to be a parking ticket. No such luck. It's the third note, handwritten in capitals as were the others, the message the only difference.

### YOU DON'T DESERVE TO HAVE CHILDREN

A chill creeps over my body. It's as if the sender has been listening in to my conversation with Becky, not only heard the words but seen into the deepest recesses of my mind.

# 2006

The house she was going to was one of the posh ones on the other side of the street. The children who lived there didn't go to Lancaster High like she was forced to, where teachers had to fight through each day as if taking part in a battle, armed with reinforcements and tactics to get through the hour. School would have been alright if she'd been able to go to the Montgomery school, the large Edwardian building surrounded by acres of grounds and proper sports facilities. The children who lived in the houses on the hill went there, obviously. She was bright; her teachers were forever telling her if only she would apply herself more she could get into one of the best universities. Her parents wanted that for her. She did too, but somewhere in the middle of year nine she'd given up trying. What was the point in paying attention in lessons when the teachers spent the whole time dealing with a handful of idiots who refused to behave. Darren Baker – everyone knew his parents were druggies, what was the point of him learning about Henry VIII and his hundreds of wives? That's where she had learned about Anne Boleyn, and attracted by her character had sought out novels written about her in the library which brought her vividly to life, revealing a fiery woman who stood up for what she believed in. But that wasn't enough. When Darren Baker was inevitably excluded, Gary Bird took over as the resident clown. Making complaints didn't get her anywhere and she was picked on when she was found out for being the snitch, because Angie Sutton fancied Gary and wouldn't leave her alone after that. Much as she enjoyed learning, it was impossible, easier to become one of the clowns instead of fighting them.

No, if she'd been able to go to the Montgomery school, where she presumed they didn't have to put up with idiots in the classroom getting away with murder just because they could, she would be going to Oxford or Cambridge and making her parents proud. Instead she was going out with Mike, who came from the rough estate in a worse part of town than that in which they lived.

'Going out with' wasn't strictly true. They'd talked for over an hour at the party a couple weekends ago, and he'd topped up her cider three times. The cider made her head feel sparkly and instead of being tongue-tied like she usually was she hadn't had to think about what to say, or look for the right words like she usually did and end up blurting out embarrassing sentences and being laughed at. Who could have known that Mike would be into the same bands as her? He'd even been at the summer festival and she had no idea. He'd taken her number and suggested they could hang out some time. She shied away from contacting him, but after a week of not hearing anything she sent him a text, overseen by Gemma, kept it really casual and asking if he fancied hooking up and he said yes. They'd met at the ice cream parlour in town and afterwards they'd gone for a walk in the woods and he'd pushed her against a tree and kissed her. A proper French kiss. She'd grazed her back on the tree bark when he pressed against her and she could feel an alarming hardness against her groin. It wasn't the first time she'd kissed anyone and he was a better kisser than frog-faced Jason, who'd not given her much choice about being kissed in the first place. 'Masterful' was the word she used to describe the encounter with Mike to Gemma; it made it feel like something out of one of the large-print romance novels her grandmother got from the mobile library. She didn't tell her about the purple bruise on her back where the tree had dug into her spine.

Their paths had crossed a couple of times the following week at school, but he wasn't in her year or her house and he was usually with his mates, some of who towered over her even though she was a respectable five foot five. They'd said hi and when she'd turned back to look at him after a suitable pause she'd caught him looking back too. He'd winked. She'd had a smile on her face all through double geography after that.

She decided not to tell Gemma about the text she'd sent him casually informing him where she was going to be on Saturday night, thanks to her favourite uncle giving her a glowing reference. She hoped he'd take her up on it and they could watch a film together on the enormous television screen. When she read the text back, she realised she had deliberately omitted to say that she wouldn't be in her house. The crazy thought she'd had about letting him think she actually lived in a house in such an exclusive postcode like that wasn't going away. Would she dare to follow it through? Definitely not one to confide in Gemma about. If only she'd known then how she would live to regret the whole episode.

# THIRTEEN

I shove the note back in the rack and pour myself a large glass of water, which I drink in huge gulps, staring into space. Somebody is terrorising me. That note was left on my car, which means that any one of the people inside of my house right at this moment could want to do me harm. I grip the edge of the kitchen counter and take huge breaths.

'Harriet, what's wrong?'

I whirl round, startled out of my reverie but relieved it's Martin standing there and not Gabi seeking me out for a girly chat like she normally would. She finds these meetups somewhat claustrophobic with me her only 'kindred spirit'. Ordinarily I'd be like-minded, finding comfort in our closeness. Another lie, no doubt.

'Nothing.'

'You're not worried about what Sienna said about Danni being attractive, I hope?'

'No, of course not.' I muster a laugh. 'Oliver's at work during the week; he's hardly going to see her. She's been great so far.'

I give him a bright smile, but he doesn't look convinced, watching me intently. Gabi appears in the doorway.

'What are you two chatting about? They're talking about their favourite romance writers in there and it's not really my thing. I like a good murder, something to get the mind going. I know exactly what I'm going to choose when it's my turn.'

I put the glass in the sink. 'I was just taking a breather. We'd better go back and join the others – it looks rude.'

Gabi leads the way and Martin pulls me back.

'Come round for a coffee some time if ever you want to talk. It will be good to have a proper chat.' His kind eyes crinkle and I squeeze his arm.

'Thanks.'

The rest of the evening passes in a blur. As more empty wine bottles appear on the table, the conversation gets louder and more raucous and after a couple of large glasses of red, I'm hoping to be able to relax myself, but my thoughts get darker and every person around the table becomes a potential enemy. Both Sienna and Asha are regular spa goers, so it's possible either one of them could have left the note, but then so are Oliver and Gabi. I have no way of knowing who else was at the gym yesterday. Besides, every household on Prospect Close has an automatic membership.

'What do you think, Harriet?' Gabi's voice pulls me out of my head. She's seated across from me, a deliberate choice on my part, to avoid her drawing me into private conversations, which is how we'd normally operate.

'Sorry, I was daydreaming. About what?'

'We were just saying that the husband shouldn't have got away with it.' My throat feels tight; what is she talking about? 'You know, in the book. He didn't deserve the happy ending.'

'I agree totally,' says Sienna. 'If you do wrong then you should atone for it somehow. People get away with far too much these days.'

I grip hold of my wine glass tight, my fingers white. 'Ah, the book, yes of course. It depends. I like to give people a second chance.'

'It depends what they've done,' Becky says.

I stand up. 'Let me clear away some of these glasses.'

I breathe a sigh of relief when I get out of the room. Everyone is watching me, keen to know my thoughts. My heartbeat is pulsing fast and I drink some water to calm myself. Once I've composed myself, I re-join the others.

'How many people are you expecting at your party?' Sienna asks. 'Any of Edward's celebrity friends?' Edward appeared on a television series earlier this year, on which he was one of a panel of judges overseeing a competition in which couples designed their own houses. The show was a huge hit, and the celebrity version is being aired next year. Edward's wit and eccentricity are making him a bit of a household name.

'I'm in charge of the guest list,' Martin says, 'and it's mostly only people from the immediate area, plus a few close friends.'

'That's a shame,' Sienna says. 'I was hoping you were going to invite the judges. Dean Ludlow specifically.'

Everyone laughs. Except me. I'm convinced the person who has it in for me is in our immediate community, never mind Oliver cheating on me with the woman next door. Who else knows about the affair? I'm on my guard with everyone now; it's the only way.

'Will Elliott be there?' Becky asks.

'He's been invited,' Martin says. 'But I doubt he'll come.'

'I heard his divorce is finally going through,' Asha says, 'but that was from Celia, Daisy and Chantal's mother. I swear she makes a lot of stuff up.'

'It's a shame he doesn't mix more,' Gabi says. 'I've barely said two words to him.'

'He certainly stepped up when I needed him,' I say. 'Before that I'd only ever spoken to him in a professional capacity but I understand why he can't really mix with us. He's keeping a distance as is expected. He's excellent at his job, which is what's important to me, and he's always perfectly pleasant. Not everybody wants to have the neighbours knowing their business.'

Gabi laughs. 'Well, we all know you'd rather be in a redeveloped barn miles deep in the countryside, far away from your nearest neighbours.'

'Spare me,' Sienna says. 'I can't think of anything worse. Is that what Oliver wants?'

'She's exaggerating,' I say, shifting on my seat, uncomfortable at being the centre of attention, despising Gabi for sitting in my house, eating my food, drinking my drink, knowing what she's doing to me. 'Does anyone want any more food or drink?'

Becky wants some more water and I fetch the bottle from the fridge. Gabi follows me.

'What was that about back there? You're always on about moving to the countryside.'

I sigh, keeping my temper in check. I have to be sure before I challenge her. 'It's just that you touched a nerve; you know how frustrated I am about still being here.'

'I thought you were going to sort it out over Christmas.'

I nod. 'We are and I'm just being an idiot. Too much wine and I find these evenings stressful at the best of times, but the past few days have been hectic and I could have done without being the hostess.'

'I totally get that. So we're good, me and you.'

*Oh, you're good, Gabi, but I'll get the better of you. Wait until I find my proof, then I'll show you just how good I am. You won't know what has hit you.*

'Of course we are.' I squeeze her arm. In my mind I'm digging my fingernails into her skin, piercing her flesh until she screams. Only then will I know she feels the same pain I do. 'Why ever would you think otherwise?'

· · ·

The book long since abandoned, and party conversation dwindling, Asha gets up and announces it's time she got back home.

'Mo's on early tomorrow, so he'll need his sleep.'

'It's time I went too,' Becky says, and suddenly everyone is standing and making their excuses, thanking me and hugging me and I'm wondering which one of them sees a target on my back. Gabi is the last to go.

'Speak tomorrow?'

I nod, wanting her out of my sight and away before Oliver turns up and I have to see them putting on a charade for my benefit.

Oliver comes downstairs as I'm closing the door and I breathe a sigh of relief, desperate for sleep, doubting I'll get any.

'Have fun?' he asks, putting his arm around me. This time I fight against the inclination to stiffen and pull away from him. These two won't get the upper hand with me.

'The usual. I could have done without it to be honest but I've got my turn out of the way.'

'Fancy a night cap?'

I shake my head. 'I can't wait to crawl into bed.'

'I'll be up to join you shortly.'

If Oliver hadn't been here, I'd have no doubt had several night caps while trying to make sense of the note Sienna found on my car.

*YOU DON'T DESERVE TO HAVE CHILDREN*

I've wanted to be a mother for so long. My life is divided into two halves, the first before I had Tess, my firstborn, only a few minutes before Tilly followed. In that moment, when I first held them both in my arms, their soft skin against my sweaty body, with Oliver holding my hand and gazing adoringly at us with tears in his eyes, the second half of my life had begun. These two small beings dominate my every thought. The fear that had played along in the background during the first half of my life had been kept safely at a distance, but doing press-ups in the background, waiting, ready to pounce. It arrived with Tess and Tilly and intensified with Lucy. Tilly's disappearance brought it sharply to the fore again.

And Oliver knows nothing about it.

Oliver crawls into bed as my mind whirrs and my body vibrates with fatigue.

He spoons up against me, whispering into my ear.

'You awake?'

I grunt, incapable of conversation, let alone anything else, desperate for the oblivion of sleep.

'Only a few more days to go.' He pulls the duvet over himself and settles down.

Why do the holidays, which I've waited so long for now, loom ahead like a threat? I should be looking forward to them. Instead I pull the duvet over my head and wish I didn't have to resurface.

# FOURTEEN

The following day a strange light glows behind the bedroom blinds and when I open them I'm confronted with Prospect Close covered in a few inches of snow. Proper snow. Thick and settled with footprints wending trails around the close. For a second I marvel at the beauty of it, before memories of last night cast a cloud over the morning. Not only has my husband betrayed me with my best friend, but the note left on my car brings me out in a cold sweat.

Oliver is nowhere to be seen, and the house is curiously quiet, considering the children have an inset day at preschool. I roll over to check on Lucy, to be faced with an empty cot. Perplexed, I jump out of bed, cursing as my ankle twists, but not stopping to ease out the pain. I hobble downstairs two steps at a time, ears straining for any baby sounds, but silence envelops the ground floor too. What if the sender of the note has swooped in the night and taken my babies away? I come to an abrupt halt in the kitchen; Danni and the twins are playing out in the back garden. The relief is overwhelming. Tess is hurling snowballs and shrieking with excitement. Tilly is building a snowman, her forehead scrunched up with concentration under her favourite red hat with the huge pompom knitted by her grandmother last winter. A nice bright colour so I can always see her. I wrench the bifold doors open, letting in a blast of cold air and the noise from Tess raising several decibels.

'Where's Lucy?'

'Oliver's taken her out for a walk. He's amazing, isn't he?'

The thudding in my heart recedes and I lean against the door frame.

'Yes, isn't he?' I smile through gritted teeth.

'I hope you didn't mind them coming out here.'

'Not at all. I was just surprised for a minute when Lucy wasn't there. Do you want a coffee?'

'Ooh that would be wonderful.'

It's been ages since Oliver has taken care of Lucy in the morning, so it's natural to be thrown. I mull over Danni's offhand remark. He was amazing when the twins were little, when he was a proud new father and we were terrified, teetering on the edge of a void, not knowing what to do with these two small beings we'd miraculously made together. Everything was scary but also exciting and wonderful and the best thing about it was that we were in it together. This time around I feel like a single parent, navigating parenthood alone. I wasn't even going to bother getting a nanny, until Oliver insisted, once his job became increasingly more demanding of his time and my business took off. That had never been part of the plan, which is why we'd come to the agreement we had. Two years here, then a big change, and my chance to move my business to the next level, to move on to the next rung of the ladder before eventually opening my own clothes shop. Watching Tess, who has joined Tilly in building a snowman, and seeing the identical expressions of determination on their faces, gives me a jolt. They get their determination from me and I am not going to lose myself. Oliver must bear responsibility for his actions. Next year is going to be different; I make that resolve, calmed by the smooth white carpet of snow which obscures the obstacles I normally see in front of me.

An hour later, the twins are back inside and a snowman watches from the back garden, his dark stone eyes fixed on me over his stubbly carrot of a nose. Oliver's bottle-green cashmere scarf is draped around his neck. Danni is making breakfast. Oliver has returned with Lucy and headed off to a meeting. She bounces on my lap, her cheeks flushed from the fresh air and her face not betraying a trace of the tiredness she should be feeling after the little sleep she got last night. It has made a change for Oliver to be there and help with her. I can't wait until he starts his leave. Having him at home means I'll be able to keep an eye on him.

'What are you doing this afternoon?' Danni asks.

'I'm visiting my neighbour for coffee.' That is another decision I've made. Talking to Martin will help and so what if I have to break Oliver's confidence? Oliver hates anyone knowing his business, but he's brought this on himself.

'Leave Lucy with me,' she says. 'We're not going anywhere.'

'We?'

'Me and the girls.'

Of course. For a second I'd imagined she was talking about Oliver. Damn Sienna for slipping that tiny doubt into my mind last night. I hesitate. 'If you're sure.'

---

I text Martin to check that he's free and he says he is and he's just baked a cake, so I get ready to leave.

It feels odd not to have Lucy in her sling, keeping my front warm, and I hug my puffy jacket tighter. My boots leave large tracks in the snow as it's been falling again since late morning.

The playground looks bizarre, with the swings and slide covered in white, strange geometric shapes sticking out of the ground. I think about Martin as I make my way to the penthouse. His uncomplicated life appeals to me, but I wouldn't be without the children for anything. And my husband? For that my answer is less clear.

The thought terrifies me.

I'm so engrossed in what my husband might be up to that I literally bump into Becky, who is walking towards me. She's dressed down for her in a sports jacket and her hair is pulled back into a loose ponytail. Normally it's sleek and glossy and she usually wears jeans and smart boots.

'So sorry,' I say. 'I'm miles away. Where are you off to?'

'Just to pick Dolly up from preschool. I know it's way too early, but after what happened to you the other day, I like to get there in plenty of time. I'm a bit of a nervous wreck when she's there to be honest. Ryan keeps telling me to get a grip. I don't understand why he doesn't take it as seriously as me... I'm sorry, I'm being totally insensitive.'

'It's fine. Don't be so hard on yourself. Is that what Ryan is telling you?'

She nods.

'Typical man.'

'Look, why don't I bring Dolly over to play tomorrow afternoon if you're free, and we can have a chat.'

'Thanks, I'd like that. Talking will help, I'm sure. Otherwise I just sit indoors while everything goes round in my head. It's alright for Oliver, he's busy at work. He says he's still upset, but he seems completely over it to me.'

'Everyone is different. So what if it takes you longer. It's different for mothers, no matter what anyone says.'

'I'd better go, but I'll see you tomorrow. The girls will be thrilled.'

'So will Dolly. Hyper I expect. Bye.'

———

The penthouse opens into one vast open space with luxurious polished concrete floors and the latest Farrow and Ball shade of paint, with bifold doors running the whole length of the flat, offering an almost panoramic view of the courtyard at one end and the normally green hills on the other side. Today the hills are white, and the sky is luminous. The view takes my breath.

'It looks wonderful, doesn't it?'

Martin stands at my side.

'You're not talking about Edward's new design, are you?'

'I've forgotten how it looked before. Fabulous artworks.' I look around the room, at the sleek new furniture and the stunning wall of wallpaper at the end of the living space. 'It's amazing too. Although if I lived here there would be children's toys everywhere.'

'Don't lie, your house is always immaculate.'

While he makes coffee and takes his cake out of the oven, I wander around inspecting the room. Edward collects art from his travels around the world, and there is a painting I haven't seen before of a beach paradise, clear blue water and palm trees. The artworks are lit by subtle light fittings to show them off at their best.

'This painting is new; it's gorgeous.'

'Isn't it? I like to lie on the chaise longue opposite and imagine I'm lying on that beach with the sun on my skin.'

Last time I was lying on a couch I was with my therapist and she was trying to make me relive the nightmares that were turning my life upside down. The sea looks beautiful in the painting but I know the dangers that lurk underneath the water, waiting to suck me down.

'That cake smells fantastic.' I switch my focus to the cinnamon and coffee smells that fill the room.

'It's a new recipe I'm trying for coffee and walnut cake. You can be my guinea pig. I hope you've got more of an appetite than you had last night. After you laid on such a delicious spread as well. I didn't see you eat a thing.'

'I get nervous being the host. I have to focus on everyone else's needs being met.'

'Is that all it is?'

Martin carries a tray with large slices of cake and cups of coffee on it over to the huge L-shaped couch in front of the window looking over the snowy peaks. The cup warms my hands.

'I'm OK, but ever since Tilly went missing I've been on edge.'

'That's understandable. You were a bit quieter than usual last night, which is also to be expected. I thought you might cancel, actually, and I'm sure everyone would have understood.'

'I wanted to, but I decided to get it over with.'

'That bad, eh?

I put my cup down on the table, shaking my head, biting my lip to stop myself from crying.

'It's Oliver; I think he's having an affair.' Everything tumbles out, finding the lipstick on the shirt, through to over-hearing Asha and Sienna at the gym. 'That's why it was so hard to face them last night. They said *everyone* knows. And I had to invite them all into my home where they can laugh at me, knowing Gabi was sitting there and what she's been doing behind my back. You'd think one of them would tell me to my face. Female solidarity and all that. Women are supposed to stick together. They're always saying how women come first.'

'That's Sienna exaggerating; she has a tendency to over-dramatise. It's the first I've heard of it so not *everyone* knows. If it's even true. There are two separate issues here, Oliver having an affair, and that it might be with Gabi. I find that *very* hard to believe.'

'How could he? It's bad enough knowing he has a mistress,

but to find out she's living next door, and she's my best friend...
It's almost as if he wants to get caught. When I assumed this
other woman was living in London, at least that made some
kind of sense; being stuck over there, far from me and the children, he might even have been missing us, missing me, not that
it would justify his behaviour, but... Oh Martin, what can I do?'

'First of all you need to establish the facts. Are you going to
confront him?'

'No. I mean yes, but not until I have concrete proof. I don't
want Gabi to know I've found out either, but pretending is so
hard; last night proved that. She knew something was up. But
I'd not long found out and I was feeling pretty fragile. Still am.'

'I would too in your position.'

For a moment I consider telling Martin everything, but that
would mean no going back. I trust him one hundred per cent
but he's part of the community. And any one of them could be
out to get me.

'How will you establish the truth?'

'I don't know yet. I haven't had a chance to think about it.'

'So at the spa you overheard Asha and Sienna talking about
a meal at a restaurant. Couldn't you ask them about it outright?'

'I could maybe speak to one of them, Asha probably, as we
see a lot more of one another because our children get on so
well. If I could swear her to secrecy. There was something else I
was suspicious about.' I explain what happened the night Oliver
was playing squash.

'Talk about making me feel stupid. At first I thought I'd got
it completely wrong, but since I found out about Gabi, I'm
convinced he uses that as a cover to see her. She had plenty of
time to warn him. Is he actually next door, carrying out this
affair right under my nose? I bet Ben knows all about it, and
maybe Holly too...' I let out a groan. 'I'm so angry, Martin.'

'Oh I can see that. But I might be able to help.'

He pours himself some more coffee and takes a bite of a fondant fancy, thinking as he chews.

'What time was he playing squash on Wednesday?'

'Eight to nine.'

'Come with me.' He crosses to the bifold door, pulling it open and stepping outside. 'Look what a marvellous view I have of Prospect Close. We have the best vantage point up here. Some days I sit and watch the comings and goings. Nothing goes on in that quadrangle that doesn't escape me. Edward is even worse. You know how he sees himself as the keeper of the castle? In a good way, of course.' He laughs.

I've often waved to them from down below, but I hadn't given much thought to what they can see. They have a bird's eye view not only of the quadrangle, but of some of the houses and the opposite block which contains Elliott's penthouse and Sienna's apartment below.

'On Wednesday evening I was reading out here with a glass of wine. Edward was cooking supper. I must admit I didn't see Oliver going out, but I did notice something interesting.'

'Oh?' I turn to face him.

'Yes. Gabi came out of your house and went into her flat. It was after nine, I'm not sure of the exact time. Shortly after somebody joined her. But it wasn't Oliver.'

I grip hold of the railings, feeling lightheaded.

'It was Ben.'

Oliver's brother, my brother-in-law.

# FIFTEEN

'What are you doing? The cleaner's due tomorrow.' Oliver frowns at me as he downs a glass of water. The kitchen island is covered with the contents of the cupboards and I'm scrubbing at the insides of the units, washing away non-existent stains.

'I can't help myself. You're back early.'

'My meeting was cancelled so I thought I'd make the most of having a free afternoon.'

'Have you had lunch?' Seeing him here is disorienting. If he was having an affair, wouldn't he have taken this unexpected opportunity to see his mistress? And if it's not Gabi, then who is it? Feeling like I don't know my own husband has taken away my sense of stability, as if I'm in freefall down a mountain, with nothing to hold onto. Cleaning brings a sense of order.

'Not yet. Have you?'

'I ate with the kids. I wasn't expecting you home so early.'

'No worries, I'll fix myself something. A sandwich will do.'

My phone pings. Gabi.

*Can we talk after I get home this evening?*

Gabi seeing Ben makes me almost as furious. She knows how fond I am of Holly, her concerns about being a good mother. No wonder she's kept that quiet.

*I'm busy with my husband.*

*My* husband.

'Problem?'

'It's Gabi, nothing important.' I put everything back in the cupboard and wash my hands. 'How was Ben on Wednesday?'

'What?'

'Ben. Your brother, when you played squash.' Maybe they didn't actually play, but it was Ben who needed an alibi. If it is Ben who's having the affair then Oliver is still lying to me to cover for him. Flashbacks from before I had children and I found out Oliver was having an affair have been haunting me ever since Martin's revelation. Does Oliver know that Ben went to see Gabi after? Presumably he was in on this and Ben used him as his cover. How can I find out whether it's true or not? Martin could be wrong.

'He was fine, same as usual. He's got a lot of work on at the moment. He's heading up a build over in Redbrook. He's having the usual problems with supplies but... why are you interested?'

'I was just wondering how he's finding being a new father. Holly was looking exhausted last night, didn't you notice?'

'I barely saw her. I was too busy with the children.'

And Danni.

'Is something wrong?' he asks. 'And why the sudden interest in Ben?'

'Just making conversation.'

'Shall we make the most of my afternoon off? I thought we could take the kids outside to the playground.'

I hesitate. 'O-K.'

'You don't sound that keen.'

'It's just I haven't been out there since the other week, you know when Tilly disappeared.'

'All the more reason to get back out there, I'd say. I can take them on my own if you want, but it would be a shame not to use the facilities anymore. I don't believe in hiding from things. It only makes them worse.'

*If only he knew.*

'Also, I'll be there. Nothing bad is going to happen to them and we won't let them out of our sight – not that we do usually.'

'Yes, you're right. Let's round them up. I'll sort Lucy out and you get the twins. They're upstairs with Danni.'

Oliver takes the stairs two at a time.

'I'm coming to get you,' he says. Excited squeals follow and little feet clatter across the floorboards above. Voices murmur and Danni laughs loudly. I wonder what the twins are doing to make her laugh. Oliver's voice rumbles and they both laugh again. Ah. Maybe it's not the twins who are making her laugh. I lift Lucy out from her cot and stick her into a papoose. Oliver is talking to Danni as they come downstairs, each carrying a twin. Tilly wriggles in Danni's arms and stretches her arms towards me.

'Mummy carry,' she says and I experience a flicker of satisfaction. I cup her face in my hands.

'I can't carry you *and* Lucy, darling, but hold my hand. We're going to the playground. That's exciting, isn't it, especially with Daddy here.'

'I can't wait to see who can swing the highest,' Oliver says.

'We don't swing high,' I say, giving him a look. 'Silly Daddy.'

'Do you want me to come?' Danni asks.

Oliver goes to answer but I jump in.

'No thanks,' I say. Kate would have never asked that question. I admonish myself for the thought. Danni's hardly been here five minutes, of course she can't anticipate my needs, but I want my husband all to myself.

As usual it takes longer than it should to get out of the house, Tess declaring she needs a wee just when we're about to go, then Oliver's phone ringing at the last minute – but he sends it to voicemail.

'Work,' he says, and I wish I didn't experience a twinge of suspicion.

At last we cross the icy quadrangle, Oliver holding a twin by each hand. Tess runs to the horse and gets Tilly to sit on the zebra, moving slowly forward and back. Tess bounces on hers, trying to make it go faster than it can, as if she's trying to get somewhere. They like to sit for ages on these, playing some private game where they babble away to one another in a language only they understand.

'She was on the zebra.' My tearful voice replays in my head. With my eyes I follow the path Tilly must have taken, only a few steps to the gate in the small wooden fence that separates the play area from the path leading out of Prospect Close into the street behind, where the noise of traffic increases and people wait at a bus stop. How easy it would have been for someone to take her tiny hand and sweep her up onto a bus. I cross the playground and make sure the gate is firmly closed.

'Tilly is fine,' Oliver says, putting his arm around my back. 'Look at her.' We sit on the bench and watch the girls. 'Do you want me to take Lucy?' He peers into the papoose.

'She's asleep again.' I stroke her head. 'She's such a good baby.'

'That's because you're a good mother.'

'Daddy, swings.'

Oliver pushes the girls on the swings and they shriek with delight, as he pushes them higher and my stomach lurches, seeing their little bodies leaning backwards over the stony ground.

'Not too high,' I call, and Lucy stirs. I stroke her face and she sighs in her sleep. Prospect Close is slumbering too as the afternoon slips by, the sky greying and lights going on in the houses around us. Such a contrast to the other evening when the sky was dark and anxious faces waited for news. The girls are on the climbing structure now, holding onto ropes and crawling over netting. The wind is picking up and I rummage around in my bag for Lucy's hat. I pull out a piece of paper, wondering what it is. It's the note, shoved out of sight the other day. I feel sick, push it back to the bottom and locate the hat.

'Let's go and see Daddy,' I murmur to Lucy.

'They're so confident,' Oliver says. 'I wish adults didn't develop that sense of danger, that prevents you taking physical risks. I used to be exactly the same as them.'

An emergency siren sounds in the distance, transporting me back to the other evening, when this area was full of adults all focused on the dangers around us.

'Come on, girls,' I say. 'It's getting cold. Let's go inside and get some hot chocolate and marshmallows.'

'Yummy mallows,' Tess says.

'Ooh yes,' Oliver says, 'I haven't had hot chocolate for ages.'

A car pulls into the close. It's an SUV belonging to Elliott. I wonder if being a head teacher he ever gets to switch off completely during the holidays, or whether he's always thinking about the hundreds of pupils he's responsible for. He doesn't have any children of his own as far as I know. He pulls into his drive before getting out and opening his boot. I wave but he doesn't notice us. The dark has crept up around the square, but the streetlights aren't yet illuminated. A red car drives in, not a car I recognise. It pulls up at an angle in the road where parking isn't allowed and a woman gets out. She's wearing smart jeans and a short jacket but her hair is uncombed and she's thin, unnaturally so, her skin sallow. She slams the car door behind her and doesn't lock the car. Elliott looks up and his face clouds over. I recognise the woman as being the one who spoke to him when he was organising the search for Tilly. He didn't appear pleased to see her then and he certainly doesn't look overjoyed now.

'That woman was here the other night,' I say to Oliver. 'Do you recognise her?'

'No, never seen her before.'

The girls take advantage of our inattention and sit on the floor, whispering to one another.

Elliott leaves the car boot open and approaches the woman.

'I told you not to come here,' he says, his voice firm but resigned. Their voices carry across the close. I hunch down in the seat, not wanting him to see us unwittingly bearing witness to his private life.

'You can't stop me,' she says. 'How else am I supposed to speak to you? You ignore my texts, never answer your phone. We need to talk.'

'We've said all we have to.'

Oliver points towards the exit and I shake my head. We don't want to hear this conversation but to leave the play area we'd have to cross in front of them. Elliott is such a private person I'd rather he didn't know we were here.

'Let's wait a minute.'

He nods.

The woman's voice is getting louder and soon we won't be the only ones to hear them.

'You might have. I want to know why you're sending me letters.'

'If you mean the documents from my solicitor, you must know what they are. You aren't stupid, Victoria, you're an intelligent woman. Have you read them?'

'No, I haven't opened them. I don't want you to communicate through documents. We don't need a solicitor. I have no money because you stopped giving me any. How am I supposed to live?'

'We've been through this. You have a good salary. We're separated and I want a divorce. I'm not having this conversation again. If you don't stop bugging me I will have to report you to the police. I don't want to go down that road but you aren't giving me much choice. I need to start again – we both do. It's for the best; you must know that after the last year we've had.'

'It's because of her, isn't it?'

'That's enough, Victoria, I'm calling the police.' He slams his boot closed and takes out his mobile.

'Why are you doing this to me?' Victoria says. 'You'll be sorry.' She gets back into her car and reverses perilously close to the fence, the girls looking up at the loud noise of the engine. 'And so will she,' she yells out of the window as she drives too fast out of the close.

'That was something,' Oliver says. 'Poor Elliott. I had no idea his divorce was so acrimonious.'

'It doesn't sound like she's very happy, but we don't know what he's done,' I say, 'she's certainly upset about something.' I tell him about the other night. We get the girls up and by the time we head for home there is no sign of Elliott and the close is quiet. We talk in low voices.

'Did you know he was married?'

'No. I hardly know anything about him. I don't think he wears a ring, he's very private.'

Back at home Oliver heats up some milk while I get the children out of their coats and shoes. Danni comes downstairs when she hears us.

'Have a good time, girls?' she asks.

The girls chatter excitedly.

'That was nice,' I say to Oliver. 'I'm so looking forward to the holidays.'

'Me too.' He pulls me towards him. 'I'm going to be working

late for a few nights next week, remember, but once that's over...'

I pull away. 'You didn't say.'

He frowns. 'I'm sure I did.'

Danni's presence stops me pressing the point. I'm sure he hasn't mentioned this before as I'm so aware of his movements at the moment. I have to be. Is that why he suggested the playground? To put me in a good mood so I wouldn't mind when he told me he'd be out late. Again. The warm cosy feeling I had on returning from our afternoon dissipates. All my concerns that had been temporarily cast aside in our family outing come rushing back.

'Hot chocolate, everyone,' Oliver says, and we all sit around the table. Oliver has made Danni a hot chocolate too and she rewards him with a beautiful smile. I remember what Sienna said about seeing her around here before. The thought makes me shiver. If it's not Gabi Oliver is seeing, but someone else from nearby, maybe it's closer to home than I feared.

My hot chocolate tastes bitter when I take the first sip.

# SIXTEEN

Oliver's back at work on Monday for the next five days before his leave begins. He was wearing his suit this morning, which made Tilly cry because she knows that means he's going to work and won't be back to read her a story this evening. He was standing in the kitchen leaning against the counter eating a piece of toast, holding his hand under it so as not to drop crumbs on his suit and I wanted to stop him going and stay and talk and just get to being the two of us against the world again. But he washes his hands, kisses us all goodbye and disappears off to London and who knows what.

Danni comes downstairs just after he's left, wearing a yellow top that makes me think of sunshine but it's white and sludgy outside. Tess, who up until that point has been pushing her cereal around the bowl and insisting she doesn't like it when I try and cajole her into eating, immediately tells Danni about Daddy going to work and tucks into her breakfast when Danni asks her to. Then she's wiping faces and clearing the table looking like a goddess the whole time and I feel like a spare part in my own home.

Once Danni has taken them off to soft play for the morning, I decide to have a look at Oliver's laptop. We share the same passwords. I justify it by telling myself I wouldn't mind if he was logging into my laptop – after all I have nothing to hide on mine. I key in the password details, tapping my fingers impatiently on the table waiting for the screen to open when I'm confronted with an error message. He's changed his password.

My stomach sinks. Clearly, he has stuff he wants to hide from me. I slam the laptop shut.

––––––

Becky and Dolly arrive early in the afternoon. Dolly squirms as her mother takes her boots off; she's impatient to join the twins, who are playing in the living room.

'Has she said any more about the other day?' she asks, as we watch them playing together.

'I haven't asked. I'm trying to forget it ever happened. The police made enquiries but haven't been able to find out any more information about the man who took her across the road. I'm just making sure to watch her like a hawk when she's outside anywhere, and obviously I've told Danni the same.'

'It must be hard to trust them with a new person after that.'

'It is, but I can't smother them.'

'It's so hard to get the right balance, isn't it? Edward's contacting the council to get more CCTV put up in the area, which is a good idea.'

'Coffee?'

'Yes please.'

'Are you looking forward to Christmas?'

She sits at the kitchen island while I put the machine on.

'Normally it's my favourite time of the year, but Ryan's really stressed at the moment. He had a family bereavement which hit him hard and I don't think his plumbing business is going as well as he would like. He bottles everything up and leaves me to guess what's bothering him. Is Oliver like that?'

'He doesn't talk about his work to me very much, but because he works such long hours, when he is home we have a lot of catching up to do with day-to-day stuff. And then he'll get involved in a new work project and so the cycle recommences. I'm looking forward to the holiday and having some family time.'

I put the mugs of coffee on the table.

'Would you like a piece of cake?'

'Yes please.'

I open the cake tin to reveal the fluffy-looking coffee cake decorated with frosting and walnuts Danni made yesterday. She really is making herself indispensable.

'That looks amazing. Did you make it?'

'I wish I could say yes, but no, that was Danni, our new nanny.' I cut her a slice.

The doorbell rings.

'Excuse me a minute.'

I open the front door to a man holding a huge bouquet of flowers. Deep red roses with velvet petals.

'Mrs Carlton?'

'Yes, wow. I wasn't expecting these.'

'Somebody loves you,' he says.

'Thanks.' I take the flowers through to the kitchen.

'Oh how gorgeous,' Becky says. 'From Oliver?'

'I suppose they must be.' Oliver used to send me flowers all the time but hasn't for ages now. I'd assumed this was the normal pattern of married life, but now I wonder. Guilty conscience?

'There's a card here,' Becky says, plucking an envelope out of the box which contains the flowers. 'Oh.'

'What is it?'

She's staring at the envelope.

'Actually,' she says, handing me the envelope, 'I'm so sorry. I've just remembered I have to be somewhere.' The chair scrapes against the floor as she gets up. 'Dolly,' she calls. 'We have to go now.'

Dolly stamps her foot and complains. Tess joins the protest.

'You can leave her with me if you want.'

'No, she's got an appointment. I can't believe I forgot. Come on, Dolly, stop fussing.' She bundles her into her coat and whisks her out of the front door, apologising as she goes.

'Why is Dolly going home?' Tess asks.

'I'm not sure, darling.' The generous slice of coffee cake lies on the plate, untouched. Their departure seems very sudden. 'I think she had to go to the doctor's.' Becky doesn't look back as she crosses the road and I wonder what really made her leave. It must be the flowers. Ryan doesn't strike me as the romantic type. The delivery must have struck a nerve. I turn my attention back to the card, frowning as I look at the envelope. My name is written in block capitals and I recognise the particular slant of the writing. The room suddenly feels cold. These flowers aren't from Oliver.

I open the envelope and slide out a small card, hesitating before I turn it over.

HOW DID YOU FEEL WHEN TILLY WENT MISSING? ARE YOU WONDERING WHO IS NEXT?

Something is grabbing at my arm. The flowers are a red blur.

'Mummy.' Tess is pulling at my sleeve. 'Pretty flowers, Mummy.'

'Yes.' The roses blur out of focus again, the colour like a wash of blood. I sit down to steady myself.

'Are they from Daddy?'

'Yes, darling.'

But I don't know who they are from and the thought terrifies me.

Danni arrives home at that moment to find me staring at the flowers. I want to fling them in the bin but haven't the energy.

'Gorgeous flowers,' she says. 'What a romantic husband you have.'

'Can we just have a chat for a minute? I want to sort out arrangements for Christmas. Has Oliver mentioned it to you at all?'

'He told me he's got some leave to take. Will you need me here?'

'No. You can take those two weeks off if you want.'

'I'm easy, I don't have any plans, apart from visiting my mum for the Christmas weekend.'

'That's nice. Where does she live?'

'In Brighton.'

'Lovely. Take as long as you like. I'm just so grateful you stepped in at such short notice to help us out.' I imagine the scene of our kitchen through Danni's eyes: her cake in the middle of the table, sliced and surrounded by crumbs, the plates evidence of Becky's visit, the uneaten slice. The flowers still in their box. 'Things are pretty hectic here as you've probably gathered.'

'The flowers smell heavenly,' Danni says. 'Do you want me to put them into a vase?'

*I'd rather you threw them in the bin.*

'Yes, please. There's one in the cupboard under the sink, a large, blue one. Mum made it in her pottery class. It's very good, actually, she's surprised us all with her hidden talent.' I'm rambling to blot out the terror that is coursing through my veins.

*ARE YOU WONDERING WHO IS NEXT?*

I'm pretty sure it's going to be me.

# 2006

Frances and Tim Freud were going to an Italian restaurant in town for a fortieth birthday party. Her uncle was going to the same party as it happened. Mrs Freud was looking like something out of *Vogue* magazine, dressed up in her designer dress and dripping with diamonds. Their au pair had been unexpectedly called back to France for a family emergency, otherwise she'd have been looking after their daughters. The elder child was staying with her grandmother, so she'd only have the six-month-old baby to look after. The first time she'd babysat, Mrs Freud had asked her how old she was when she stood nervously on the front doorstep in her new jeans and leather jacket. She thought she looked older than her fifteen years and told Mrs Freud she was sixteen because she nearly was, only two months and a bit to go. You could get married then, with parental approval, but Mum and Dad were set on her going to university and for once they shared the same goal, although she didn't tell them her real motivation for getting a degree was being able to leave home and have more freedom. The evening had gone well, anyway, and she'd passed the test.

Mrs Freud liked a list. She'd written a list which she'd left on the kitchen island, containing all the phone numbers she could possibly need: hers, Tim's, the restaurant, the friend whose party it was and the local police station. In the kitchen she'd left a list about Lydia, detailing her feeds and her sleep pattern. That was way over the top but Harriet paid attention as she wanted to get everything right. That way more babysitting gigs might lie, especially if she recommended her to all her rich friends.

The Freuds left at seven o'clock and Mike texted at seven-fifteen. Three words which made her heart jump.

*I'm coming over.*

She rushed upstairs to check her makeup in the mirror. The fake eyelashes looked good and she liked the smoky eye she'd spent ages perfecting, watching videos on YouTube, and the dark flick was perfectly symmetrical and at just the right angle. Next she checked on Lydia, who was still fast asleep and, according to the normal timetable left by Mrs Freud, she wouldn't wake again until around midnight, by which time they expected to be back, and Mr Freud would run her home in the jeep. Living your life according to a timetable must be reassuring, Harriet knew they would be back when they said because Mrs Freud was that sort of person.

*I'm outside.*

The text made her jump. She sprinted downstairs, her feet not making a sound on the plush carpet, which felt like stepping into cotton wool, and patted her hair down in front of the mirror and checked her eyes hadn't smudged before she opened the door.

'Nice gaff,' Mike said, waving a bottle of cider at her and walking in as if he'd been here many times before and headed for the kitchen. 'And would you just look at this.' He went straight over to the bar area, stocked with bottles in the corner of the living room. 'Check it out!'

'I'm babysitting,' she said, unable to go through with the pretence that she lived here as she'd have to keep checking on Lydia and inventing a baby sister was too problematic. One little lie only led into a nasty tangle that was impossible to pick your way out of. She wiped her palms on her jeans to stop them sweating, immediately worrying about leaving a mark. The baby monitor sat on the mantelpiece over the real log fire, with a stack of logs forming part of the earthy design of the living room. She'd only ever seen that on television before. One day she planned to own a house like this.

'How many kids? They're not going to wake up and interrupt us, are they?'

'No, only one, a baby girl. I'm not expecting her to wake up. She's really cute; do you want to have a look at her?'

'Not particularly. I'd rather look for the bottle opener; do you know where it is?'

She opened a couple of kitchen drawers. It didn't take long to find it. Mrs Freud had said she could eat what she liked from the fridge but she hadn't mentioned the alcohol. Harriet had no plans to touch it.

'Smart glasses,' Mike said when she took two champagne flutes from the cupboard. The others were out of her reach. He poured them both a glass.

'Cheers.' They clinked glasses and each took a sip. Mike smacked his lips with pleasure. 'Come here,' he said, and with his free hand pulled her to him and kissed her. He was more ardent this time and she tried to make herself relax and follow his lead. It went on for quite a long time and made her feel all funny inside.

'I thought we could watch a film,' she said, when the kiss

eventually ended. She wasn't sure whether she'd enjoyed it or not.

'Whatever,' he said, 'as long as we're nice and cosy.' Mike sank into the soft leather sofa. He was taller than she remembered and his chin was covered in dark stubble. She glanced at the baby monitor. The light was on as it should be.

'Maybe I should run upstairs and check on Lydia,' she said.

'Not yet,' he said, pulling her down onto the sofa. 'Where are the DVDs?'

She passed the pile to him and he selected a film without asking her opinion. The one now playing definitely wasn't one she would have chosen. It was fast-paced with cars driving at top speed and a lot of shooting and men running around shouting. Bloody scenes played out in front of her, the graphic images making her feel nauseous. She kept glancing at the baby monitor, worried the noise level would wake the baby, although Mrs Freud had said she'd sleep through anything.

'Let's get comfy,' he said, putting his arm around her. He was holding her very tight and for the first time she wondered if she'd done the right thing by inviting him here.

The light on the baby monitor flashed red.

# SEVENTEEN

Somehow I get through the week by focusing on my work. A direct threat has been made against my children. I break out in a sweat just thinking about it and despite Danni's protestations I insist on taking the girls to and from preschool myself. The rest of the time I spend at home. Making clothes has always been my way of destressing: using my energy in a positive way to create something beautiful. Only the machine keeps snagging, needles snapping and the sharp point breaks through my skin when I'm changing the machine, sending me into floods of tears. But not from the pain; it's pure terror. I want to talk to Gabi, but I can't. She's texted me a couple of times asking me to meet and I've fobbed her off.

To date I've received four notes. Whoever sent them knows where I live, where I go to exercise, what car I drive. That's everyone on the close, plus... it could be anyone. But an outsider would stand out. The community here is notoriously inquisitive, stemming from a sense of neighbourliness, I'd always assumed, but it could be for any number of reasons. Like getting at me. I check the WhatsApp group but there is no mention of suspicious people.

I give up on trying to work and write out a list of everyone who lives on the close and anyone I've seen hanging around. The woman arguing with Elliott springs to mind. But she won't be interested in me. Still, I can't rule her out.

Oliver arrives home that Friday evening, depositing his bag in the hall with a definitive air. That's symbolic to me. Next time that bag leaves the house, not only will it be a new year, but changes will have been made in our relationship. When the bag next departs it will take the air of uncertainty with it.

Oliver smells of coffee and his face is lined with fatigue as he brushes his bristly face against me for a kiss.

'You look shattered.'

He runs his hands through his hair, the edges of which are peppered with grey. Does he know his life is catching up with him?

'We had to tie up a transaction before I left. It was touch and go but we made the deadline.' He pulls his tie off and hurls it onto the sofa. 'I can forget all that for the next two weeks,' he says, 'focus on my family instead. How's it been?'

'Fine. Danni's great and the children love her. She's going home for a few days over Christmas, to her family in Brighton.'

'Have you done the food shopping yet?'

'No, I thought we could do that on the Wednesday, the day before the party.'

'Party?'

'At the penthouse.'

'Oh, of course. Lovely flowers by the way. Who are they from?'

'Becky.' It's the first name that comes into my head. 'She called round.' I wanted to chuck them on sight, but Danni would have noticed.

'How is she doing?'

'She's fine. Have you eaten?'

'No.'

'I'll cook something.'

'I must get out of this suit. Have I got time to grab a quick shower?'

'Sure.'

He goes upstairs, leaving his bag on the chair. I wait until I hear the sound of the water running, the pipes burbling, and then I take his phone out of his bag. If he's changed the passcode of this too then I've had it but the code works and I'm in. I open WhatsApp and scroll through his recent messages. Several to colleagues I recognise, the banking group made up of his French colleagues, Ben, his parents. I pause, alert to any change in sound but the boiler continues to rumble, indicating use. No women apart from Nadine, those messages all in French. The name Patrick I don't recognise. I run through the names of his colleagues but can't place a Patrick. The water is still running upstairs, but I'm jumpy, not wanting to be caught with his phone. I read through the messages to Patrick. They're in constant contact and I open the thread, frowning, the latest message of which is today. In fact there are several today. Too many. My eyes blur as I see how early they begin this morning and I realise what this is.

*I'm missing you already*

                                                                *Same*

*It won't be long until the next time*

                *Indeed! We'll be in touching distance but it will be harder to touch*

*Don't make me think about touching you. I have to go into a meeting and it wouldn't be appropriate*

*I hate it when you're so close yet so far*

There's a clunk from upstairs as the shower switches off. My heart is thumping and I grab my own phone and take a screenshot of 'Patrick's' number. I clear the screen and drop his phone back into his bag as if it's scalding my skin. I get some pasta from the cupboard and switch on the kettle, willing my hands to stop shaking.

*So close yet so far.*

How dare they? Could they be any more blatant? Anger pours off me in a cold sweat.

I take a larger knife than usual to slice the garlic, driving the blade into the chopping board, slicing faster with each chop, gripping the knife so hard it hurts. I've had enough. With each slice I take out my stress on the board. By the time he comes back down, hair damp and dressed in a soft sweatshirt and jeans, I'm stirring a carbonara sauce on the stove.

'Smells good,' he says, nuzzling my hair and I try not to flinch.

I switch the television on and we eat with trays on our laps. He falls asleep soon after eating and I wonder if he's dreaming of 'Patrick'. Patricia? I can't think of anyone I know called Patricia and it has to be a code name. I need to know. Or is it one of my neighbours? The thought makes me want to cry. Would it be easier if it was a woman I didn't know? I deposit our plates in the dishwasher and go around the house making sure all the windows and doors are locked. I stand in front of the window and look down over Prospect Close. Lights are on in some of the houses, and I can make out a glow from Elliott's penthouse. Is his ex-wife going through similar emotions? I wonder who betrayed who. I scan the houses and think about the flowers, and wonder who it is that is tormenting me. I should go to bed but I know I won't be able to switch off my mind.

The children are asleep; their father is asleep. I'm too alert to relax, not sure I'll be able to sleep again since the arrival of the flowers.

Downstairs I rummage around in the dresser drawer until I find my old mobile phone. I keep a pay as you go SIM card with it just in case of emergency and setting up the phone helps me focus. Unexpectedly, Patrick's number isn't a French one. A pain stabs my chest. It's late, but so what if it's late, spoiling someone's sleep? I've barely slept since I found out about her.

The dial tone rings out and I stab at the close button to end the call, my heartbeat elevated. What am I going to say? Before I lose my nerve I redial, deciding to remain silent, I just want to know who this Patrick is. Maybe it will be a voice I recognise. I pace up and down and a scenario comes to mind: I will say Oliver has had an accident and this number was the last one dialled from his phone, I'll ask them who they are and what their relationship is to Oliver. Perfect. The phone rings and nobody is answering and I'm sure it's about to switch to voice-mail when somebody answers.

'Hello.'

A woman's voice. English accent. I sink to the floor, grip-ping the phone.

'Hello,' she repeats. 'Hello. Who is this?'

I press the red button to end the call and grip my head in my hands.

Everything I feared is true.

'Patrick' is the mistress. But she definitely isn't Gabi. I'm relieved to have that confirmed.

And she's definitely in the UK, but just how close is she?

# EIGHTEEN

Danni and I go through the calendar on what is the first day of the school holidays. The twins are wriggling around on the sofa; Lucy is asleep beside me. The knot of anxiety in my stomach only lessens when the three of them are within my sights, safe inside my home. Thank goodness for the holidays. Oliver being home too adds to the sense of security. At least I can keep my eye on him here. I woke up this morning and made a decision to speak to Gabi as soon as I can, ask her outright about Ben. The call last night has convinced me she's not seeing Oliver, but I have to know about Ben. I have avoided Holly since, worried she'd know something was up, and I want Martin to be wrong. I mark in the time when Danni will be away, working out in my head when the best time to talk to Oliver will be. I can't do it while she's here, and I still need more evidence. Who can this woman be?

*So close yet so far*

The irony of needing a calendar to make an appointment with my husband doesn't escape me. The temptation to hurl accusations at him the minute he steps through the door is strong, but I need to find out more about 'Patrick' before I do.

Danni clears her throat and I switch off the running commentary in my head.

'So you're leaving for Brighton on Tuesday?'

'Yes. I'll go in the morning, early; I'm hoping there won't be too much traffic.'

The evening of the 21st, then, I decide, the day before the party. In three days' time.

Oliver comes in through the back door, removing his muddy shoes and leaving them on the doormat. His face is flushed and his hair windswept.

'You've been running,' Danni says. 'You know so often I go to bed telling myself I'll get up extra early and go out for a run, but the minute the alarm goes off I switch it straight off and go back to sleep. I just can't face it.'

'Come with me one morning,' Oliver says, helping himself to a large glass of water. 'I have no problem getting up.'

'He forgets we have breakfast to sort out for the children.' I gather our used plates together with a clatter. Oliver going running with the nanny is not factored into my timetable.

'I didn't mean when I was here,' Danni says. 'Obviously.'

I fill the sink with hot water, too hot, flinching as it burns my skin, grateful to be turned away from them. I blame Oliver for making me feel side-lined.

'Let me do that,' he says. 'And I'll take Lucy out for a walk this morning. It's about time I got to know the new lady in my life better.'

'Go together,' Danni says. 'I'm taking the twins out this morning.'

————

Oliver pushes the pram out of the close and over to the woodland area, near where Tilly wandered off. Seeing the trees looming over dark hidden spaces makes me shudder. Oliver asks me questions about it as we go. We stick to the path and bypass the wood, ending up at a little street with a café. I answer his questions while biting my tongue, refraining from challenging him outright. If he knows I'm suspicious, he'll double his efforts to cover his tracks, and I have to be sure this time. I've always clung onto our family, believing two parents are best for my children, but if he is having an affair, then it's time to step out on my own. I deserve better than second place.

'Fancy a sit-down?' Oliver suggests.

'It's too cold.' I'm not sure I can sit and look at him with this bubbling rage inside me.

'Come on,' he says. 'You're always saying how little time we get to spend together.'

'OK.' I select a table and tuck the pram in beside me while Oliver goes in to get our drinks. I watch him at the counter, making the young waitress behind the counter laugh, laying on the charm no doubt, as he always does with the opposite sex. It never used to bother me until he had his affair; maybe warning bells should have been ringing the first time it occurred, saving me all this heartache. He reappears with our drinks and two slices of cake. I give Lucy some milk to drink and Oliver demolishes his cake in a few bites.

'I didn't have breakfast,' he says. 'Can I get Lucy out of the pram?'

'You don't have to ask.'

'I wasn't sure of her routine.' He uncovers Lucy and takes her onto his lap. She stares at his face with her serious blue eyes. 'She's growing so quickly. Is Danni working out OK? You still seem a bit stressed.'

'She's fine. I'm just tired.'

His phone beeps with a message. He ignores it.

'Aren't you going to get that?'

'It won't be important.'

My fists are clenched under the table, restraining myself

from unleashing the anger inside me. I just need one concrete piece of proof and then I'll let rip. Make him wish he'd never dare cheat on me. I wonder how 'Patrick' is this morning, how important Oliver is to her. I imagine her sitting outside a café wherever she might be, a tiny coffee cup in front of her, a man smoking a cigarette at the adjacent table; she's frowning as the smoke reaches her eyes and tapping out a text with her neatly polished nails. Is the unanswered call she received last night of any significance to her? That will depend on the importance of her relationship with Oliver. If he's always on her mind then everything will relate back to him. Could it be a suspicious wife catching up with her, or will it be relegated to discarded memories, an insignificant misdialled number, or a cold call, filed under nuisance and the number blocked?

'You're not eating that,' Oliver says.

'I'm not hungry. You have it.'

His phone beeps again. *Is it her?*

'Take it, I don't mind.'

He pulls his phone from his pocket and frowns at the screen.

'It's work. I told them not to contact me unless it was urgent.'

'So it must be urgent.'

'They can wait. I'm not going to rush back to the office even if a crisis is unfurling. I've been looking forward to spending time with you and nothing is going to stop that. Not even a financial crash.'

He's lying to me. I feel hot. I loosen my scarf, wrench off my jacket. My hand is shaking and I try to pick my cup up but I fumble and knock it over, spilling coffee on the table.

'Careful,' he says.

Something breaks inside me.

'Are you sure it's work calling?'

I imagine 'Patrick' flapping a hand in front of her face, irritated at the smoke and the lack of response to her messages, slapping some coins into the little tray containing the receipt and smoothing her pencil skirt down before leaving the café, her high heels clicking as she passes her inconsiderate neighbour, whose mouth is an oblivious pout.

He turns the mobile to face me. Nadine's name is showing next to the missed call message.

I feel stupid. The phone rings again: Nadine.

'Answer it.' I cut my cake into pieces. He talks for a few moments about a file she's mislaid. I'm going to speak to Gabi. Otherwise I'll go mad. Then I'll confront him. My focus needs to be the threats against me, and finding out who is behind them, and keeping my children safe. If he's betraying me, he doesn't deserve my energy.

Oliver ends the call. 'It wasn't important. Are you eating that?' He finishes my slice of cake. 'I won't eat any lunch now. It wasn't exactly the healthy start to the week I had in mind.'

I shrug. 'You're on holiday.'

'Remind me when the Penthouse Party is again.'

'The twenty-third.'

'Danni will have gone home by then so we'll need a babysitter. Have you organised anything?'

'Not yet. I'm going to see if Mum's free.'

'Why don't we just get a babysitter? Your mum's always looking after them and she doesn't exactly live nearby.'

'She doesn't mind.'

'I know, but she'll want to have them at her house so we'll have to go and get them the next day. You know what traffic's like over Christmas. More snow is forecast. It's not like she lives on the doorstep. I'll ask Ryan, see what they're doing with Dolly. Maybe they could all stay together.'

'Let me check with Becky. Martin mentioned his niece babysits and lives very close to us.' I try and ignore the way my stomach is churning at the thought of leaving my children in unknown hands.

'OK.' He wrinkles his nose. 'I think this one might need changing. I'll do it.' He takes the baby bag from the pram and heads inside, only to reappear moments later, pulling a face. 'The bathroom is closed, flooded. Typical. I've paid the bill. We'd better head back before this little one gets too grizzly.'

'Keep Tuesday night free,' I say, as we hurry back. 'I'm going to cook something special. I want to talk to you about my work plans. I've got some ideas on how I can expand.'

'Great. I was hoping having Danni here would help.'

Oliver has always been supportive of my business, my cheerleader yelling from the side lines, but wanting to get involved. Now I wonder whether he just wants me preoccupied, out of the way. The image of the other woman returns as she pauses outside the café terrace, glancing back over her shoulder to see me standing watching her. Our eyes meet before she spins on her elegant ankle and walks away, leaving a trail of expensive perfume behind.

# NINETEEN

'There's Gabi,' Oliver says, pointing towards her balcony as we turn back to the close. 'Shouldn't she be at work?' He waves back. She's too far away for me to read her expression.

'I don't know.'

'Have you two had words?'

'What makes you say that?'

'I don't know, something's up with you.'

'Harriet,' Gabi calls as we come level with her building. 'Can you come up for a minute?' She's in her loungewear.

'I need to get lunch.'

'No, you go ahead,' Oliver says. 'I'll get some lunch ready.'

'Great,' Gabi says. 'I'll make some coffee.'

Danni opens our front door and the twins run out.

'Go on,' Oliver says. He pushes the pram down the path and Danni says something. Her laughter rings out as I go next door. I stop, watching them together. They look good, like a couple... If it isn't Gabi, who else is he interested in? He found Danni after all. And Sienna thought she'd seen her around here before.

I can't stand this.

Gabi's flat door stands open.

'Hi.' I hover in the doorway, anxious now, not wanting to face her. She beckons me over.

Two cups of coffee are on the table.

'Have you been avoiding me?'

I take a sip of coffee and it burns my tongue.

'Last time I saw you at the book group, you barely spoke to me.'

'I was hosting; you know I hate that.'

'It was more than that. You didn't have a problem with Martin; you were chatting away to him. You were definitely being weird with me. And ever since you say no when I ask you over. I know you're busy with the family but I can sense a weird atmosphere. If there's anything bothering you I'd rather you came out and say it. Tell me what's wrong.'

I sigh. I can't hide my feelings. I perch on the edge of the sofa whereas ordinarily I'd kick my shoes off and sprawl across it, legs slung over the side.

'You're right. I've been worrying about something.'

'With Oliver?'

'No, indirectly it was, but... I'll just say it, OK. Are you having an affair with my brother-in-law?'

Gabi's mouth gapes open, and she flushes red then white with anger. 'Ben? No! Of course I'm not. How could you even think that?'

I explain to her what happened at the gym, the conversation I overheard, and Martin's revelation.

'My first reaction was disbelief, I didn't think you would do that to me, but you have been very secretive about this man you're obviously seeing but won't speak about, and then last night I looked at Oliver's phone and called this woman he's been texting, and obviously it wasn't you.'

'Of course it wasn't.' Her cheeks are flushed red. 'I can't

believe you would think that. Ben is bad enough, but Oliver, you really don't know me at all.'

'Asha also mentioned Mo seeing him at a restaurant.'

'That wasn't me either, of course it wasn't.' She looks upset and I know she's telling me the truth.

'I should have known not to trust gossip. It's been so awful, these last few days, imagining you and Ben together, then worrying about Holly.'

Her eyes flash. 'How dare they say that about me? I've a good mind to go round to Sienna's...'

'No, you can't.'

Gabi shakes her head, lips pressed together.

'This is so ridiculous. Ben came round one evening to give me a quote for my ensuite; I want to upgrade my shower. You can ask Holly; she knows all about it as she was the one who suggested he could do it. It was quite late, but he's busy and that was the only time he could fit me in. I can ring him now, if you want, whatever it takes. Bloody Sienna and Asha, honestly. I will put them straight, you know. They can't go round spreading rumours like that. Gossip hurts, I should know. I'm so glad you told me, though; I just want everything to be alright between us.' She goes to the fridge. 'I need some water. Do you want one too?'

'Yes please.'

She takes out a bottle of sparkling water and removes the top, dropping it in the bin, and pours two glasses. 'Did you seriously think I was seeing Oliver behind your back? I can't believe you think I'd do that.'

'I'm so sorry.'

She slams the glass down on the table. 'Seriously, though, how could you think I would do that to you?'

'It's only because of your secrecy about whoever it is you're seeing. You must understand my logic in that? Otherwise, no, you're a fantastic friend and I don't really think you have it in you to do that. Honestly. Please forgive me, my head's been all over the place. Oliver *has* been cheating on me, I found evidence of that.' I tell her about the conversation I discovered on his phone. 'I don't know what to think, honestly. I've even started wondering about Danni. Oliver put me in touch with her, and as Sienna so kindly pointed out she's extremely attractive.'

'Don't listen to Sienna. I couldn't believe it when she said that. So insensitive. Yes, she could be a supermodel,' Gabi says, 'but no offence – she's way out of Oliver's league.'

I can't help laughing; it's relief more than anything.

'Sienna likes to stir up trouble.'

'I should just confront her, or ask Asha – she's more straightforward.'

'Asha would hate to think she'd upset you. I think you're wrong about Danni. Would Oliver really be so brazen as to introduce his mistress into your house?'

'I doubt it.'

'The thing is, this is my fault because of all the secrecy. That's why I wanted to talk to you. I can't expect us to be close friends if I'm keeping secrets from you. If I tell you who I'm seeing, you promise you won't tell anyone? That includes Oliver. It's really important. You'll see why when I tell you.'

'I don't feel like confiding anything to Oliver at the moment. He's still having an affair, even though it's not with you.'

Gabi laughs. I laugh too, relief at having my ally back.

'I'm so relieved it isn't. Honestly, I was going out of my mind. So come on, who is it?'

'It's Elliott.'

'Elliott? Really?' Elliott with his smart suits and smooth exterior, the kindly head teacher who is a pillar of our community. Who keeps himself at a respectable distance for fear of overstepping the mark and being over-familiar with anyone who has anything to do with the local school. Until the unfortunate incident the other day.

'Yes, really. Oh it's such a relief to be able to tell you. He's so paranoid about it, he made me swear not to tell you and I've wanted to for ages. But now it's coming between us, it's the right decision.'

'He doesn't need to know you've told me. Tell me everything. I actually know nothing about him.'

'Exactly. That's what he's like.'

'Well, apart from...' I hesitate.

'What?'

'Oliver and I witnessed him having an unfortunate encounter with a woman the other day. His wife.'

Gabi sighs, nodding.

'His wife won't accept the separation. I encountered her the first time we met. I was driving home from work one day when my car broke down. Elliott happened to be driving behind me, and he helped me move the car and insisted on waiting with me as it was dark and there weren't many people around on that desolate stretch of road. The recovery service arrived an hour later, but my car had to be towed to a garage so he drove me back to Prospect Close. He invited me up to the penthouse and while I was there Victoria rang the entry phone, wanting to come up. She'd been sitting in her car outside his flat wanting to talk, saw him come home with me and jumped to the wrong conclusion. At that time. This intrusion proved to be a step too far, and he threatened her with a restraining order.

'He told me all about his situation; he's been separated for years and was trying to get divorced and Victoria has been hounding him ever since. His career is so important to him, you've seen how he cares about the children but he's paranoid about keeping his reputation blemish free. Half the governors and parents were willing him to fail, forever testing him, after he replaced an extremely popular head who had suddenly died.

Leaving the family home devastated his wife. He keeps himself to himself partly for professional reasons, given that half the residents are involved with the local school in some way and his wife has slowly turned their friends against him after spreading lies about him to anyone who would listen.

'That's why when we started seeing one another he had to keep it secret. If his wife found out – I don't know what she's capable of. I wish she didn't cast such a dark shadow over our relationship. I really like him.

'It was probably a mistake moving here, he told me, living so close to the school, but it's perfect for his needs. Being a head leaves you with virtually no free time and he didn't want to waste time travelling.

'I told him he can't let his wife affect him in this way. I even suggested the police, but he doesn't want to involve them. He is entitled to have a relationship,' Gabi says.

She tells me they've fallen in love. He assured her the secrecy wouldn't last forever, but as time has gone by, she's started to despair that Victoria would never move on.

'I don't get why he doesn't just brazen it out,' I say. 'She's blackmailing him with her deranged behaviour.'

'He'd rather she didn't have anything to reproach him with, so it's essential that she doesn't know about our relationship.'

'No! No wonder you're paranoid about keeping it quiet. I'm so sorry, I didn't really believe that you would go behind my back like that. I should have just confronted them. I've been a terrible friend. I promise you can trust me, though. I certainly don't want to give the neighbours anything else to gossip about. They don't mean to hurt anyone but fail to think about the consequences.'

'I've been terrified one of them will find out about Elliott. I've never met Victoria, I haven't even seen her, but she sounds so unpredictable.'

'She was there when Tilly went missing.'

'No way.'

I tell her what I saw.

'Glad I wasn't around then. I'd rather stay off her radar.'

'I don't blame you. But you seem to be happy, that's the most important thing.'

'Oh I am. It's the best, most equal relationship I've ever had. But we can't carry on like this forever. You know I've never stayed at the penthouse. We always go out, far away where nobody knows us. It's exciting, but also draining. Sometimes I just want to put my feet up in front of the fire and snuggle up to him. In my own front room, not in a fancy hotel where I'm living out of a suitcase and don't have my home comforts around me.'

'Life is never straightforward. I don't feel as if I can do that either. Because of Oliver working so much, and having the nanny with us whenever he is home I've been so looking forward to these two weeks with him. But having an affair changes everything.'

'What are you going to do? You said you want evidence, and you have the phone conversation as proof.'

'I know, but I have to know who she is.'

'How could you find out?'

'Apart from looking at his phone, or following him' – Gabi pulls a face – 'which rather smacks of Victoria's behaviour.'

'I don't know. He's off the next couple of weeks and Danni will be away for Christmas so we'll talk then. I can't live like this any longer. I need to know exactly what I'm up against. If he is having an affair then I'm going to leave him, and make a new life for me and the children.'

'Gosh. That's huge.'

'I know.' My eyes fill with tears at this realisation. 'You know our move here was meant to be short term but I hadn't expected to find such a sense of community and to make friends, good friends like you and Martin. I still have that dream of setting up my craft shop in a country village, but it's looking increasingly like I'll have to do that without my husband.'

'Would he fight you for custody?'

'Most probably. The thought makes me feel sick. But if I can prove the adultery then that should go in my favour.'

Unless my past is dredged up. Should I tell her about the notes? It would help so much just to be able to share my burden with one other person, but I already know it's impossible. How many times before have I wanted to share, only to remind myself of my vow of silence and the reasons behind it. Anyone could be responsible, and secrets always get whispered around, flying from house to house. Besides, I'm trusting everything she's told me, and the protective part of me is telling me that I need to check out her story and make sure it adds up.

I push the notes from my mind momentarily. 'At least we've got each other.'

'It's such a relief to be able to talk to you about this. I've wanted to for so long.'

We hug.

Gabi isn't the mistress next door. So who is?

# TWENTY

Danni comes into the kitchen, not her usually composed self. She's looking at her phone, a worried expression on her face. Tilly presses against her legs and she absent-mindedly strokes her hair.

'Is everything OK?' I ask.

She shakes her head, her face pinched. 'My mum's had an accident.'

'Oh no.'

'She fell down the stairs and broke her leg. It happened early this morning. I can't believe I've only just found out. She can't stay at home because she lives on the third floor and the lift has been out of order for weeks. She's had to go to my sister in Halifax so I won't be able to go to her for Christmas. Poor Mum, I was so looking forward to it.'

Oliver has come in halfway through the conversation.

'Can't you go to your sister's instead?' I suggest.

She pulls a face. 'She doesn't have much room but even if she did I wouldn't go. I can't stand her husband.' She looks away from me as she says this.

'You can't spend Christmas on your own,' Oliver says. 'Stay here with us. It's not a problem.'

I open my mouth to protest but close it immediately. Danni looks so relieved and she rewards Oliver with a dazzling smile.

'Thanks, that's amazing. As long as I'm not imposing.' She looks at me.

'Not at all.'

'I'll help with the children, cooking, whatever you need. I can make a Christmas cake.'

'Great,' Oliver says, 'everybody's happy.'

———

When I next get Oliver on his own, I close the bedroom door. Danni is playing in the garden with the children but I can't risk being overheard.

'What did you say that for?'

'What?'

'About her staying here. You know how much I was looking forward to spending time just the two of us.'

'I was too, but she's upset about her mother. We can't just turf her out.'

'We've only just met her. She must have other people she can stay with.'

'You're not normally so heartless. I didn't realise it was such a big deal. It's only one day.'

'But it's not, is it? I have plans for Tuesday night.'

'You do?'

'A meal, I told you.'

'Her being here won't make any difference. We can fit that in easily. She'll most likely stay in her room.'

I stare out of the window, frustrated. Out in the back garden, Tess and Tilly are shrieking with delight. Danni has Lucy in her arms, watching them with a smile on her face. With her long skirt and loose hair, she looks quite the earth mother. With my children. I turn to face Oliver, deflated.

'I can't do this anymore.'

'Do what?'

'This.' I sweep my hand around to encompass the outside and the room we're in. 'It's too claustrophobic living here. I want to move and we have to make it happen next year. Two years, you promised me we'd live here. Next year it will be our sixth year here.'

'I don't understand you. You've got so many friends, a beautiful house.'

'I know, and I'm not saying it will be easy, it will definitely be a wrench, but I'm increasingly worried about the children's safety. I'd rather they grew up in the country. And it's my dream, you know that.' If only I trusted him, I could tell him the real reason I have to go, the mounting threats against our children. I steady myself by leaning against the wall. I'm aware my argument sounds weak.

'You mean the one where you live miles away from anywhere and run your sustainable baby clothes shop? I'm not entirely against it, but it would have to be within commuting distance of London.'

'I thought you wanted to give up working for the bank; you always said you'd burn yourself out if you stayed much longer.'

'I love my job.' The words hit me like bullets. 'I'm not sure I could give it all up, I just didn't know how to tell you. I love all of it. The buzz of the boardroom, experiencing different countries, even the travelling. And I love my family just as much. I'm willing to talk about working less but don't make me give it up because I won't. I don't mind a long commute and most places are accessible to London.'

'It's because of her, isn't it?'

'Her?'

'I know you've been seeing someone else. I know the conference only lasted a day but you made out it was for a weekend; I spoke to Nadine.'

'What?'

'I wouldn't have minded but why not mention it to me? That makes me suspicious. You must have something to hide.'

He's pacing up and down now. 'I go away all the time. You know I do. It was a bonding experience with the team; I had to be there. I didn't realise I had to share my work diary with you.'

'What about all those restaurant meals for two, both here and on that weekend in Paris? If it was a team event, why are there only two of you?'

'Those are work meetings too; taking clients out for lunch is a frequent occurrence. I don't understand why you are saying all this.'

'I saw your credit card bill. Some of the dates and times are when you've told me you were elsewhere.'

The colour has drained from Oliver's face.

'You've been looking at my post. How dare you?'

'I don't think you have the right to say that. I know the signs and I had to make sure. I've also seen the conversations on your phone. It wouldn't be the first time, would it?'

'We said we wouldn't bring that up again,' he says, his teeth clenched. 'Our marriage is never going to work if you can't get over that one indiscretion. Never mind that other false accusation you made. We went through all that at marriage guidance. You reassured me that you would be able to put it behind you.'

'That promise no longer means anything when you're back up to your old tricks. How could you do this to me again? And were you ever going to tell me, or were you just going to string me along? Lucy is only six months old for god's sake. You were sleeping with someone else while I was carrying your child. And it's still carrying on. Who is she?'

'She doesn't exist. Lack of sleep is making you imagine things.'

Oliver runs his hands over his face, raking his hair back, no longer his usual composed self. I can't look at him, don't want to watch him tell me more lies. Outside, Tilly trips as she runs forward and lets out a howl. Danni reaches out to her but she's hampered by Lucy, cradling her head with her free hand. She looks back at the house.

'I've got to go and help Danni. This conversation will have to wait.'

I push past him, my eyes dry, determined. My children come first and they need me now.

# TWENTY-ONE

Oliver and I barely speak for the rest of the weekend. Having Danni around makes it easier. I go to bed early and feign sleep when he comes up much later. He falls straight asleep and I lie seething with resentment for what feels like hours before sliding into an agitated dream. I'm on the Eurostar, and the train flies past Paris, not stopping as it traverses France. When it stops at Nice the doors are locked and Oliver sits at the terrace of the station café with the woman who haunts my imagination. She smirks at me as I hammer on the glass. Lucy wakes me in the early hours and once I've fed her and got her back to sleep, I lie on the couch next to her cot. She's only been in this room for a couple of weeks and leaving her on her own still makes me anxious, even though I've been through it before with the twins.

Over breakfast on Monday morning, Oliver reminds me he's visiting his parents today. They live a ninety-minute drive away and he's taking the twins with him.

'What time will you be back?'

'Hopefully by six.'

I raise a sardonic eyebrow. 'OK.'

'I'll be back in time to eat.'

When the car has driven off and the front door is closed, I lean against the wall with relief, thankful to have a few hours to myself. Mum is taking Lucy this afternoon so I can go into town and get some shopping. I decide to treat myself to a new dress for the Penthouse Party. Several hours later when I'm looking at myself from all angles, trying to ascertain whether the slinky back dress I've selected makes me look huge from the back, I wrench a muscle in my neck. Who am I trying to kid? Wearing a new outfit may well camouflage my state of mind but it won't take away the pitiful mess that is my marriage. In the end I select an inoffensive dress that I'll feel comfortable in. Next I go to the food shops and pick up some ingredients for this evening's meal. Everywhere there are reminders of Christmas and New Year approaching, and the imminence of a new year beginning makes me determined to sort out a plan for it. If it means Oliver and I splitting up... I'm so lost in my thoughts I walk right into a woman who's approaching from the other direction.

'I'm so sorry,' I say, looking at the woman. 'Oh.' It's Kate. I freeze. Kate's normally friendly face has a decidedly awkward expression on it. She's dressed in jeans, ankle boots and a furry jacket, a bag over her shoulder.

'Harriet. You've been shopping.' She looks at my bags, the chic cardboard one containing my dress and an Orla Kiely reusable bag full of fresh vegetables and a rye loaf.

It's so unexpected, my feet are rooted to the spot and I'm gazing at her open-mouthed. She angles her body away from me and is looking around her as if she's about to make a dash for a train.

'Yes. How are you?'

'Fine,' she says, her eyes looking anywhere but at me, her hand clutched around the strap of her bag.

'Don't go. I was about to get a coffee. Do you fancy one?'

'I can't,' she says, 'I have to be somewhere.'

She moves to the side as we're centre pavement. I follow her, my pulse racing, anxious not to let her go, but swamped by sadness at seeing someone I was close to so obviously uncomfortable in my presence.

'What's the matter, Kate? Why did you leave so suddenly?'

She pulls her bag to her chest. 'I'm sorry, I have to go.' She stumbles as she moves so quickly to get away, leaving me watching her, and a wave of shock washes over me. I've missed her, but something is clearly wrong. I stand on the pavement for ages, stunned that she was so desperate to get away from me. Something must have happened to make her like this. A woman tuts as she manoeuvres her shopping trolley around me and I pull myself together and move to the side of the pavement while I compose myself before I'm ready to head home.

———

When I get back, I dump the shopping on the kitchen island and pull up Kate's social media accounts. I'm still shaking. She isn't one for posting constant updates on her life, but she is a keen photographer and posts photos two or three times a week. She hasn't posted anything for the last few weeks – since she left us. On her Facebook account, her relationship status is the same, 'in a relationship', but whoever she is in a relationship with is not featured on her page. I think back on our friendship. She alluded to her partner, but never spoke about him directly. That's assuming it was a him. I'd wondered whether she was seeing a woman, but she'd have known she didn't have to keep that from us. Was there some other reason for her to be so secretive? What with her and Gabi keeping everything secret from me, it makes me think my friends don't trust me. Suddenly it hits me and it's so obvious. Has she been having an affair with Oliver and that's why she had to leave without warning? It would explain why she can't even look me in the eye. I feel sick at the thought of what that would mean.

But she wasn't the woman who answered the phone. At least I didn't recognise her voice but then I wasn't expecting anyone to actually pick up. And she could have been wary, or recognised my number. I have to find her again, if only so that I can rule her out. Could there be more than one other woman? Before we got together, Oliver had a reputation as a womaniser and my friends warned me against him at the time. At first we kept our dates secret, which merely added to the excitement. It took me a long time to trust him, and he had to earn that trust.

I check the time, wanting to speak to someone, to stop myself from driving myself mad. Gabi is the obvious candidate and she knows the background but she'll be at work. Martin will no doubt be busy with party preparations and I know he would drop everything for me but I don't want to impose on him. Oliver and the children are due back in an hour. I'd planned to prepare the meal before they get back so that all I have to do is get the children to bed and then we can talk, instead of waiting until Tuesday as I'd planned. They will be tired after spending a day with their father and their grandparents. Having their father to themselves is a novelty and it shouldn't be. The reality is, the only person I can fully trust is myself.

When Mum rings the doorbell half an hour later, Lucy is asleep in her car seat and Mum hands her to me.

'Aren't you coming in?'

'I can't stop, I'm meeting Jean for a meal.'

'How was Lucy?'

'Good as gold. I fed and changed her before I left.'

'I hope she hasn't slept all afternoon.'

'Not at all, she's kept me busy the whole time and as soon as we got in the car she went straight to sleep. I think we were both exhausted.'

'I'd better wake her; I want her to sleep tonight. Oliver's not back with the twins yet.'

'I wonder how he's got on with those two. Has Tilly been OK since the other week?'

'Yes, still nothing, thankfully. And Oliver will be fine. His mother will have taken over. She doesn't get to see them as much as you do. I bet you anything she'll have played with the children and he'll have sat in the garden chatting to his dad.'

'As long as they're having fun, which I'm sure they will be. Enjoy your evening, love.'

'You too.'

# TWENTY-TWO

Oliver fetches a bottle of wine from the wine rack while he updates me on his afternoon. We're both being polite, taking gentle steps around one another, not yet willing to address the elephant in the room. I showered and changed before he got back and I've put a dress on and refreshed my makeup. I got out of the habit of dressing up for Oliver but with the thought that I have competition out there it's a matter of pride. Besides, I'm doing it for my benefit, to drag my self-esteem up out of the gutter. Upstairs, all is quiet and I'm hoping the busy day will have knocked all the children out. I'd woken Lucy as soon as Mum left to make sure of an uninterrupted evening. Once the food is finished, Oliver removes our used plates from the table and tops up our wine glasses. The silence isn't a comfortable one. Asking him about 'Patrick' is on the tip of my tongue but we have to talk about our living situation first. Once he knows I've spoken to her, I doubt we'll be capable of a civil conversation.

'I need to know what your intentions are. Last night you said you don't want to move. You know I don't want to stay here. I want to tell you where I'm at. When we bought this house in

Prospect Close it was supposed to be for about two years. Do you remember that conversation?'

'I do.'

'Good. Since then obviously we've had children and we've barely had time to breathe, let alone think about moving. But it's been five years now and I'm making a stand. I don't want to live here anymore.'

'What don't you like about it?'

I've been planning what to say when he asks all afternoon. If I could tell him about the notes, it would be an easy conversation and he'd most likely want to move as much as I do. Fear does that, makes your behaviour appear rational to other people. But I can't tell him that, so hope he'll believe the reasons I give.

'It's too claustrophobic. I'm a country girl; where I grew up, I thought our nearest market town was busy. Every time I step out of the door I bump into someone I know, everyone knows everyone else's business and it's too small-minded. Every property is overlooking us; it's like I'm being watched. Do you know how I really found out about your affair? I overheard some of the neighbours gossiping in the steam room; they'd seen what they thought was you slipping into Gabi's flat. That's why I was avoiding her – maybe you didn't notice although I assumed you would as anything to do with her would be on your radar.'

'Me and Gabi? That's a load of nonsense. Don't tell me you believed them.'

'Why wouldn't I? They were half right, weren't they?'

'It's not true, I swear it isn't.'

'I know it isn't. They were talking about Ben, they mistook him for you – you know you look alike from behind, and he'd gone to speak to her about a new shower. But the point is, gossip is dangerous and I don't want to live like this anymore.

'Then there's the issue of my work. My business doing so well recently means it has real potential, but I have to take it to the next level and for that I need more space. That would be too expensive around here, or anywhere within commuting distance of London. Aside from work, I want my children to experience living in the countryside, away from all this pollution. And after what happened to Tilly the other day I'm worried about security too. There are too many dodgy people around here.'

'You don't know that. Tilly was fine; she didn't meet anyone *dodgy*. There are strange people everywhere, being surrounded by fields doesn't necessarily mean you'll be safe. I'd say it makes us more of a target.'

The way he says the word in a slightly mocking tone infuriates me. It also scares me. Could that be true? But I'm convinced the person who is taunting me with the notes is close by, connected to Prospect Close.

'It's a chance I'm willing to take.'

'I want to stay here. I think you're deluding yourself. Prospect Close is a wonderful place to live. You've made really good friends, the house is gorgeous and we're surrounded by people who care about us.'

'They don't. Obviously Ben and Holly do, but they're family. The others are good neighbours, admittedly, but could you say you really care about them? You're not here enough to know.' I sip some wine. 'I want to know whether you still want to stick to our original plan. I have three questions. Are you ever going to give up working in London?'

'Honestly? I can't answer that. Situations change in life. Nothing can be guaranteed. None of us know what will happen from one day until the next. I meant it when I originally agreed, but I really enjoy it. I need more time to think.'

That means no.

'Are you willing to move to the countryside?'

He looks away from me. I didn't think so.

'I won't rule it out, but again, I need time to mull it over. I like it here; I like the community. I thought you did too.'

'You've had five years.'

He sighs and runs his hands through his hair. 'That's two; what's the third question?'

I pause to take a large drink from my wine glass.

'Who's Patrick?' My heart thuds in my chest.

'Patrick?' He screws up his forehead. 'I don't know anyone called Patrick. Should I?'

'Your phone rang when you were in the shower the other day.' It's a half truth but since when did he bother about telling me the truth? 'After I spoke to Patrick, I looked at your history to see how often you are in touch and the evidence is pretty damning.'

'Patrick?' he repeats, like a stupid parrot.

'Your lover! Your mistress. The one on your phone who pretends to be Patrick. Do you think I'm stupid? I've seen what you write to each other. And don't tell me you're gay – not that an affair with a man wouldn't matter as much but I've spoken to her and she's definitely a woman. Who is she?'

Oliver drains his wine glass and tops it up again. He tugs at the neck of his top. I stare at him the whole time. He closes his eyes as if preparing himself and takes a deep breath.

'Her name's Pascale. She works at our Nice branch and she was at the conference. It didn't mean anything to me. It was a stupid fling but it's over between us, I swear. I finished with her this afternoon. You can look at the messages on my phone if you want.'

'This afternoon? While you were with the girls?'

He shrugs. 'It had to be done and I couldn't do it here. I wouldn't do that to you.'

I laugh. 'Bit late to think about my feelings, isn't it? How did she take it?' *Assuming this is true.*

'Not well. But she won't be a problem. Our paths shouldn't cross again. The messages you saw were all build-up, a flirtation. I'm so sorry. I understand if you won't forgive me. I want us to try and work it out. I know I haven't been as attentive lately, or here for you and the children as I should be, but I can change that, I promise.'

'It's too late for promises; you made one after the last affair, remember, and I won't do it again. I've made a decision. I won't put up with another affair. I'm moving out next year, and it's up to you to decide whether you want to come with me or not.' I'm relieved now that I never confided in him about my past, or the notes. If he knows it's me who's attracting potential danger to the children, he'd use it against me to get custody. Sweat pours down my back just at the thought of it.

'What about the children?'

'They come with me.'

He shakes his head. 'You can't do this. I've made a mistake but it doesn't mean we have to split up.'

'Aren't you listening to me? I've had enough. Your affair has catapulted me into gear. I should have done this ages ago.'

'Do you think you might have postnatal depression?'

I stare at him. 'I can't believe you said that. I'm not depressed. Far from it.'

'I don't think you'd cope as well as you think in the country. You haven't mentioned the real reason you want to go. You don't think the children are safe here. I don't want our children to be swaddled in cotton wool. I want them to be assertive, streetwise, to understand about the world and how to protect themselves. Hiding them away and isolating them won't be good for their mental development.'

His words send a chill right through me. He's closer to the truth than he realises. He can't know, can he?

'They'll be at school. I'm not saying we won't be part of a community, but it won't be right on top of us. This feels more like a commune to me at times.'

'Now you're exaggerating. You need help.'

'Don't you dare. I see what you're doing. You want to take

the kids away from me. Make out I've lost the plot, that I'm having some kind of breakdown. I won't let that happen. Nobody will separate me from my children.'

'That's not what I'm saying.'

'You would never get custody anyway; no court would rule in your favour. I'm not sure you'd know how to look after the three of them. Unless you're lying about your girlfriend, and she's waiting to step into my place. Am I right?'

'No.' He looks defeated. 'We're not splitting up, OK? All this talk about custody is way too premature. I want us to work this out.'

'Then you have to take my needs into consideration. I've told you what I want from the start. I'm going to have to make a choice if you don't want the same life as me. And I think you've already made that choice.'

'No,' he says, 'but give me a few days. Let's get Christmas over, then we can talk again before I go back to work.' He pours himself another glass of wine, offers me some, but my head is spinning enough already with all the words we've said this evening. I go into the bathroom and lock the door behind me. Apart from working out for definite whether I really want to lose him, a terrible thought has entered my head.

What if the person he's been seeing is somehow connected to the notes?

# TWENTY-THREE

On the day of the party, I wake up in Lucy's room, having gone to her in the night and not wanting to go back to our room, to lie facing Oliver's back – the wall confronting me with everything that is wrong in our relationship. A noise awakens me, the whirring of the treadmill, and I imagine Oliver running hard, setting the dial ever higher, pounding away, each tread of his foot thumping out his tension. My whole body is tense with anxiety. He's admitted the affair; it's no longer only in the realms of the possible. I mull over our conversation from the other night. Do I believe him about the woman in Nice, this casual affair as he made it out to be? The text *'so near yet so far'* is preying on my mind. I'm convinced his mistress is closer to home, living somewhere in Prospect Close, literally next door. What if his lover flew to France to be with him? The thought makes me feel cold. Now it's definitely time to make a decision and get on with the rest of my life.

I take Lucy downstairs and feed her. When it's warm enough to sit outside, I like to make the most of the early mornings; I've always appreciated the peacefulness at that hour, listening to birdsong which isn't drowned out by traffic and building works, watching the sky change as the morning weather reveals itself. The past few mornings I've barely noticed the outside world, the turmoil in my head making any sense of tranquillity out of the question. Lucy is a bit sniffly; I make sure she's well wrapped up. Cuddling her is comforting, her sturdy body warm against my cold one. Today, excited squeals filter down from upstairs where Oliver has surprised the twins and is playing a boisterous game. Usually I play with them before breakfast so this will be a nice change for them.

Once breakfast is over and the children are occupied, Oliver asks me about the party.

'What time will we be leaving this evening?'

I open the dishwasher to unload it. 'I'm not sure I still want to go.'

'Please,' he says. 'I want us to get through this, and we will. It was a terrible mistake, a one-off and I really am sorry. How can I make it up to you?'

I take cups and plates out of the dishwasher, making a lot of noise. A cup slides out of my hand and smashes on the floor.

'Let me get it,' he says, crouching down to the floor.

'It will take a lot more than that.'

He tries to take my hand and I swat at him, like I would at an irritating fly. He looks crestfallen.

'Please come to the party. Everyone will wonder where we are otherwise and you don't want that, do you? I know you hate other people knowing our business.'

'Which is why an affair is so hurtful.' I close the dishwasher with a bang. 'But yes, I don't want people asking questions any more than you do so I'll go to the party, as long as I can sort out childcare. Mum can't make it and I only found out the other night.'

I cross to the window. Martin is outside watering his front garden.

'Oh look, Martin's outside; he mentioned his niece may be

available so I'll just pop down and ask him, and check that she's suitable. Can you keep an eye on Lucy for me? I don't want to take her out in the cold unnecessarily.'

'Anything,' he says. Would he really try and take the children from me if I decided to leave? My chest tightens at the thought. I slam the door behind me and take a few deep breaths, welcoming the fresh air, despite the cold, grateful for the chance to get away from him, although the uncomfortable feelings are always with me. I no longer know how to act around my own husband. A noise makes me look up. Sienna is calling my name from across the road. I'd normally be pleased to see her, but I still haven't spoken to her about the incident at the gym and my cheeks colour at the thought.

'Harriet! How's it going?'

I attempt a smile.

'Cold,' I say, 'how are you?'

'I'm great. I've got four days off work and I'm going for a pampering at the health centre later this morning. Treat myself like I deserve. I was just saying to Asha how we haven't had a catch-up in ages. Do you want to come in for a coffee? I've got a bit of time before I need to go out.'

'I can't, I've left Oliver with Lucy and I said I wouldn't be long.'

'He's such a good father.'

'Isn't he?' I hope my smile hides my real thoughts on the matter.

'Is Tilly alright?'

'Yes, thanks, she's completely fine. I'm glad I ran into you, though; I wanted to put you straight on something.'

Her smile falters a little. 'Oh? Am I in trouble?'

'No. It's just a bit of an awkward situation. I was in the steam room the other day, and it was so thick with steam, you know how it gets, and I didn't realise you and Asha were in there. I overheard you talking about me.'

Sienna claps her hands over her mouth, two pink spots appearing on her cheeks.

'Oh my god, I'm mortified,' she says, 'honestly, if I'd known you were there... Why didn't you just come and talk to me?'

'Would you if you heard someone talking about you and your partner?'

Her face reddens and she looks at the ground. 'I guess not.'

'I had to hear what you were going to say, and good job I did because now I can put you straight. It's not true, Oliver is not seeing Gabi; I have to put you straight on that. Or anyone for that matter. It was Ben you saw going into Gabi's house, and his reason for being there was legitimate. He went round to look at her ensuite; Holly actually sent him over to give her a quote for a new shower.'

Sienna widens her eyes. 'Oh no, I feel so dreadful now. Please tell me you didn't tell Gabi.'

'Well – I had to check for Holly's sake, and I didn't want to ask her for obvious reasons. Don't worry, honestly, Holly would probably find it amusing, you know what's she's like. You also talked about seeing him a restaurant.'

'That was Asha. But now you've explained I should have realised, I'm such an idiot. Can you imagine Gabi going out with Ben, really, in his work overalls?' She bites her lip and her mouth twitches. 'He's way out of her league.'

'Watch it, he is my brother-in-law. Just be more careful what you say in future.'

'I know, I know, you're totally right. Me and my big mouth. I'll keep it zipped from now on. Until I forget.' She laughs. 'I can't wait for the party tonight,' she says, 'Oliver is going with you, isn't he?'

'Provided I can sort out a babysitter; that's where I'm off to now.'

'Don't let me stop you.' She gives me a hug. 'It's so good to see you. And I'm truly truly sorry. Catch you later.'

I head over to the penthouse where Martin is still watering his plants.

'Hey,' he says. 'Want to come up for a coffee?'

'I won't, thanks. Oliver is home with the children.' I tell him about my predicament. 'You mentioned your niece might be available, so I was wondering...'

'Of course. I'll ring her now.'

'It's really short notice, I know, but...'

'Stop fretting.' He listens as the phone rings, before giving her a thumbs-up.

'Hi, Kelly, Uncle Martin here.' He explains the situation and smiles as she answers him. Harriet can hear the tone of her voice but can't make out what she's saying. 'Fab, I'll text you the details.

'She's thrilled,' he says. 'She wants to go to a New Year's Eve party at a West End club and the tickets are expensive. Her friend has a spare one but needs to know by tomorrow, so she's very keen. This is her number...' He texts it to me with a flourish of his hand. 'And she's expecting to hear from you.'

'Thank you so much. I'll pay her generously. I think Becky might be stuck for someone too. Do you think Kelly would be OK with having Dolly as well?'

'Of course.' He makes a dismissive gesture. 'She said "the more the merrier". Honestly, she's mad about children. In fact she's of those babysitters who'll be disappointed if the children aren't awake when she comes over. Don't look so worried, she's very sensible. I'm sending you her number now.'

My phone pings. 'The thing is we'll be only along the road, so if there's any problem...'

'Exactly. As long as we don't all get too drunk.'

'Don't.' Thinking about what might go wrong is setting my nerves on edge. An image flashes in front of me and I shift my feet to steady myself.

'Is something bothering you? I'm only joking, you should

know me better – as if I'd try and scare you. I wish you'd relax and enjoy yourself.'

Martin is being so kind and I'm tempted to tell him everything that's going on. I'd be like a tap that's been left on, my worries gushing out. I open my mouth to speak when my phone buzzes. It's Oliver.

*Where are you?*

'I've got to go. No doubt Lucy is going crazy and he can't cope.'

'I thought you had a new nanny?'

'We have, but she's not supposed to be here.' I explain about her mother. 'At least if she'd been able to babysit tonight that would have helped but she's already got plans.'

'Well, you don't need to worry about that anymore.'

'I don't. I can't thank you enough.'

'Seeing you enjoying yourself later will be all the thanks I need.'

Martin heads back inside and I cross over to Becky's and ring the doorbell. Ryan answers the door wearing a paint-splattered T-shirt. Dolly runs down the passageway and hides behind his legs. The hall smells of paint and a hint of burnt toast from the kitchen.

'Is Becky in?'

'No, she's gone to the shops. Can I help?'

'Have you got a babysitter for this evening? Becky mentioned she hadn't arranged anything to me.'

'Funny you should say that. My brother was going to come over, but he's been called away for work.'

'I've just arranged for Martin's niece to babysit. She's happy to have Dolly too if you want to bring her over to our house.'

'Bring them over here if you want.'

'No it's fine, I've already arranged it. But thanks.'

'Suit yourself. I'm looking forward to the party. See what that fancy penthouse is like. How the other half live, eh?'

'You're not doing so badly here; it's beautiful.'

'Yeah, but it's Becky's house, isn't it? How are you doing anyway?'

'I'm fine thanks.'

'I'm impressed. I'm not sure I would be if someone tried to take my kid.'

'They didn't; she just wandered off.'

He pulls a face. 'I'm not sure the police are telling you the whole story. Catch you later.'

I'm closing the garden gate when he calls my name.

'It just shows you, doesn't it, you can't be too vigilant, even in Prospect Close.'

Wind whips my hair as I hurry across the street, my stomach churning at his words which have awakened my fear. I can hear Lucy screaming as I approach the house. Her face is red and she's roaring and Oliver has her over his shoulder and is rubbing her back. His face is almost as pink and he has sweat on his forehead.

'There you are,' he says, thrusting her towards me as if her clothes are on fire. 'You've been ages.'

'I wasn't that long. Come on, darling.' I take her into my arms, noticing a distinct aroma. 'She needs changing, hadn't you noticed?'

'I've only just picked her up. Tilly dropped her orange juice on the floor and got upset and it was basically pandemonium.' He gestures towards the ceiling with his head. 'I was hoping Danni would hear and come to my rescue but...'

'She isn't even supposed to be here. Come on, darling, let's go and get you changed.'

'How did you get on? Any luck?' He follows me into the downstairs bathroom, where I lay Lucy on a mat.

'Watch her for a second while I get the stuff.' I rummage in the cupboard with my back to them. 'And yes, Martin has arranged for his niece to babysit, I just need to call her to confirm. But she's very young. I wonder if I should stay at home after all, or whether we should go in relays.'

'It's important we go to the party together. Don't forget Gavin Lord and his wife are going, and it's crucial I don't give him a bad impression of me. He's involved in the panel who will be discussing roles in the company next year.'

'Is that the only reason you want me there?'

'Of course it isn't, but my financial prospects are important for our family, whatever happens. Let's try and enjoy it as much as we can given the circumstances.'

'How can I enjoy it? I don't know I can trust you anymore.'

'It will take time but I'll prove it to you. Have faith in me, please.'

He looks pensive as he goes upstairs.

I hear him talking to Danni and they laugh. Oliver never dwells on things, unlike me. He and Danni are always laughing together. Does he care? Or does he think he's got away with it? I go to the bottom of the stairs and try and listen to the conversation but it's too muffled.

I text Kelly with my details and ask her to come over at seven; that will give us some time to help familiarise her with our routines. I'm not convinced I've made the right decision. Leaving the children makes me anxious. Next I call Becky to let her know. Ryan answers and he asks me to hold on and I hear a muffled conversation in the background. He's gone for what seems like a while and the tone of their voices is agitated.

'That's sorted,' he says.

'Are you sure? Can I speak to Becky as she's there?'

'She's busy; she'll see you later.'

I'm left frowning at the phone. Becky's normally friendly and chatty and always up for conversation. She'd been quite anxious about her own children the other day, but it's not surprising with Ryan's attitude towards the police. Maybe he is right; there's more to Tilly's disappearance than the police are letting on. And obviously they don't know about the notes. I scoop Lucy up from the playmat and hold her tight. Her skin smells of peaches and I stroke her hair.

'I'll never let anyone hurt you,' I murmur, my breath hot against her skin. I would never hurt my child, or any child. If only I could make other people believe this.

# TWENTY-FOUR

Danni leaves around midday to meet a friend. Perfume wafts into the room and she's dressed up in a floral jumpsuit and carrying a clutch bag. Her hair is loose and silky and I can't help being struck by how pretty she is every time I see her. Conventionally pretty, that is, unlike me who has an 'interesting' face according to my husband when pressed once on the subject after a few glasses of gin. 'You're you,' he'd said, 'I wouldn't say pretty exactly but you have a gorgeous smile and your eyes are a piercing blue. I'd describe your look as interesting.' It had amused me at the time, but now it appears more as a casual put-down.

He hasn't seen much of my 'gorgeous smile' lately. I wonder how he's described me to his mistress, or does he not mention me at all? It's depressing not knowing what depths of deception my husband is capable of going to, whether I can believe his insistence that the affair is over.

'I'll see you guys tomorrow.' She hoists her bag onto her shoulder.

'Gorgeous bag,' I say.

'Thanks, I got it in Paris the other weekend.'

'I thought you went to the Seychelles.'

'Oh I did, but I travelled back via France and spent the weekend there.'

Oliver comes into the kitchen. 'Where are you off to?' he asks.

'I'm meeting a friend in Covent Garden.'

He pulls a face. 'You'll have trouble parking in Central London.'

Danni laughs. 'I'm not driving. I'm catching the midday train. And if I don't hurry I'm not going to make it.'

'I'll give you a lift,' Oliver says. 'It only takes a few minutes in the car. And you won't be able to run in those heels.'

Good to know he's noticed her heels. Now my attention is drawn to her high-heeled court shoes.

'Gosh, that would be fabulous, but only if you're sure.'

'I won't be long. You don't need me for anything?' he asks, looking at me, although he's already grabbing his car keys as if he can't wait to get out fast enough. I don't bother to answer, concentrating on feeding Lucy, who is currently resisting the spoonful of apple puree I'm trying to feed her.

'Have a great time at the party,' Danni says. 'And see you tomorrow. I'll help you with the Christmas lunch. If there's anything you need me to do, last-minute shopping or whatever, it's the least I can do to thank you for letting me gate-crash your Christmas dinner.'

'Thanks,' I say, giving her a hug. Oliver is already outside and opening the garage. It's hard to resent her when she's being so sweet and it's Oliver who's making me fume. But her comment about being in Paris reverberates in my mind – that could have been the weekend Oliver was there. I chew on my lip. I'm not sure how we'll get through this afternoon, pretending everything is fine just to be able to cope with this evening in one piece.

It turns out we don't have to. Oliver texts me half an hour

later to say he's gone to help Ben pick up his Christmas tree as his car has broken down.

'Where's Daddy?' asks Tess, clambering onto the sofa to look out of the window.

'He's gone out with Uncle Ben. How about you girls help me with some Christmas wrapping?'

My suggestion is met with squeals of excitement and we spend a productive couple of hours wrapping up everything I've bought for the family, although I'm subjected to their *Kiddie Christmas* album which involves cartoon characters from their favourite television programme warbling out festive tunes in high-pitched voices. Tess mostly dances around while Tilly folds wrapping paper along the lines I've indicated, breathing hard as she concentrates. They buy my explanation that Father Christmas only delivers to children, hence me buying and wrapping presents for the adults so they don't feel left out. These white lies would normally prickle at my conscience but when Oliver is telling whopping scarlet ones, mine don't bear comparison. Applying myself to the task helps settle my mind as I'm good at wrapping and enjoy creating beautiful-looking packages which Tess arranges in piles under the tree. Ordinarily I'd have completed the wrapping over a week ago. I've never left it so late before. After that they help me bake some mince pies so that we'll have plenty for when Father Christmas squeezes down our chimney and has a rest by the fire with the obligatory tumbler of whisky.

'Father Christmas is so fat,' Tess says, making Tilly giggle and she copies her, and they repeat the refrain, getting louder and louder. 'What if he gets stuck?' The image delights them and makes them laugh even harder, Tilly wobbling and falling against the pile of presents, which teeters but manage to stay upright.

'That's enough, you're getting overexcited. Let's make sure your rooms are tidy now for when Kelly comes.'

The thought of Kelly has them skipping eagerly upstairs. I don't hear any more from Oliver and he doesn't reply to my texts asking him what is taking so long. I start preparing some food for the girls, wanting to get them ready nice and early for when Kelly arrives. For the past hour I've been constantly looking out of the window for signs of Oliver or Ben. Finally, Oliver's car pulls into the drive.

'You've been ages,' I say. 'What took so long? Didn't you see my texts?'

'It was a nightmare. The tree place had sold out and we had to drive to that shop over near the cricket ground. Turns out we weren't the only ones doing everything last minute and there was a massive snake of traffic leading up to the garden centre.' He drops his keys onto the sideboard. 'I thought it would be easier for you if I wasn't here.'

'It's not about me. The children missed you.'

'I'll take over now if you want to get ready, have a bath and pamper yourself. I know you'll want to get all dolled up.'

Usually I enjoy getting dressed up for a night out, spending time on the process which is a huge part of the enjoyment. Tonight, how I look matters more, as if all the other women are competition for Oliver to eye up; I've seen the way he looks at Danni and jumps to help her whenever she needs. I wonder what they said to one another in the car. A voice keeps whispering suspicious thoughts about them, returning no matter how I try to convince myself I'm fabricating things. Tonight will be torture. All the women will be in their finery and I'll be watching his every move, to see who he might know better than he should.

'What time is the babysitter coming?' Oliver asks.

'Seven.'

'I bet the girls are excited. It's the first time we're leaving them with someone they haven't met before. How old is she again?'

'Sixteen.' *Too young. Too young to be responsible.* Angry words from the past rain down on me like hailstones. Cold sweat covers my back.

'Actually, I'm having second thoughts. I'm not in the mood for a party. Why don't you go and enjoy yourself; I'll stay with the children.'

'No.' I'm surprised by the force with which he spits out the word. 'I won't let you punish me by not going. What will the neighbours think? And you know the Lords will be there. They'd be bound to ask questions. We should be presenting a united front.'

He opens the fridge and pulls a bottle of lager out from inside the door. 'I won't let you give up on us that easily. I need time to think about your ultimatum but avoiding each other won't help and I don't want other people gossiping about the state of our marriage. I want you by my side, looking beautiful at this party.'

'That's not what this is about. I'm unsure about Kelly, that's all. I've never met her and she's very young. I haven't left Lucy with anyone apart from Mum. After what happened with Tilly, I'm not sure it's a good idea.'

He rolls his eyes.

'Not this again. You can't live your life being so anxious. Martin wouldn't have recommended her if he didn't think she was reliable. I won't let you mollycoddle the children. They need to be able to stand up for themselves in life, not hide under their grandmother's skirts.'

'You're being ridiculous.'

'Hardly. You said it had made Becky extra careful with Dolly but is she fretting about going, worried about leaving Dolly? I bet she isn't.'

'Her daughter didn't go missing.'

'And our daughter is fine.' He sighs with exasperation. 'Go and get ready, please. I want us to try.'

Oliver's lack of understanding touches a nerve. It's not his fault he doesn't know all the facts. I lock the bathroom door and run myself a bath. Despite the steam from the bath and the glorious peachy smell of the bath lotion which is now filling the water with bubbles of different sizes, I can't stop my rising anxiety. I believe in karma, which means something bad will happen to my children tonight. It's what I deserve. Sitting in the bath shivering and waiting to feel the effect of the hot water on my skin, which is already turning pink, I think back to those past sessions with the counsellor, who taught me to look at my situation with a different perspective. I repeat the mantras she taught me to recite to myself when panic was rising and threatening to take over my life, while imagining what an objective observer would make of my fears. I'd be laughed at. Oliver is just being sensible.

My skin prickles now as the heat seeps into it and I stretch myself out and submerge my whole head and body under the water. Images flicker, like the beginning of an old black and white film, and the familiar sequence of events plays out under my eyelids.

*The baby is crying. It sounds as if she is a long way from where I am. What starts as a solitary wail is followed by a few seconds of silence where I hope I've imagined it, followed by a full-blown bellowing where she doesn't sound as if she has time to take a breath and the cries are like nails scraping down a blackboard. Why does she sound as if she is so far away? Someone must have closed the door because I deliberately left it open so that I would be able to hear her. There's only one other person here so that means it must have been him.*

*The next part is blurry, like a rain-spattered windscreen; no matter how fast the wipers go, you can't quite see what is happening. What I do know is that my pulse is racing and I'm frantic to get to the baby, desperate to find out why she is crying and to relieve her pain. The raindrops are ever heavier and large bursts of water blur my vision and I don't understand why I left her in the first place. There's no chance of being able to see what lies ahead; if I could I'd never have arranged to meet him, never have come to this house. I don't know how long this goes on for or whether I'm dreaming but the next thing I remember is a banging on the door and my life as I know it becomes irretrievably altered.*

*How I wish I could go back and undo the last few months. Everyone else wishes that too, and that I didn't exist.*

The bath water is getting cold. When I get those flashbacks I lose track of time. No doubt Oliver thinks I'm deliberately avoiding him, leaving him with the children, but I want him to spend time with them; I want them to have a good relationship with their father. My own father worked long hours, beginning very early and consequentially arriving home exhausted and retreating to bed, without time for playing or stories or hearing about our day at school. 'Don't disturb your father' was a familiar refrain.

'Are you still in the bath?' Oliver's voice floats up from the hall. I have no idea how long I've been in here. My watch is on the side – too long. It's too late to cancel Kelly even if it had been an option. Oliver's right, we don't want to give the residents any more fodder for their gossiping; as it is, my ears are constantly tingling and I'm convinced they are talking about me. Or are they speculating about him?

I wrap myself in a towel and go onto the landing.

'I'll be down in a minute.'

Kelly arrives bang on seven, by which time I'm dressed and fully made up. Despite everything I'm pleased with the reflection that looks back at me from the full-length mirror. I was right to keep it simple. I throw a shawl over my bare shoulders as no doubt we'll be spending time on the terrace. Gabi likes a 'cheeky' cigarette on this kind of occasion. Despite the outdoor heaters, it can't possibly be very warm up there.

Kelly is about five-two, dressed in jeans and a hooded sweat-shirt, her long brown hair tied back in a high ponytail. She looks very young, but has an air of capability about her. Her face is covered in freckles and she has large eyes and dimples in her cheeks when she smiles, which she does a lot. I warm to her instantly. She swoops down to the floor where Lucy is sitting in her carry chair, wide eyed and alert to everything that is going on around her, looking from side to side and kicking her legs.

'What a gorgeous baby,' she says. 'Uncle Martin said she was cute but not this cute.' She strokes her cheek. 'I adore babies. I can't wait to have one of my own. I want four children; I'm not bothered about gender.'

'Yes, she's cute but she's far too awake for my liking. I tried to get her to sleep this afternoon but she wasn't having any of it.'

'It doesn't bother me, Mrs Carlton,' she says.

'Harriet, please.'

'Harriet. Where are the other two?'

'Their father is reading them a story.' On cue, rapid foot-steps shuffle across the landing and down the stairs, followed by Oliver's heavier tread. Tess bursts into the room followed by Tilly, who hangs back in the doorway when she sees a stranger.

'Hello, I'm Kelly.'

'My name is Tess and my sister is Tilly and she's shy.'

'That's OK. Hello, Tess and Tilly. I sometimes get shy. I bet Tilly is glad she's got you for a sister.'

'Hi.' Oliver comes into the room and holds out his hand for Kelly to shake. He's wearing a patterned shirt in black and turquoise which I haven't seen before, and smart black jeans. His hair is slicked back with product and I'm reminded of the first time I set eyes on him and knew he was exactly what I'd been searching for.

'Kelly,' she says.

'Oliver.'

'Come into the kitchen with me, Kelly, and I'll show you

what's what,' I say. I talk her through the children's require-
ments and routine, and show her where everything is. 'Help
yourself to anything from the fridge. There's a delicious chocolate cake which needs finishing.'

'Your house is gorgeous,' she says. 'Prospect Close is such a
lovely area. I'd feel like I'd died and gone to heaven if I lived
here. Uncle Martin living here is the next best thing.'

I laugh. 'Our house doesn't compare to your uncle's
penthouse.'

'It is a bit fabulous, I must admit. I went up there before I
came here. They've got caterers serving food and drink and
everything. I almost wished I was staying for the party.'

'Almost?'

'No offence, but everyone is a lot older than me. It's not
really my thing. Anyway, I adore children, I expect Uncle
Martin told you, and I couldn't wait to meet your three. I want
to be a paediatrician, always have done ever since I was little
and used to practise medicine on my dolls.'

'Are you studying at the moment?'

She nods. 'A levels. This is only the start. It's a long haul,
years of study and practice.' She watches the children as she
talks. 'But that's way off yet, and I need to get my grades first.'

'Have you done much babysitting?'

'Not masses. People don't seem to go out as much anymore;
everything's so expensive. I've got a little sister, though, and I
have to look after her a lot. Not that I get paid, mind.'

The doorbell rings. 'Excuse me, that will be Becky and
Dolly. Have you met them before?'

'I'll get it.' Oliver leaves the room.

'No, I don't know her at all. I feel as if I know you, though;
Uncle Martin's always talking about you.'

'Good things I hope,' I say, blushing. 'He's a good friend.'

'Hello.' Becky comes in holding Dolly's hand, looking at
Kelly. Ryan is behind her. 'You must be Kelly. Thank you so

much for stepping in at the last minute. I couldn't bear to miss this party.'

'I'm just showing my face so you know who I am,' Ryan says. 'Alright Becky?' He glares at her. 'I've got to get back.' He goes back into the hall with Oliver.

'She's a life saver, isn't she?' I look at Becky but she's unbuttoning Dolly's coat.

'Hmm,' she says. 'Dolly, this is Kelly. You're going to be a good girl, aren't you? She gets a bit excited when she sees the twins. I hope you won't regret this.'

'Trust me, you don't need to worry. We're going to get along just fine, aren't we, girls? I hope you're going to want me to read you all a story because I love doing that.'

'Yes, yes.' The girls clamour around her, Tilly forgetting her shyness and Tess leads Kelly over to the bookcase to show her their favourite books.

I turn to Becky, taking in her blue silk dress and matching stilettos, a fur stole over her shoulder.

'You look nice; I love your dress.'

'I'm going to have to rush back home because Ryan's not ready yet. I'll see you at the party. Thanks again, Kelly, this is my mobile number and you know where we are.' The smile she gives Kelly is in contrast to the glacial feeling I'm picking up from her towards me. She hasn't looked at me once.

'I'll show you out,' Oliver says. He's been standing behind us the whole time when I assumed he'd gone upstairs. I expect him to come back straight away but they have what seems like a lengthy conversation on the doorstep.

'The girls want me to read them a story up in their bedroom,' Kelly says, reminding me of her presence. 'Is there anything else you need to tell me?'

'No. I'll let you know when we're leaving and you can take over with Lucy.' The three of them disappear upstairs. Oliver comes back in.

'What were you talking about for so long?'

Oliver narrows his eyes. 'Am I not allowed to speak to another woman now?'

'No,' I say in an exasperated tone. 'But I was going to ask you if you'd noticed how she was with me. She was a bit off.'

'No I didn't, but I wasn't particularly paying attention. She was telling me Ryan was in a mood and didn't want to go to the party but he didn't want to babysit either and how he's driving her mad. She was just letting off steam, I think.'

'It's weird, though; normally she'd have said that to me. I get on really well with her – at least up until the other day when she left so abruptly. But that can't have had anything to do with me.'

'What else could have made her leave?'

'I'd just received those flowers.' My voice tails off as I remember the note and how I don't want Oliver to know about it. 'I don't know what was the matter. It was strange.'

'I thought you said she gave you them.'

'Did I? No, it was Gabi.' I avoid looking at him.

He frowns. 'Perhaps they hit a nerve. Ryan not sending her flowers, behaving like an idiot. She sounded pretty fed up with him.'

I shrug. 'I guess. I hope I haven't done something to upset her.'

'I'm sure you haven't,' Oliver says, 'you always overthink everything. You've got enough on your mind as it is.'

His comment surprises me, and reminds me how well he knows me and how hard it is going to be if we separate.

'Try not to worry about the children. They're in safe hands, she has our numbers and we'll only be a few steps away.'

I nod and glance at the kitchen clock. 'It's time we left.' Lucy is now asleep in her carry chair. 'I'll take Lucy up to bed and speak to Kelly before we go. Can you grab a bottle of champagne to take with us? One of the boxed ones, as a gift.'

'Sure.'

Upstairs in the twins' bedroom, Kelly is sitting on the bed, resting against the headboard with the twins one side, Dolly on the other, all leaning against her, engrossed in the book. Tilly has her thumb in her mouth. Kelly grins at me.

'This is such a good book.' She holds it up to show me the cover. '*Mr Pea*.'

I roll my eyes. 'It is the first few times but then it gets a bit old, night after night of *Mr Pea*.'

She laughs.

'We're heading off now. Lucy's asleep in her cot. She shouldn't wake up until the early hours and we'll be back by then, but the baby monitor is where I showed you. And you've got our numbers?'

'Yes, honestly, everything is good. You don't need to worry, I promise. Uncle Martin told me what happened the other evening and I understand and you honestly have nothing to worry about. I can see us three are going to get on like a house on fire.'

'Is the house on fire?' Tilly says.

'No, darling.' I indicate to Kelly that we'll be off without saying goodbye to the girls, not wanting to unsettle them, although I doubt they'd be the slightest bit bothered, as Kelly is far too interesting. I use the bathroom, checking my makeup in the mirror, I look better than I have all week. I smile at my reflection. Oliver's right, it's going to be a good evening. The power of positive thinking and all that. I run downstairs, careful to keep my tread light and collect my bag from the entrance hall, making sure that I have everything I need. I check my phone to find a text message from an unknown number.

'Are you ready?' Oliver appears.

'Yes,' I say, distracted, the back of my neck tingling. The text is written in capital letters.

'I'll make sure the back door is locked.' He disappears again.

I lean against the bannister, take in a deep breath, not wanting to see, but compelled to open the text, which instantly dispels my uplift in mood.

*I KNOW WHO YOU ARE AND SOON EVERYONE ELSE WILL TOO. ENJOY THE PARTY. MIDNIGHT BECKONS.*

## 2006

'The baby alarm's gone off.' She pointed at the monitor and tried to untangle herself from him. He was like an octopus, with hands everywhere. 'I've got to go upstairs.' She had to tug at her arm before he would let go of her.

'Be quick, then.' She left him scowling at the television where bullets pelted into a target and blood seeped onto a man's shirt. The crying baby had done her a favour.

Upstairs Lydia was grizzling, her face scrunchy and pink. She picked her up and hugged her, grimacing as the dampness of her nappy touched her skin and the unmistakable smell of urine tickled her nose.

'Poor thing, let's get you changed.'

Now she thanked Mrs Freud for being so thorough about where everything was. It shouldn't take long to change the nappy, but her fingers kept slipping as she tried to work as quickly as possible, conscious the whole time that Mike was waiting for her downstairs. Finally the nappy was on. He had to understand that the baby came first this evening. If only it were Gemma downstairs instead of Mike, they'd be laughing at a rom com and tucking into a box of chocolates. Instead, Mike was getting slowly intoxicated. She had no idea how well he could take his drink, really, she barely knew him, and with Gemma she could just be herself.

She tucked Lydia back into her cot and watched over her, rocking the mobile over her bed, which Lydia followed with her eyes until they drooped and closed. On the landing she thought she could smell smoke. Her pulse quickened and she ran downstairs. Mike wasn't in the living room where she'd left him but in the kitchen, smoking a cigarette. A thick cloud of smoke hung over him, but it was no ordinary cigarette, the acrid herby smell tickling her throat.

'You can't smoke in this house,' she said, opening the back door.

'I was bored,' he said, 'waiting for you. Why did you invite me here? Saturday night I always go out with my mates. I'm beginning to wish I was with them. I thought you liked me.'

'I do,' she said. 'Let's go back and finish the film.'

He blew a cloud of smoke straight at her and hurled the cigarette butt towards the open back door. He put his arms around her and kissed her again. She made a mental note to retrieve the cigarette end before the Freuds got back.

In the living room the film was paused on a shot of an ambulance and she picked up the remote control. Mike threw himself over the arm of the sofa before sprawling on his back, a lazy grin on his face. 'Come here,' he said, 'let's get comfy.' He pulled her down and she leaned back against him and he put his arms around her waist. She pressed play and they watched the rest of the film although she hadn't a clue what was going on. The cider had given her a headache and her attention was fixed on Mike's hands, which were wandering higher and higher under her top. Plus the aroma of smoke clinging to his clothes was making her throat itch. When his hands started fumbling with her bra strap, she tried to sit up but he pulled her back down.

'Don't move,' he said, 'just relax.'

Her phone beeped. She wrenched herself away, reaching for it and jumping to her feet.

'Mrs Freud,' she said, 'the woman who lives here. They're on their way back. You'd better go,' she said. 'They mustn't find you here.' Her hands shook as she shoved the phone in her pocket, not wanting him to see Gemma's name on the screen. Mike stared at her.

'You're kicking me out?' Sprawled on the sofa, he made no effort to move. 'Unbelievable.' When she didn't respond he drained the rest of his cider before getting to his feet as if he was weighed down by a heavy load and the effort was just too much. 'Guess I'll have to see what the guys are up to.' He pulled his phone out, sent a message, waiting for a reply. When it came, he laughed. She switched from one foot to the other. It had been a while since she checked on Lydia and now she wanted him to go. 'They're all down the Red Lion chatting up some hot girls. Most likely hit the nightclubs after. Guess I'll have to check out your competition seeing as there's not much going on here. And you wouldn't get in. You're just a kid.'

She clenched her fists at her side, her cheeks burning. With his sweaty forehead and dishevelled shirt, she couldn't imagine what she had seen in him. She'd heard that boys were only after one thing but hadn't wanted to believe it of him. It turned out he was as bad as the boys in her class who tried it on with girls and then bragged about how far they'd got.

She fetched his jacket to hurry him up and he stared at her as he snatched it out of her hands, his eyes boring into her as he shrugged it over his shoulders.

'I thought you were different.'

*Same.*

She kept quiet, not wanting him to prolong his departure. Upstairs was silent, a good sign.

Or was it?

## TWENTY-FIVE

'What is it now?' Oliver is holding a bottle of Dom Pérignon in its black box. Dark, like my thoughts.

'I can't go.'

'We've been through this, what's made you change your mind?'

I glance back at my phone.

'What is it?'

'Someone is threatening me.'

'Show me,' he says.

I hold the phone out for him to read.

'What does it mean?'

'I've no idea, but Tilly going missing may be connected.'

'Tilly wandered off, we've established that now.'

'What about the man she talked about?'

'I don't think there ever was a man. The police told me there was nothing on CCTV; I forgot to tell you.'

'There is no CCTV once you get past the main road.'

He sighs. 'We can't live our lives in fear. The message is most likely a scam.'

'Scam?'

'Prank, a mistake, I don't know. You can't seriously be afraid to go to this party because of that. You know how important it is to me.'

'I'd rather stay with the children.'

'The children are safe with Kelly. We can be home in two minutes if necessary. Nothing in that text is threatening them. If I thought for a minute they were under threat, do you really think I'd leave them behind? Surely you can't think that little of me just because of an affair.'

'So it is an affair. Is it Danni? Are you sure you've only just met?'

'What?' He looks incredulous. 'Of course not. I've told you the details. Don't do this, please, not now. It's crucial I make a good impression on Gavin. Have you received any other texts like this?'

I shake my head. I can't tell him, not here, not now.

'No.'

'Look, if it helps you could get home by midnight, that way avoiding any threat, although I really don't think it's serious. If I did, I'd be ringing the police.'

'OK.' I drop the phone into my bag and fake a smile. 'Let's go.' I pull my pashmina over my bare shoulders as we leave the house, the cold air hitting my lungs. It's only a few paces down the road but my neck tingles as if eyes are watching me from across the street. Stepping into the party feels like walking the plank. The sender of the note is in there, waiting for me. Four and a half hours until midnight. I'm reluctant to move, but Oliver puts his hand on my back and escorts me forward. I'm not sure I'd have been able to move without that small bit of pressure. For a second I waver. Maybe I should tell Oliver about the text, it looks like he's about to find out who I really am soon enough, but he's blissfully unaware of the horror I'm experiencing; now is not the time for revelations. If I keep my wits about me, perhaps I can work out who is out to get me and expose them, challenge them when I'm surrounded by people.

Oliver is grinning, waving to someone who's already up on the penthouse terrace, music pumping around the quadrangle. 'It's Sienna,' he says, and I look up, straight at the full moon to the left of the terrace where Sienna is waving a bottle. The bright light makes me blink. A premonition of madness – what lies in store for us tonight? I shiver, my heart still pounding as it has been since I opened the text.

'Hurry up, you two, or I'll have drunk the whole bottle before you get here.'

'No chance of that,' Oliver says, taking my arm. 'We've got reinforcements.' I lean against him; slushy snow lies on the ground, hiding treacherous patches of black ice, and as my stilettos stick I picture myself sliding, falling, my leg twisting, breaking, my whole body snapping into pieces as a dark figure leers down at me from the penthouse terrace, cackling.

*For goodness' sake, it's not Halloween.*

'You're a bit unsteady this evening. That glass of wine must have gone to your head. You'd better eat something when you get there.' Oliver sounds as if he cares, but I won't be swayed. He's cheated on me, and I can't get past that. The thought of eating makes my stomach lurch, and my foot slips on an icy patch.

'Careful.' Oliver grips my arm hard, steadying me.

The lift glides upwards and my stomach turns over with it. The lift walls are mirrors and our reflection watches us. We stand together, awkward, like shop mannequins.

'We'll get through this, I promise you,' Oliver says.

The messages I read on his phone drift before my eyes.

*I hate it when you're so close yet so far*

Is there a clue in those words, 'so close'? What if his lover isn't in London, but here, now, at this party? I squeeze my fists to stop myself from throwing his arm off me, a snake coiled around my waist. The lift doors slide open and the music which had disappeared in the lift greets us as we step out. The penthouse door is open, music spilling out. A few people are dotted about, standing around making conversation; it's early for a party and I imagine most people will arrive later. At a quick glance, I see that neither Gabi nor Asha are here yet. Edward walks towards us, glass of something pink in his hand, the drink full of crushed ice and a raspberry on top.

'Come in, come in,' he says, waving the glass. 'I've made the most fabulous cocktails if I do say so myself. I hired a professional and he's given me a lesson.' He's wearing a deep green velvet waistcoat over a white collarless shirt, and beautifully pressed trousers. He air-kisses me on both cheeks and shakes Oliver's hand. 'Sophie.' He motions to a girl who is wearing a white shirt and black trousers, as are several of the people who are dispersed amongst the guests in the vast open-plan lounge and kitchen. 'Take their coats, will you, darling,' he says, giving her a dazzling smile. I hand the young woman my pashmina. A young man in identical black and white garb appears at our side proffering a tray of champagne flutes. Oliver looks around.

'I can't see the Lords yet. Oh look, there's Ben,' Oliver says, as he takes a glass from the tray and crosses the room where his brother is with Holly and a few others. Ben breaks away from the group and the two of them move aside, plunging straight into conversation which looks like anything but small talk. Someone touches my shoulder and I turn to see Martin, who gives me a warm hug.

'I hear you've got Kelly looking after your brood. I'm glad you took me up on it. I wasn't sure you were going to. And she's thrilled, she's desperate for cash, and if she's with small children then she's happy.'

'She seems lovely. I left her reading them stories. They'll have her reading all night if she doesn't put her foot down.'

'Oh she will. She'll see through all their little tricks. Let me get you a drink,' he says. 'I'd advise against one of Edward's cocktails unless you want to knock yourself out.'

'That sounds like exactly what I need.'

Martin gives me a sharp look.

I laugh to dismiss it, and opt for a glass of white wine, but he must notice the way my hand shakes when I pick up the glass.

'Come and see the terrace,' he says. 'It will take your breath away.'

I take the opportunity to glance at my watch; it's almost eight. Four hours until midnight. We step onto the terrace. Martin is right. Tiny white lights are strung up all around the sides of the space and the area has been divided into separate zones. The spa pool is hidden by a circle of plants, which creates the illusion of a pond; a long wooden table occupies another zone and several people are sitting around it chatting. On the other side is a pair of comfy-looking benches strewn with cushions, but the eye is drawn to the view. Rising behind the lower buildings on the other side of Prospect Close is a vast expanse of green that stretches for miles. The edge of this area is where Tilly was found. She could so easily have got lost.

Martin is looking at me expectantly.

'It's stunning,' I say.

'Pretty special, isn't it? Edward's extremely chuffed with himself; he's like a proud peacock.'

'In that gorgeous green waistcoat.'

'Well spotted. That was a gift from me. It's the first time he's worn it.'

'Harriet.' The sound of my name being called echoes up from below. Both Martin and I peer over the edge. Gabi is down in the courtyard, the shiny fabric of her dress gleaming under the streetlight. Next to her a blonde woman is kneeling down, fiddling with the buckle of her shoe strap.

'Look who I found,' Gabi says. 'I hope you don't mind me inviting her along.'

The woman stands up and waves. It's Danni. She's wearing a shimmering jumpsuit that she wasn't wearing when she left our house earlier and I wonder when she got changed.

'Danni, what happened? I thought you were out seeing your friend.' My voice echoes around the quadrangle.

'She was taken ill, so I decided to come back. I left a message with Oliver. He said it was OK.'

She texted Oliver? I stiffen, unsure how to reply but Martin gets in before me.

'Of course it's OK. You're officially invited to my party,' Martin says. 'Come inside and get a drink and we can introduce ourselves properly. You don't mind, do you?' he says, as he takes my elbow and leads me to the sofa.

'No, it's just unexpected. She was supposed to spend the night with a friend.'

'That's a shame, but she's welcome here. Let's take advantage of this quiet time to have a chat; I'm sure I won't get a moment to myself once the rest of the guests arrive. Edward has invited far too many people. You know Gavin Lord is going to be here, don't you?'

'I do. Oliver's desperate to make a good impression; he wants me on my best behaviour.'

He laughs. 'I can't imagine you behaving badly.'

The bench is as comfortable as it looks, the leather soft as I sit down, but I'm too on edge to sink into it. I can see Oliver and Ben still in conversation and I wonder if Ben knows about Oliver's affairs, whether he sees me as someone to pity or laugh at. Whichever it is, I've had enough.

'Have you told him?' Martin has picked up on my sarcasm. I grip onto my glass as if I'm holding onto a rope and will crash to the floor if I lessen my grip. 'You're not yourself tonight.'

I sigh. 'Is it that obvious?'

'Maybe not to anyone who doesn't know you, but to me you look like someone who carries the weight of the world on her shoulders. And if you're worrying that I'll tell Edward, his mind is on loftier planes; he's not interested in local gossip. Unless it's to do with neighbourhood security, obviously. I guessed it was to do with your husband.'

I manage a weak smile and put my glass down, my mind made up. I check no one is in immediate earshot, before taking a deep breath.

'Yes, it's Oliver, obviously. He knows about the shirt I found with lipstick on and he admitted it. He said it was a one-off that weekend. It was one of his colleagues from Nice. I only half believe him, though.' I explain about the texts.

'What makes you think he isn't telling the whole truth?'

'Because it's not the first time.' It all comes tumbling out, the words in a fast torrent because now I've opened the tap, I want to get it all out there before something stops me and I'm back to carrying all this stuff around in my head, feeling as if I'm about to burst. 'He's insisted it's over, of course, but you know when you just know, in here.' I tap my heart, where it feels as if it's knocking back against my breastbone in response. He's hiding something, I'm sure he is.

'But I've made my mind up. I'll wait until after Christmas is over, and then we're leaving. You know how much I've always wanted to go and live in the countryside, open a shop, how Oliver is always delaying it, *just one more year,* well, I realise now that one more year is going to be a decade if I don't make a stand. That's what I'm doing now.' I drain my glass of wine, place it firmly back down. A waiter is standing in the doorway and I beckon him over, take a glass of champagne, no longer caring about being sensible, not mixing drinks. I've spent too long being careful. 'I'll move out, take the children and I'll make it happen. I can divorce him on grounds of infidelity. Even if he is telling the truth about this recent liaison, he's done it in the past and I can prove it. Our marriage was never going to succeed with him being away all the time.' And if I get through tonight unscathed I'm going to get as far away from the threats as I can, with or without Oliver.

'Are you sure that's what you want?' Martin asks. 'You'd be working plus sorting out a new school; it would be a lot to cope with on your own. I'm not sure how realistic this countryside dream is. You'd be very isolated. You have friends here, and those that aren't friends are good neighbours, people who you could turn to in a crisis. Help on your doorstep. And the children have friends here too. Imagine for a minute you were here alone with the children, without Oliver, wouldn't you be happy?'

I try to imagine how it would feel if Oliver's absences were permanent. If that omnipresent sense of ill ease were removed, if I didn't have to work around his timetable and his secrets. The house is lovely, the gym is on the doorstep, and yes, I've got a few friends but I hate the gossiping. What I don't tell him is how the layout of Prospect Close makes me feel claustrophobic, the way all the houses look at one another. 'I'd make friends elsewhere, through the school, through other parents, and hopefully I'd meet customers who come into my shop and meet like-minded people that way.'

'What about the children? You wouldn't have Oliver or – I assume – the nanny, and your mother is so close geographically here. You rely on her a huge amount. Unless you're planning on moving her with you?'

I picture Mum with her busy social life, failing to imagine her isolated from all her friends.

'That would never happen. She loves it here. And as for work, I'd continue to make my products at home and I'd hope to appoint a manager for the shop eventually, if it takes off in the way I hope it will. I'd make it work.'

'I'm not saying it couldn't work, but it would take time to establish new roots and with the emotional backlash that's bound to happen it's going to be extremely tough – as it would be for anyone. Your reasons for leaving need to be pretty compelling.'

'They are.' If only he knew.

I drink half of my champagne down in one go. Martin is astute and I'm sure he knows I'm hiding something. The alcohol ignites a thought that has been trying to break through since we came out here.

What if I confided in Martin?

'What is it?'

If I've learned one thing about Martin, it is that he is utterly trustworthy. Given the direct threat I've had about this party it makes sense to take somebody into my confidence. But to break the habit of a lifetime... I could tell him about the notes, at least. I don't have to explain the background.

The sound of a woman shrieking with laughter bursts out from the party, and the high-pitched tone goes right through me.

'I haven't told you everything. Somebody has been threatening me.'

I take my phone out and show him the recent text. 'I've had notes too.'

'This is awful,' he gasps, 'I can't believe you've kept this to yourself! When did it start?'

'The first one arrived the evening Tilly went missing. That in itself was pretty weird if you think about it. Nobody really knows the details of what happened to her. Aside from that, Becky's acting strangely with me and I have no idea why. The result is I'm terrified.'

'As are all the other parents, you've seen that.'

'But how do you explain the notes?' My voice has risen and I apologise. 'Sorry, I know you're only trying to help. I'm terrified whenever I'm away from my children. I tried to get out of coming but Oliver insisted, especially as his employer is invited. Not that he's paid me any attention since we got here; he's only interested in talking to his brother, and making sure he looks good in front of the Lords.'

'What did the police say?'

'I haven't told them.'

Martin looks startled. 'Whyever not?'

'I wasn't sure they'd take it seriously.'

'I'm sure they would, especially after what happened with Tilly. Has anyone else received notes?'

'I don't know. I haven't told a soul, not even Oliver. I can't trust him at the moment. I'm not convinced by his explanation about the woman from Nice; I'm beginning to think his partner is much closer to home and I won't tell him anything.'

'The police would know if more people had been threatened.'

'I can't tell the police.'

'OK. But you shouldn't hide away. I'm glad you came. And you don't need to worry about Kelly. She's brilliant and so sensible. I'd never have recommended her if she wasn't.'

'It's not her I'm worried about.'

'Then what is?'

Inside the apartment, from where I'm sitting and the way the light is falling, I can make out shapes of people, some standing, some seated; one person is dancing. Is it you? Or her? Or him? They were at a party back then, drinking, dancing, making the most of a well-deserved night off, the people I was supposed to be helping. Blissfully unaware their lives were about to be ruined.

'Somebody at this party wants to do me harm, and I have no idea who it is.'

## 2006

She opened the door, avoiding looking at Mike.

'Tease,' he muttered under his breath as she stood back to let him past.

She closed the door and leaned against it, closing her eyes. Her heart was thumping. She slid the chain on the lock. Her body itched from the way he'd pawed at her and she'd hated every second of it. What was she thinking by inviting him here? How was she going to explain the smell of smoke?

Upstairs was silent.

She took the stairs two at a time. Lydia hadn't moved since she last checked, and she paused in the doorway not wanting to wake her but to listen to her breathing. Nothing. The room was completely silent. She was too far away. She crept closer. Lydia lay on her back, the yellow blanket up to her neck. Her face was pale. Too pale. Her lips had a bluish tinge. She knelt down beside her and pulled off the cover. The tiny body was cold.

# TWENTY-SIX

'I don't deserve to have children.'

'What makes you say that?' Martin waves to somebody over my shoulder before turning his attention to me.

'I did something terrible. A long time ago. It's what I deserve.'

'I can't imagine you doing anything bad to anyone.' He watches me drain my champagne and look around for the waiter. 'I'd go easy on that if I were you. In the mood you're in it will only make everything worse. Life gets exaggerated when one is under the influence. Tell me what's wrong and I'm sure I can put your mind at ease.'

He's so sure of himself. Why is that? A chill runs through me. Should I watch what I say in front of Martin? What if he's the one I should be scared of? I get to my feet, my ankle twisting in my haste.

'These shoes! I'm not used to wearing stilettos. You're right, Martin. I'm imagining things. Worrying about Oliver is making my mind play tricks on me. Let's go and see who else has arrived.' From this side of the terrace I can see my house, the lights on both upstairs and downstairs. If only I could see through the walls, know for sure my children are OK. The quadrangle is in darkness, no loners out on the street, everyone up here, celebrating. I quickly check my phone before we head inside but there's no message from Kelly. *No news is good news.* Or is it? I'll stay for an hour, make my excuses. I doubt Oliver will even notice I've gone.

Back inside I hear Sienna's laugh. She's with Asha and wearing a gorgeous gold dress, slit low at the front but positioned perfectly with invisible tape to hide her modesty, high-heeled sandals to match and a short-sleeve white jacket. Asha is in electric blue. A man I've never seen before watches the women from across the room, his eyes appraising them. I'm taken back to the steam room, where I skulked around the corner listening to their conversation. I'm glad I had the opportunity to sort that out with Sienna otherwise I'd be feeling uncomfortable. I'm about to go and speak to them when Gabi appears brandishing a bottle of champagne.

'You need a top-up,' she says. 'I've just been outside. The view is breathtaking.' I follow her gaze back to where I was just sitting with Martin. Oliver and Ben are out there now, still deep in conversation. I scan the crowds, but can't see the Lords.

'I hope you don't mind me rescuing your nanny. She's lovely, isn't she?'

'Yes, she is.'

'Try telling your face to believe you. What is it?'

'This thing with Oliver is driving me mad. We agreed to try and forget about it this evening but how can I? I'm not so sure I believe his story about a one-night stand. I'm beginning to suspect his lover is closer to home, as in someone here. Danni revealed earlier that she was in Paris around the same time as Oliver's conference. It's a bit of a coincidence. But he swears they only just met when she came to work for us. She's stunning.'

'And so are you. That dress is gorgeous on you. So what if she was in Paris that weekend? It's a big city.'

'Yes, you're right. But he could have invited me; that's preying on my mind. Instead I had a hectic weekend as Kate had just quit. You weren't around that weekend either, so I couldn't talk to you about it. I have to be sure about Danni.'

'Why don't you speak to her about it?'

I pull a face. 'She's my employee and I want to keep it professional. And I might be overheard; you know what the others are like.'

'Are you going to have it out with Sienna about what happened at the gym?'

'No need, we had a chat about it the other day. She was extremely apologetic. I should go and say hello, actually. Coming?'

'If you don't mind, I'd rather stay here. That gorgeous young man over by the fireplace looks like he needs some company.' I don't recognise the man she is talking about. Who is he and what is he doing here? As she goes over, Elliott appears in the doorway. I'm taken aback; it's the first time he's been to one of our social events. He looks straight past Gabi and heads towards Edward, shakes his hand. He's dressed in an expensive-looking black jacket and trousers with a white polo neck sweater underneath. His short dark hair is peppered with white and he has a trim beard. Gabi doesn't react to seeing him; she's good.

'Why is it that men look better as they get older, without putting any effort in,' a middle-aged woman standing next to me says, 'while us women spend a fortune on expensive creams and treatments and put ourselves through gruelling regimes to stay in shape?' Her own face looks suspiciously line free.

'Things are changing,' the woman next to her says. 'Young men are equally obsessed these days. An ex of mine used to spend way longer than I did in the bathroom. And he spent serious money on skincare.'

'Are they really?' the woman says. 'My husband…'

I slip away from them and move through the room, which is filling up as more guests arrive and I wave to Becky, who's just come in but she doesn't appear to see me.

'Hi, Harriet,' Sienna says, moving aside for me to join their huddle.

'I'm so sorry about the steam room episode,' Asha says. 'Sienna put me straight. I grilled Mo about it after talking to Sienna, and he's not so sure now. I really am sorry. I know Oliver is often away but that's no reason to make assumptions.'

I take a large gulp of my drink to hide the reddening of my cheeks. Why would she say that?

Over her shoulder Oliver appears with a young woman at his side, his face lit up in that friendly, engaged way he has, when his attention is entirely focused on the other person. A stab of pain winds me. He hasn't looked at me like that in so long, and I miss him. I miss my own husband who is standing mere feet away from me.

Asha notices me staring and turns to see what I'm looking at.

'Do you know her?' I ask.

'No,' she says. 'Is everything OK with you and Oliver?'

'Yes, of course it is. Have you spoken to Becky at all recently?'

'Not since book club.'

Oliver's loud laugh catches my attention. He's still with the woman. He's removing two glasses of champagne from the tray being offered to him, and his eyes catch mine watching him. He hesitates, drinks held mid-air, then nods before turning away from me. As if I'm just another guest.

'Harriet.' A woman's voice interrupts my thoughts. 'It's so good to see you.' It takes me a moment to realise the woman in front of me is Audrey Lord, the wife of Gavin, Oliver's boss.

'How are you? We haven't seen you for ages. It's a

wonderful apartment,' she says. 'I'm so pleased we were invited. Have you been outside? The views are phenomenal.'

'Yes, Martin gave me a tour.'

'How are the children? Gavin says Oliver appears to be taking the upheaval of having a new baby in his stride. Although if he's anything like Gavin was when our children were small, it was me who did all the work.' She gives a tinkling laugh.

'That's exactly how it is. Oliver works such long hours, and what with the added commute...Then there's the odd weekend in France. It all adds up, not that I'm complaining, of course.'

'Oh.' She looks surprised. 'I thought Gavin said Oliver didn't need to travel as part of his new role,' she says. 'He thought it would suit him better since you had your last baby. I must be mistaken.'

Her words kindle a surge of anxiety. Has Oliver been lying to me about his work commitments too?

'The most recent was the conference. Did Gavin go?'

'Yes, he did. As it was just for a day I joined him for the rest of the weekend and we travelled down to Nice for a few days. Gavin visited the branch there but apart from that I had him all to myself.' She takes a sip of her drink and I take a quick glance at my watch as midnight ticks closer. Little time has passed since I last looked.

'Oliver was telling us about your new nanny. Really singing her praises, he was.'

I smile stiffly. 'Yes, she is doing well so far. Have you any plans for the holidays?'

'The family are descending as usual. I do so love Christmas. How about you?'

'Just a quiet one with the family.' It won't be, though, will it, now that Danni is with us too. I'll look for her, find out what her plans are. 'It's been lovely talking to you, but will you excuse me, there's someone I need to find.'

'Of course.'

Speaking to Audrey has helped confirm my perspective. He insisted the affair was a brief fling over one weekend; what with the texts and now this, I'm even more convinced that he's still seeing another woman. Why should I put up with a husband who doesn't appreciate what he has? Work is the most important part of his life. Family is mine, the children in particular. Which reminds me. Kelly answers her phone immediately, and assures me that all is well.

'You enjoy your party,' she says. 'You don't need to worry about the children.'

*If only.*

A passing waiter sees my glass is almost empty and tops it up. I look around to see if I can spot Danni and locate her with Oliver over by the kitchen. They're standing close together, and she laughs, putting her hand on his arm. I'm about to go over when Elliott appears in front of me.

'Mrs Carlton,' he says.

'Oh please, call me Harriet. It's good to see you here.' I wonder if Gabi talks to him about me.

He nods. 'Edward insisted. I'm not a great one for socialising as you've probably realised, but I was interested to see the work he's carried out here. Most impressive. It's given me some ideas for my apartment, if only I had the time.'

'Being a head teacher must be incredibly stressful.' Over his shoulder I keep my eye on Danni and Oliver.

'Yes, but rewarding too. Helping young people gives me such pleasure.'

'It was good of you to organise the search the other day, for Tilly.'

'It was the natural thing to do. Such a relief that she was returned unscathed. I hope you're recovered from the shock.'

'I have, thanks.'

'Any plans for Christmas?'

'Nothing special, Oliver's got time off for work and we'll see my mother at some point. The girls are hugely excited.'

'I imagine they are. That's what Christmas is all about, isn't it?' He looks wistful.

'Do you have plans?'

'Just a quiet one, as you say, making the most of the school holidays.'

A young couple are hovering and I make my excuses and leave Elliott to speak to them. Oliver is still talking to Danni and the woman he was with before, only Edward and a couple of others have joined them. Holly and I chat for a while, and I tell her about the misunderstanding with Ben and Gabi, which makes her laugh aloud.

'Can you imagine those two together?'

'What's so funny?' Sienna joins us.

'You,' Holly says. 'Apparently I shouldn't allow my husband to fix Gabi's shower.'

'I'll never live this down, will I? I saw you talking to Elliott,' she says. 'Any gossip?'

I roll my eyes, in an exaggerated fashion. 'No, Sienna, no gossip, remember.'

Somebody laughs loudly, and I look to see who it is. It's the young woman who is still talking to Oliver. Because I'm continually checking my watch, I know they've been talking for a good while.

'Who is that woman?' Sienna asks. I experience a flash of anger. If my friends are noticing the inordinate amount of time Oliver is chatting to an attractive woman then it has to be out of the ordinary. And he wanted me to make a good impression on his employers. As far as I can tell he hasn't spent much time with them. A quick look around the room tells me Audrey is talking to Gabi now, and Gavin is with Martin. Maybe Martin knows who she is.

'She's behaving strangely,' Sienna says, 'I reckon she's been hitting the vodka hard.' I look again to see what she means, realising she isn't talking about the woman with Oliver, but an older woman. She's wearing jeans and an oversize shirt, contrasting with the cocktail dresses and suits surrounding her, and her hair is pulled back into a ponytail, loose tendrils springing out over her face. 'And she clearly doesn't understand the meaning of formal attire.' As if she senses us talking about her, she turns and looks towards us, glaring, and I feel a jolt of recognition. It's Victoria, Elliott's wife. I doubt very much she should be here.

'I think I know her,' I say. 'I won't be a minute.' I join Gabi, who is now alone, moving around to the music.

'Gabi,' I hiss, 'is that Victoria over by the fireplace?' Up close, I recognise her as the woman who was arguing with Elliott and now I realise she was the woman in the café when Martin and I were in there. She must have been hanging around the close for ages.

She looks across to where she stands, finishing one glass of red wine while a waiter hovers, waiting for her to take another.

'Shit,' she says. 'I've seen her in photos and it most certainly is. Where's Elliott?'

'He's over there.'

'I can't approach him, not here. I'll text him.'

'Will he hear through this music?'

'He's got a smartwatch; it will alert him.'

Sure enough, a few seconds later, Elliott checks his phone, looking up and scanning the room.

'This is a nightmare,' Gabi says. 'The last thing he will want is a confrontation. I wish I could be with him.'

'Get him to meet you outside? I could tell Martin if you like, without going into detail. He's very discreet.'

'Would you? That might work. I'll text Elliott.'

I tap Martin on the shoulder to get his attention, seeing Elliott move away from the group towards the terrace.

'Don't look now,' I say, 'but Elliott's wife is here and she's very volatile. She isn't supposed to go near him. I can't say too much but is there anything you can do?'

Sienna appears at my side. 'What's going on? Who is that woman? Do you know her?' Her voice is loud and the woman looks over. Martin groans.

'Are you talking about me?' she says, coming over to us, her glass held in front of her. She trips and takes an involuntary step forward, her drink tilting at a precarious angle and sending drops of red liquid onto Sienna's pristine sleeve. She lets out a cry of dismay.

'Look what you've done. My new jacket.'

'Do you know my husband?' Victoria asks.

'Never mind your husband, look what you've done to my jacket. This was new; I treated myself when I was last away.'

'You were away with my husband. I knew it! It's you, isn't it, you're the one who's been running around with him.'

Sienna's mouth drops open in shock.

'Come with me,' Martin says, taking Victoria's arm. 'Let's see if we can find him. I'm not sure we've met – I'm Martin; I live here.' He catches my eye with a reassuring look. Gabi appears next to me.

'What's going on?' she asks.

'There was an accident; some wine was spilled. It's only a few drops, Sienna,' I say, 'don't make a fuss.' Anyone would think the whole bottle had covered her from the way she's reacting. 'That woman spilled it,' I say pointedly to Gabi, indicating Victoria. 'Martin's sorting her out, she's a bit drunk.'

'What does she mean? Who is she?' Asha has joined Sienna now.

'Elliott's gone home,' Gabi says quietly, 'thank god.'

'Don't take any notice of her,' Asha says. 'She's a bit tipsy, that's all. Let's go to the bathroom and rinse your jacket; I'm sure it will come out.'

Once she's gone, I tell Gabi what Victoria said. 'I didn't give anything away. All I mentioned to Martin was that she shouldn't be here.'

'If anyone can calm her down, it's him. I need a drink, come on.'

I follow her to the kitchen. People are dancing now, Gavin and Audrey Lord at the centre, Holly and Ben alongside them, holding onto one another and laughing. I still haven't spoken to Danni or Oliver since we arrived. Oliver was so keen for me to come to the party, yet he's spent the whole night elsewhere. I have a flashback to a New Year's Eve party we went to once, where we agreed beforehand we'd make an effort to be sociable, chat to our friends, as we'd been holed up in our flat for weeks, not needing the company of anyone else. We tried, but it was as if we were connected by a magnetic force, and even when he was on the opposite side of the room, I was drawn to him, slinking up to his side, taking his hand. 'Don't leave me again,' he'd said, desire in his eyes. We'd crossed to the dancefloor and spent the rest of the night watching and touching one another, before running down the street hand in hand, the short distance to our flat, before closing the outside world off, and glued back together again. The magnetic force is long gone.

Anger flares inside me. Gabi hands me a drink.

'Are you OK?' I ask.

She nods. 'Just relieved Elliott has gone. Can you imagine if Victoria had caused a scene? I had to persuade him to come in the first place. He needs to live his life, he can't stay hidden forever, but you see how persistent she is. He's too nice and doesn't want to hurt her, but enough is enough. How are you and Oliver doing?'

'I haven't spoken to him since we arrived. He's not with his boss, despite the fuss he made about making a good example.'

Gabi bites her lip.

'What is it?'

She sighs. 'I didn't know whether to tell you.'

'You have to now. If you know anything you have to tell me.'

'He's been chatting with this woman all night. He seems very attentive.'

'You don't mean Danni?'

'No, a younger woman.'

'Still? I saw her with him ages ago. Do you know who she is?'

'Never seen her before.'

'What shall I do?'

'If it were me I'd go and join them, see what the vibe is. He's on the sofa near where the cake is displayed.'

Oliver is deep in conversation with the same woman. As I get closer I see she is younger than I realised, barely in her twenties. I've never seen her before, I'm sure of that.

'Oliver.' He looks up, startled. The woman smiles at me and reaches for her drink.

'I'm here,' I say.

'Yes, clearly.' He frowns. 'Have you met Cindy?'

'Hi,' she says.

'Hi,' I say, forcing a smile.

'My wife, Harriet.'

I nod. Silence follows.

'I think I'll get a drink,' the woman says, slipping around me. 'Can I get you anything?'

I shake my head. Oliver watches her go.

'Having fun?' he asks.

'Not as much as you are. Is that her?'

'What are you talking about?' Realisation dawns. 'No, I've told you there is no *her*. I thought we were going to try and put that aside for one evening.'

'How can I *put it aside*? I thought you wanted *us* to spend time together this evening, to impress your boss and his wife.

Yet you've spent the whole night talking to other women, first Danni, now her.'

'What are you talking about? Are you drunk?'

'No I'm not drunk. How dare you patronise me.'

'You sound jealous, which is ludicrous,' Oliver says, his voice low. 'It's a party, I'm making conversation and I've spoken to loads of people. Danni was upset because her evening plans went wrong. I'm just being friendly.'

'Yes, she told me she'd sent you a text. Why would she send it to you and not me? She hardly knows you, or am I missing something?'

'You're imagining all this. I thought we agreed to be adult about this and put our differences behind us just for this evening.'

I stare at him, a rage burning inside me. 'You're kidding me. You're the one who's having an affair. And if it's not Danni, it must be with her, right?'

'Keep your voice down. That woman is Cindy Lord, Gavin and Audrey's daughter. She's barely out of her teens, for Christ's sake. I was making her feel welcome.'

He pushes past me and disappears. Aside from a couple of people watching us, the noise of conversation fills the air and I see Edward has seamlessly rescued the situation and is drawing attention to a large cake which has miraculously materialised on the table in the middle of the room. He's making a speech and people are laughing. I can't see Martin or Sienna. Gabi is chatting to the young man she had her eye on earlier.

What am I doing here? I look around at the glitzy apartment, everyone dressed up and having a good time while I am consumed by so many feelings: jealousy, rage, fear. My bra strap is digging into my shoulder and it's so long since I've worn heels that my feet are screaming to slip into a soft pair of mules. The track playing over the speakers has a deep bass beat and the same refrain plays over and over like the throb in my head. I check the time. Not long now until midnight. Why stay here and tempt fate? If the note is a real threat then I need to be with my family, to guard them and keep them safe. I should never have left them.

I'm going home to my children.

The music continues at the same volume as I go up the wooden staircase in the centre of the room, the clatter of my heels hidden by the deafening beat, the music programmed to play in every corner of the apartment. The coats are hanging in the walk-in wardrobe adjacent to the guest bedroom, where Kelly will be staying tonight. I take out my phone and check for any messages from her but there are none. I should have asked her to let me know that everything was OK for my peace of mind. My head is throbbing from the noise and the strong cocktails I've drunk and I can't wait to get out of here. I'm scanning the row of neatly hung jackets for my silver pashmina when I hear a noise and realise I'm not alone. I stand still and listen. Did I imagine it?

I've been up here only once before, when Martin gave us a tour of the apartment at the first book club meeting he held at his house. The room is L-shaped and there is a corner around which I can't see. There's a pause in the music and a couple of seconds' silence and I hear a shuffling and a groan. I pull a face. There's no mistaking now when a man speaks in a low voice and there's more rustling. Without moving I look for my pashmina, spot it at the end of the rail. Holding my breath, I reach forward to pluck it from the hanger, not wanting to disturb the canoodling couple when I spot the mirror which is angled in such a way that I can see round the hidden corner. I have a full-length view of a golden dress covering lightly tanned skin and my breath catches in my throat. It's Sienna. I slide the shawl from the hanger as carefully as I can and step backwards, desperate not to alert her to my presence as the mirror disappears from my sightline. I tiptoe out of the room and am just about to let out a sigh of relief when I hear a man's voice from back in the closet, muffled, but unmistakable.

'We should stop,' he says. 'Anyone could come up here.'

I'm unable to move. It's Oliver.

Oliver and Sienna.

Sienna is his mistress.

# TWENTY-SEVEN

I'm no longer aware of the pounding music; all I can hear is the sound of my heart thumping and a scream stifled in my throat. Instead, ragged breaths escape my mouth as I'm consumed by panic. Of all the women at the party it had to be Sienna. How she must have been laughing at me. My marriage is definitely over. For Oliver to do this so close to home, he clearly has no feelings for me whatsoever. The humiliation is what's stopping my breath and making my pulse race. To avoid bumping into anyone in the lift I run down the stairs, no longer mindful of my heels and somehow I don't twist my ankle. I'll get the children and drive to my parents'. I never want to see this place again. Has Oliver been across the road in Sienna's house, cheating with her while I'm tearing my hair out trying to keep the children in check, wishing he was at my side, missing him? The humiliation makes my skin burn.

'Harriet.' I'm just about to open the front door when Becky calls me. Maybe she's been off with me because she knows and can't bear to look me in the eye. Does everybody know, hands clapped over their mouths behind their drawn blinds, as Oliver and Sienna sneak off together?

'Not now,' I say, 'I have to go, something's come up.'

'Please,' she says, 'it's important and I need to know what's going on.'

I'm keeping the staircase in my eyeline, in case Oliver or Sienna should appear. I don't want him to stop me leaving.

'I really do need to go, something's come up. What is it?' Becky comes closer, and she's wearing more makeup than usual, but the heat is melting her foundation and not quite masking a black eye. 'Are you OK? Your eye...'

'I'm fine. It looks worse than it is. When I was at your house the other day, and you got those flowers, I left so quickly because I didn't know what to do when I saw it.' The image of the flowers flickers behind my eyes.

'Saw what?' I really don't need to be reminded of that threat. All the more reason to get away from here.

I reach out to the door and open it. Now I've made up my mind to leave I don't really care what she has to say, I won't be coming back to this place. She doesn't take the hint.

'The writing on the card that came with the flowers. I know who sent them.'

'You do? Who?' I grab her wrist. 'You have to tell me.'

'It was Ryan.'

I'm speechless. 'I don't understand.' What would Becky's partner have to do with this? A cold fear runs through my veins and I struggle to compute this information. I'm wondering what Ryan has to do with me. Is he the one behind all this, somehow connected? Or has he been put up to it by someone else? Not knowing where the threat is coming from is putting me into a state of panic.

Her jaw is clenched. 'If it's true I want to know. Have you been seeing him?'

'No.' My voice is loud, but it's such a preposterous idea. 'I promise you, nothing could be further from the truth. Are you sure about the writing? Only the flowers are one of several strange things that have been happening to me, and the note that came with them contained a threat. It's not the first I've had.'

'I'm sure.' Becky's face is pale. 'But I don't understand. What did the note say?'

'It threatened my children. Do you know why he sent it?' I grab her arm. 'You have to tell me; it's important. I've been terrified, ever since Tilly went missing. Let me speak to him; is he here now?'

She shakes her head. 'I don't understand any of this but he has been behaving strangely lately. I'm really worried about him. He seems so preoccupied but gets defensive if I ask him what's wrong. He's not here; he wouldn't come. I don't know why. We had a big row about it.'

'Did he give you that black eye?'

She hesitates, then nods.

'Oh Becky.' I'm shaking now. Who is this man and what is he capable of? 'Is he at your house?'

'I don't know. He's not answering his mobile.'

A cold draught blows through the door, reminding me it's open.

'Where are you going?'

'Home. I've just...' The words stick in my throat.

'What's the matter?'

'It's Oliver, I've just caught him with someone else. I have to get out of here.'

'Oh no, I'm sorry.' She follows me outside. 'And here I am accusing you. Can I do anything?'

'Don't tell anyone I've gone. Especially Ryan.'

'I don't understand.'

'Neither do I. But I'm going to get the children so I'd better let Kelly know. Dolly can stay at my house until you fetch her, don't worry about that.'

'OK, if you're sure. I'd better check how Dolly is when you speak to her.'

Kelly's number is ringing; Becky fiddles with her hair, watching me, her posture awkward.

'Hello,' Kelly says, her voice lively, carefree. 'That's funny, I was just about to ring you.'

'Why? Is something wrong?' I grip my mobile and Becky edges closer to try and hear.

'No, I just wanted to say Ryan's done as you asked and he's been over and taken the children back to his house.'

'Ryan?'

'Put it on speaker,' Becky says, grabbing my arm. Kelly's voice is clear.

'Yes, he said it was a surprise to him but he didn't mind as he didn't want to go to the party anyway. Obviously I wouldn't have let him if you hadn't authorised it.'

'I didn't.'

'But...'

'Kelly, this is Becky. This is very important. Has he taken all four of the children?'

'Yes, to your house. I helped him carry the baby across. The twins held his hands.'

'How long ago was this?'

'Five minutes. I've literally just got back. I'm so sorry, have I done something wrong?'

'It's OK. Stay where you are.'

Becky looks at me. 'I'm sure everything's fine.' Her white face tells a different story. For a second I'm transfixed, as pieces of the jigsaw tumble into place. Ryan's writing, the note, the threats to my children. Adrenalin floods through me, galvanising me into action.

'I'm not. Come on. You said yourself Ryan was behaving strangely. What the hell does he think he's doing?' I run down the path, tripping over my heels.

Martin appears in the doorway, followed by Danni.

'Everything alright?' he asks. 'It's a bit cold with the door open.'

'Call the police,' I shout, 'Ryan's taken the children. Danni, go back to the house, stay with Kelly. I'll explain later.'

'Sure.' She hurries across to our house.

'What's going on?' Oliver pushes past Martin.

'Ryan's taken the children back to our house,' Becky says, 'I'm sure it's fine, but we're going over there now.'

'Over where?'

'To my house.'

'I'm coming with you.' Sienna appears at his side. Seeing her give me a flash of anger. I don't want her there but haven't time to deal with her right now. Kelly joins us as we cross the quadrangle. It only takes minutes to get to Becky's house and she fumbles in her bag to get her key.

'What's wrong?' Kelly asks. 'Was I wrong to let them go?'

'We didn't know anything about it, that's all,' I say, trying to hide my panic. Kelly starts crying.

'I'm sorry, this is all my fault.'

'Try to keep calm,' Becky says. 'Ryan wouldn't hurt the children. He adores Dolly.' She unlocks the door.

'Ryan,' she calls, 'Ryan, where are you? What are you playing at?'

Oliver runs upstairs, quickly comes back. 'They're not upstairs.' The ground floor is empty too.

'The lights are on so he must be here. I turned them off when we went out. He said he was going for a drive to clear his head.'

'I don't understand,' Oliver says. Becky slides open the bifold doors and looks outside. 'He's not here.'

The door from the hall opens and we all turn. It's Sienna. She's dared to follow Oliver. I haven't the energy to tell her she has no place here; all I care about is Lucy, the twins and Dolly and what Ryan is up to. Why is he doing this?

'Is there anywhere else he might be?' I ask.

'Only the garage – follow me.'

We go through the bifold doors round to the side of the house. The lights are on in the garage and as we enter from the back the front gate is sliding upwards, Ryan is standing by the driver's door, remote in one hand pointing it forward, a baby in his arm. It's Lucy. My throat tightens and I struggle to breathe. I find my voice and scream. 'It's my baby, he's got Lucy, help me stop him.' Inside the car the twins are strapped in. Tilly bangs on the window.

'Mummy,' she calls and I rush over to her, scrabble at the car door handle, but it's locked, as I knew it would be. My heart stops when I turn my attention back to Ryan. Lucy is motionless in his arms. Why isn't she moving?

'Give me my daughter.'

'What are you doing, Ryan?' Becky asks. Ryan swivels round and drops the remote, still holding Lucy tightly to him.

'Get out,' he says.

'Ryan? I don't understand. Where's Dolly?'

'Dolly is fine.'

'Give Lucy to me,' I yell. 'Becky, stop him, please stop him.'

Becky hesitates and Oliver pushes past her. Ryan drops the remote and pulls something from his pocket, holds his arm in the air and points it at Oliver.

'Stay right where you are, all of you, unless you want me to use this.'

# TWENTY-EIGHT

The gun glints in the dim light of the garage.

'Please don't hurt the children.' Becky and I say these words in unison.

'Shut up.'

Becky gasps.

'Give me my baby,' I shout again, my voice shaky with fear.

'Make her shut up, Becks, or I'll use this.'

Becky grips my hand. She's trembling almost as much as I am. 'Do as he says, otherwise...'

A sob bursts from my throat but I squeeze my lips together to stop myself from letting out the scream unfolding inside me. My legs wobble and I grip hold of Becky, terrified of falling. Any sudden movement and who knows what Ryan might do?

Oliver stares at the barrel of the gun and I cling to Becky's arm. Both of us are shaking.

In those few terrifying seconds, I pray that Sienna has seen what is happening and has gone for help. Oliver takes a step backwards.

'Why are you doing this?' I ignore him. I won't let him take my children. Everything I hold dear is being ripped away from me.

Ryan's eyes flick between us as the hand holding the gun wobbles. He waves it towards the three of us. Becky and I are behind Oliver, partly shielded by his body, but it's no comfort. I put a hand on Oliver's back to let him know we're here for him.

'I said don't move.'

'Why are you doing this, Ryan? I don't understand. At least let me take Lucy. She shouldn't be on her own.' Becky is trying to appeal to his reasonable side, but he ignores her.

'Shut up! She'll tell you why I'm doing this,' he says, glaring at me, his arm shifting to the side so that the gun is pointing at me. 'Tell them, Harriet, let's hear what you did. When he knows what you've done he'll understand why you don't deserve children.'

'Harriet, what's going on? Do you know what he's talking about?'

The gun transfixes me and I'm terrified lest I make an involuntary movement.

'Are you behind the notes?'

'What notes?' Oliver sounds exasperated. 'If you know what he's talking about, for god's sake tell us, Harriet. Anything to stop him waving that gun around.'

'It sounds like you've never told your husband what you did. How you ruined so many lives. This is payback time.'

'Who are you?' I ask, not daring to take my eyes off the barrel of the gun.

'He's my partner,' a voice from behind me says and Sienna steps forward.

# TWENTY-NINE

Sienna joins Ryan and takes Lucy from his arms. She's asleep, blissfully unaware of the danger she's in. I lean into Becky, my legs unsteady. The foundations I've so carefully crafted over the years are slowly crumbling.

'Your partner? You mean... your lover...?' Oliver stumbles over the word, his face pale. Sienna smirks.

'I didn't tell you a lot of things,' Sienna says. 'Like you didn't tell your wife what you were really up to on a Wednesday evening, sneaking over to my flat, even getting Ben to cover for you. Everybody knows about us, by the way; you were right about that. And soon, Harriet, they'll know who you are and what you did. Tell Oliver what you did to my little sister. I'm Sienna Lavery. Ryan and I were at school together; he grew up knowing you killed the rest of my family. Now it's payback time.'

I stumble as her words hit the spot. Sienna Lavery, Lydia's half sister. Sienna Wright must be her married name. I know she's divorced; maybe she kept her name, though.

'Tell him now or you'll never see Lucy again.' She strokes Lucy's head as she says this. 'I know people who would pay good money for a baby, no questions asked. Failing that, we could bring her up along with her sisters; why separate them? I never thought I'd be a mother but change is meant to be good, right.' A smirk snakes across her face.

'You wouldn't dare,' Oliver says, his voice cracking. 'If you know what this is about, Harriet, hurry up and speak.'

My voice when I find it is robotic.

'Lydia Freud.' I haven't said that name out loud for years, and a cold hand squeezes my heart. 'She was a baby who lived nearby. Our parents were friendly. I was sixteen, and I was asked to babysit her. What I did was wrong, but...'

'Just tell us the facts.' Sienna's voice is like ice. 'We don't care how you feel.'

'Lydia's parents went out. Lydia was asleep in her cot. I checked on her and she was fine. I invited a male friend over. He wasn't exactly my boyfriend but I hoped he might be. When he came he was different to how he'd been before; he'd been drinking and he brought some cider with him. I only had a small glass and I've never drunk it since.'

'Cut the excuses and get on with it.'

'We were watching a film, messing about kissing and stuff. The baby alarm was on and I looked at it all the time. Maybe I should have checked on Lydia regardless of that, but I didn't. When I went to her room after Mike had gone I thought she was sleeping, but...' I burst into tears. 'She wasn't moving and I know I should have checked on her but...'

'But you didn't,' Sienna cuts in. 'You didn't check because you were too busy with your boyfriend while upstairs in the same house my little sister was dying.'

'Is this true?' Oliver asks.

'It's true that Lydia died but I didn't kill her and I didn't kill anyone else.'

'You as good as killed my whole family. My parents never got over it. And neither did I, I adored my baby sister. And you, you got away with it while we were left with a death sentence.'

A face flashes into my mind, Lydia's five-year-old sister, a solemn child with dark eyes staring out from underneath a pageboy haircut. Eyes that bore into me the one time I saw her after that, when I went round to their house to try and explain. 'There isn't a day goes by that I don't regret what happened; I'm so sorry, Sienna.'

'You're sorry, ha. Not sorry enough to tell your husband, to admit what you did and who you are, trapping him into having his children when you shouldn't be allowed anywhere near a child. That's why we're taking them, me and Ryan. He's helped me with this, getting you frightened with those threats, the notes, the woman who answered the phone when you called, but that was just for starters. I'm going to destroy your life just like you destroyed mine. I've been planning it ever since Lydia died. Why should you walk free after what you did? It's the least you deserve, so here's what's going to happen.'

Ryan steps forward. His arm holding the gun hasn't wavered once, just as my eyes haven't left it. 'You three stand back against the wall.'

We do as he says, terror stealing our words. With her free hand, Sienna opens the driver's door of the car and hands Lucy to Tess. Tess is too small to hold onto her properly. Sienna doesn't understand children; she can't take mine. I won't let her even if it kills me.

'Put her under your seat belt,' she says, 'we're going for a little adventure.'

'No,' I scream, so loud Becky flinches.

'Mummy.' Tilly bangs on the window from where she can see her parents standing by.

'No, please don't do this,' I plead with Sienna. I don't want to alarm the children – the gun is out of their sight range from where they are sitting. I look at Oliver, trying to communicate with him through a look that we need to do something to stop this madness happening. He can't read my mind but I won't let Sienna drive off.

'Stop her,' I shout, pushing Becky to create a diversion, throwing myself at Ryan, knocking the gun as it goes off, narrowly missing my arm. Oliver throws a punch at Ryan, and he swipes back. A roaring noise fills the room as Sienna starts the car's engine, revving as loudly as possible. Becky stands in front of the car, screaming at Sienna to stop. A more urgent sound is wailing in the background, and I wonder if some kind of alarm has gone off in the house, when blue lights flash through the garage window and a police car pulls up outside.

2006

*What had she done?*

Terror crept through her body and her breath came out in a gasp, her chest so tight she feared it would burst. If only it would burst, then she would be the one lying still on the bed instead of the baby. Lydia, so little, so innocent.

A baby. A baby she was responsible for.

Her hands shook as she dialled the ambulance.

After she'd rung the ambulance she stayed in the room with Lydia, not wanting to leave her on her own. She'd rubbed her with her cold hands in a futile attempt to warm her up and tried CPR as the woman with the soft voice at the end of the emergency helpline had directed her but it was to no avail. The paramedics arrived before the Freuds, followed immediately by the police and she stuttered answers to their questions. Her throat seized up with shock, and she couldn't get her words out. She wouldn't mention Mike, not then. The way he'd looked at her and what he'd said when he left made her feel cold every time she thought about it.

The Freuds' return to the house happened in slow motion for Harriet. By that time she was unable to speak, or even cry, her body shaking with the enormity of what she'd done. Her throat was so painful she could barely swallow. She couldn't unsee the baby's face, still and blue. If only it was her instead of the child lying there. She knew already the image would never leave her and a future mired in pain flashed before her. It was what she deserved. She yearned for her mother to hold her yet didn't want her mother to know what a terrible thing she'd done.

The Freuds told the police she was *too* cold, *unnatural.* They took in the empty bottle, the traces of smoke in the kitchen and concluded she'd drunk herself into a stupor and forgotten their precious baby. The police bombarded her with questions, pressing her for answers. She resisted for a while but of course eventually she had to tell them about Mike coming over and they brought him in for questioning. She knew she deserved everything the Freuds said about her. Nobody understood the shame and guilt which weighed down on her as soon as she opened her eyes. Nothing could undo what she'd done.

The days following Lydia's death were horrific for so many people. No matter how her parents tried to console her she could see the real thoughts behind their eyes when they showered her with placatory words. She'd done a terrible thing; she was wicked and didn't deserve to be alive.

The media were all over the story but she was protected by dint of her age; she was a child in the eyes of the law and was granted anonymity. She read everything written like she was a hoover, sucking it all up, the dirt filling her lungs and understanding what vermin she was. Much was made in the newspapers and online; she read everything she could get hold of even though her parents tried to stop her. Back at school for only a day, she knew her anonymity had been blown. People stopped talking when she entered a room and Gemma was extra nice to her, telling her it wasn't her fault but she'd killed a baby; Lydia had died and nothing could reverse that. She walked out of school that first afternoon, unable to stand the stares in the lunch hall and refused to go back. One month later she was in hospital having a psychiatric breakdown and being taught how to live her life again. They didn't understand that was impossible because she didn't deserve it.

After months in hospital, her parents moved house so she was discharged into a completely new environment where nobody knew what she'd done. After a failed attempt at taking her own life and seeing what that did to her parents, realising they would love her whatever she did, she started taking the medication offered and responding to the talking therapy and very slowly she'd begun to learn to live again, teaching herself techniques to cope with it.

Not that she forgot Lydia, not a day went by that she didn't think about her. It was important to make amends for what she had done by being a good person. By changing her mentality and blocking out the memories of those few hours in that house, she was able to build a new life for herself, go back to school, take exams and apply to university, all the things normal young people did. It wasn't so easy when she started dating, in her late twenties, and fell in love for the first time. Then her thoughts switched to marriage and children, and that sparked off the doubts again.

She didn't deserve to have children, did she?

# THIRTY

## SIENNA

I wasn't sure what Ryan would say when I put my proposal to him; he hadn't been directly affected in the way that I had, but we'd been close friends since primary school and he saw the change in me after my sister died. As we grew older, he saw how our family suffered as a result of what she did, destroying their daughter after they'd fought so hard to have her. She was a precious jewel and she should still be shining today. When we became a couple, we vowed to get revenge, no matter how long it took.

She ruined all that.

Mum was such a loving person, I loved being with her and she made every minute we spent together fun. Being so young, I didn't have too many memories from that time but I did remember that the fun times stopped happening after the babysitter came round and took Lydia away from us.

The post-mortem was a travesty. Just thinking about them doing that to my baby sister killed me, cutting her tiny body up and looking inside her. They told my parents she had a heart condition, that it wasn't anyone's fault, but Mum and Dad didn't believe a word of it and neither did I. She was bonny and healthy, and anyone could see if she had been looked after properly that night, none of this would have happened. The findings of the post-mortem meant Harriet walked free, when she should have been locked up for the rest of her life.

After she escaped justice, Mum and my stepdad Tim couldn't bear to stay in that house anymore. For a while we stayed with Grandma and Grandpa before we moved to a different house, but it was smaller and I was now an only child. I felt as if I'd lost a limb. I carried a dull ache in my heart where my baby sister had once been. Mum and Tim changed into different people the night we lost Lydia. My grandparents were very old and they died a couple of years later, by which time we were in our new house, a boxy little square with poky rooms and hardly any outside space. We'd had a lovely garden with green grass and lots of flowers before but Mum wasn't interested in gardening after that; she wasn't interested in anything except talking about Lydia, and who she might have been.

Looking back now, I think at first it was good for her to remember Lydia, if it helped her then it could only be a good thing, but it became like an obsession, and over the years she drilled into me what a wicked thing Harriet had done, inviting a boy over, something 'only sluts did', Mum said, and she would bring me up properly with good morals and proper behaviour and I would be a responsible loving wife and mother, when I was old enough. She said Harriet didn't deserve to have children, ever.

Going to church gave Mum some comfort for a while. She started going to St Hilda's after Lydia died and she insisted on taking me with her. Back at home she studied her bible and spent a lot of time praying, praying for justice for Lydia. It was the only thing she would do. Tim tried to get her interested in other things, he wanted her to go on trips in the car and join him for long walks, take me out to the seaside for the day and eat ice cream on the beach, but she refused to go and he gave up trying.

He left us shortly after that, moving into a house not that far away. He took me out at the weekends but he was very serious and I wondered if I'd imagined the jolly man who used to tickle me and play silly games and make me laugh until my sides hurt.

Mum even stopped going to church after he left and I got used to looking after the two of us. Talking about Lydia was her only interest. Lydia and Harriet Underwood. The name Harriet Underwood is one I'll never forget, and I was sick of hearing it. Mum drummed into me how unfair it was that she got to go to university and get married and be happy – to live the life that Lydia should have had. Lydia was a clever baby, Mum said, although I wondered how she knew as she didn't live for very long. One hundred and eighty-one days. Mum said that a lot too.

Sadly Mum never got to see me deal with Harriet Underwood. She passed away six years ago and it was Mum's death that spurred me on, to get revenge on the girl who had caused our family so much grief. It didn't matter that she had been judged not deserving of any punishment; she was guilty in our eyes and the eyes of anyone we knew. I made sure I kept tabs on her, keeping up with the life that she dared to move ahead with, making sure I always knew where she was living and what she was doing. And once Ryan and I became lovers, I proposed my plan to him and he understood without much explanation as he was around at the time and saw how what happened ruined our family. I'd kept tabs on her for years, which helped, so I knew all about her marriage and her fancy house in Prospect Close. But it was when she had children that I swung into action. She didn't have the right. Ryan and I would soon put a stop to that. When an apartment became vacant, I used my savings to pay the deposit and later, when I met Oliver and we started our affair, it wasn't difficult to persuade him to contribute to my mortgage. Soon I was able to watch her every day and infiltrate the community, get into the heads of the people closest to her, and get into her mind. Ryan getting to know Becky slotted neatly into my plan. It didn't take long for him to persuade her to let him move in with her. Seeing Harriet with the baby in her arms was unforgiveable, and when I met her gorgeous husband and heard the women gossiping about his reputation for being a ladies' man it made sense to take him away from her too.

From my conversations with the other women I knew she was paranoid about her children, a super over-protective mum, and unlike them I knew exactly why. It made what we were doing seem justified – she knew she didn't deserve to have them after what she did to Lydia and that it was only a matter of time. Ryan kicked it all off by faking Tilly's kidnap; one of his mates took her for a walk. She wasn't in danger for a second; Ryan knew I just wanted her scared, and if it made her more protective in the future, well, that could only be a good thing.

Ryan wasn't happy about leaving Dolly with a teenage babysitter; we know all too well what that can lead to. I made sure to persuade Oliver he had to come to the party, offering him the added thrill of getting off with me while his wife was downstairs.

But we got caught, the plan stopped mid-track. We hadn't planned to do anything terrible to the children, quite the opposite; I was going to save them from her and Ryan and I would bring them up as our own. Not only would our taking them have given her a scare, forcing her to admit to her husband who she really was and what she'd done, he'd kick her out and she would have lost everything. Not that raising her children or punishing her would bring Lydia back; nothing could ever do that.

# THIRTY-ONE

The children and I stay with Mum that night after I've given my statement to the police. It's ironic that now Oliver knows the truth and says he can forgive me, I'm not interested in him anymore. Not only can I break free from my past, I can break away from my marriage which hasn't been making me happy for so long. Gabi helps me see that, when we meet the next day.

'You haven't been happy for ages. Catching him with Sienna is just too blatant. I don't think he's capable of being faithful to you.'

'The way forward seems so obvious now, but I don't think it would have happened if I hadn't been exposed.'

Gabi is pragmatic about that too. 'You know inviting Mike over was wrong, but you've been punished enough. I bet there isn't a day goes by that you don't think of that poor little girl.'

'There isn't. I know her face as well as I know Lucy's, only Lucy's will change and mature but Lydia's never does.'

'You were only sixteen and your emotions were all over the place. The courts didn't believe you deserved to be punished. I've been doing a little digging into your case. I requested all the files and read through everything. Lydia had a heart condition, so it would have happened even if her parents had been there. We know so much more about this condition nowadays, and there have been several cases in the media which have been well documented. Obviously, I can't prove this but I'm pretty sure this is one of those conditions that suddenly occur and the margin for taking action is incredibly short, and that's with an adult. An adult can tell you something is wrong, whereas a baby can only cry. Honestly, Harriet, it was nothing to do with you. But you must have known this? Surely they told you their findings?'

'Yes, I was told but I couldn't accept it. I was convinced that if I had been paying proper attention then she might have survived.'

'But it would have happened some other time. It was always going to happen, Harriet. You have to stop punishing yourself. What happened to your boyfriend by the way? Has he spent his life feeling terrible about this? Somehow, I think not.'

'I couldn't speak to him afterwards. I was terrified because I saw a different side to him when he left what night. My parents wouldn't have let me even if I'd wanted to, but I went into a depressive funk and didn't emerge from it for months. He moved away.'

After the conversation with Gabi there is a shift in me. My shoulders are a little lighter and I know in my heart that I wasn't to blame. I accept that now, and somehow having my awful secret out in the open enables me to heal. My real friends stand by me, and I'm no longer afraid of the shadows of my past.

———

Oliver has dark stubble on his chin and he's wearing old jeans and a sweatshirt. Two cases stand to attention in the hallway. It's the first time we've been together since that night three weeks ago when we had a gun pointed at us.

'Are you going somewhere?'

He nods. We sit in the kitchen and he pours two glasses of water, which sit on the table untouched. I don't want to make myself at home with him ever again.

'How are the children?' he asks after several awkward moments.

'They're fine. They don't know any different.' I notice there are spaces on the shelves in the living room; his books have been taken off.

'I'm going away,' he says. 'I'm moving to France.'

'With Sienna?'

'No. She's not allowed to leave the country while she's on bail awaiting trial.'

'Was she the supposed woman from Nice or was that a lie too?'

He looks at his hands. 'Yes, she came over to Paris for the weekend. Uninvited, in fact, but once she was there... I should have owned up to it, but I was trying to spare your feelings. Wrong, I know.' He puts his head in his hands before pulling himself together and looking straight into my eyes. 'I was telling the truth about her; she means nothing. I've already blocked her. I don't want anything more to do with Sienna. How could I, after she tried to take our children? I swear I knew nothing about it. And she was seeing Ryan the whole time too. I guess it serves me right.'

Yet another lie. I've made the right decision.

'I know you were helping pay her mortgage. Greenwood Lettings, that was a codename, wasn't it?'

He puts his head in his hands again, nodding.

I believe him. He looks deflated, a man who's lost everything.

'About the children,' he says. I sit upright, my case prepared, my lines learned; Gabi has briefed me on this just in case he should try anything. 'It's only right that you should have full custody; they need to be with you. Whatever you did in the past I know you wouldn't harm our children. I'd like to stay in their lives, if possible.'

'I'm sure we can work something out.'

'We need to talk about the house.'

My stomach sinks; I knew this was coming. Even though I've been desperate to move, being forced out and embarking on life as a single parent is not how I imagined it playing out.

'When do you plan to sell?' Oliver paid the bulk of the deposit with his savings and his earning power has always well exceeded mine; even when I was working full-time I couldn't compete. I'm confident enough about my business but it will take time to grow to that level.

'That's up to you. I'm moving into an apartment on my own. I'll take it from there. I presume you'll want to move to the country, now there's nothing standing in your way.'

'It's too early for me to make that kind of decision.'

'You can stay here for as long as you like. The children have a routine. I won't stand in your way. They're my children and I'll always provide for them, I can promise you that.'

'OK.' I can't bring myself to thank him after everything he's put me through.

———

Since he left that day, Oliver has only communicated through his solicitor. When I returned from the police station on the night of the party, the house was empty. No explanation, nothing. Until his visit three weeks later, and shortly after that I received a letter from his solicitor confirming he would continue to provide for the children until they reached adulthood, and I could stay in the house until I decided to move, at which point he was prepared to buy my share of it; alternatively if I wanted to stay there I could buy him out.

He's being so reasonable I wonder if there is a catch. After everything that happened I can never trust him again. Maybe being double crossed by Sienna made him see things from my point of view. His disbelief at what she did that night was all too real and she hasn't heard from him since that night either. She's been writing to Asha from jail. She and Ryan received custodial sentences for kidnapping the children, and for possessing and using an illegal weapon.

Becky dumped Ryan. Aside from his long-standing affair with Sienna and his increasing violence, she was incensed when she discovered he'd faked the kidnapping and set off the threats against me. He hasn't attempted to get in touch with her and she's pretty sure he won't.

Funnily enough, since that night I've seen Prospect Close through new eyes. It's a beautiful place to live, and the community has rallied round to support me. Asha has been a diamond; she's dragged me out for coffees when I wasn't in the mood, constantly encouraging me to talk, to get it all out, and helping me see how what happened to Lydia wasn't solely my fault. Mistakes were made, yes, but I understand and can forgive myself. Now that I no longer feel the need to escape my past and my unfaithful husband, the appeal of living in a rural retreat has lost all appeal. Good friends, outstanding schools, and a sense of belonging is worth more than gold to me.

When the case hit the press I expected a turn of opinion against me, but it didn't happen. Online, the inevitable trolls came out of their holes, but I no longer care what anonymous people think of me; the people I care about know the truth about me and that is what matters. Kate got in touch when she heard what had happened. That night has been liberating for her too, and she was able to tell me the truth about what happened. She'd come home early one afternoon when she was working for us to find a naked Oliver and Sienna in the bedroom. Oliver had threatened her and given her money to leave. She'd been too scared to go against him and devastated to leave so abruptly, and it was easier for her to cut all contact than have to face me and lie. She insisted on giving the money he gave her to the children.

Then when Danni decided to leave after a few months, Kate came back to work for me part-time.

Kelly is babysitting tonight and I'm going out to dinner with Gabi and Elliott. The children are safe in her care and the irrational fear I used to have about leaving them has gone. Gabi has been a fantastic friend to me, and as a lawyer herself she's been able to give me invaluable advice. And I've been able to help her too – seeing me relieved of the burden of secrets, she issued Elliott with an ultimatum. He didn't want to lose her and it turned out he just needed a bit of a push to get his wife to agree to a divorce. He persuaded Victoria to get some help with her mental health and since she's been having psychiatric care she's more able to accept the end of her marriage, and learning to live a different life.

'Be good for Kelly, won't you?' The twins are jumping up and down with excitement when she arrives. It's noticeably lighter when I let myself out into Prospect Close since the clocks went forward last weekend and a bed of purple crocuses brightens the border of the quadrangle. For the first time since Christmas I sense I'm being watched.

'Harriet.' I hear my name called from somewhere above and I look up to see Martin waving from his terrace, white lights twinkling around him. 'Come up for a night cap when you're done.'

'I'd love to.'

I'm still being watched, but by my friends in this community, waiting to catch me whenever I trip and fall.

# A LETTER FROM LESLEY

Thank you so much for reading *The Mistress Next Door*. I hope you enjoyed reading it as much as I enjoyed writing it. To keep up to date with the latest news on my new releases, just click on the link below to sign up for a newsletter. I promise never to share your email with anyone else.

*www.bookouture.com/lesley-sanderson*

As with my first six books *The Orchid Girls, The Woman at 46 Heath Street, The Leaving Party, I Know You Lied, Every Little Lie* and *The Widow's Husband,* I hoped to create an evocative novel about obsession, secrets and the blurred lines between love and lies.

If you enjoyed *The Mistress Next Door,* I would love it if you could write a short review. Getting reviews from readers who have enjoyed my writing is my favourite way to persuade other readers to pick up one of my books for the first time.

I'd also love to hear from you via social media: see the links below.

facebook.com/lsandersonbooks

twitter.com/LSandersonbooks

instagram.com/lesleysandersonauthor

Printed in Great Britain
by Amazon